2a

MW00938285

... ...us

and explore the
world.

love heure v

Bakewell

2/8/19

THE
SMART KIDS

JOHN THOMAS CROWLEY

Order of Characters

Anjala
Hamish
Charlie
Ephraim
Priya
Juan
Naeku
Duscha
Anaru
Dantel
Guia
Emerita
Saif and Zahid
Malaina
Yeshe
Kymana
Fadl

Also by John Thomas Crowley

Brilliant Challenges
Great Rescues
Meeting V.I.Ps

This book and the others I have written would never have come about if it was not for my closest friends, Pete Mugleston, Andy Moss and James Atkins. These guys have inspired me with what they do in their own professional lives, but their encouragement and support over the last few years has been simply amazing. Therefore as a measure of my appreciation I dedicate this book to all three of you. A huge thank you guys.

ANJALA

Home for Anjala and her brother Rajesh was a small, snow-covered village high in the Himalayan Mountains of the tiny Kingdom of Nepal. In the valley below lay the small town of Pokhara, where she and her brother attended school most days. The daily treks back and forth to school along the narrow and dangerous mountain paths were challenging, but to two Nepalese children this was the norm.

The classroom clock that hung above the board was showing 3.15pm and in a few minutes the bell would go, bringing the school day to a close. Anjala looked out of the window; the January snowstorm that had been raging all day had abated. The fresh snow that had covered the area meant it would be impossible for her and Rajesh, along with the other schoolchildren that came from the surrounding villages, to attempt the journey home. A simple text from her mother confirmed that she and Rajesh were to spend the next few days with their aunt, who lived in a large flat above one of the many ironmongers' shops scattered around the town.

Outside the air had a chilling nip to it; while waiting for Rajesh she looked up at the sparkling, snow-covered mountains, now set against a deep blue sky. The powdered snow that had recently come to rest on the summit's peaks of the Annapurna range was now being blown around by savage, vicious winds; plumes of what appeared to be white dust could clearly be seen spiralling high into the atmosphere.

Leaning against the school gate post, Anjala wondered how her snow leopard, whom she had named Heaven, and her cub had coped with the recent blizzards. Her train of thought was broken by the boisterous eruption of Rajesh and his mates from the classroom.

"What were you thinking about, Anjala?" asked Rajesh.

"I was thinking about Heaven and her cub."

"Who's Heaven?" asked one of Rajesh's mates.

"None of your business," snarled Anjala, for she knew what the villagers' reaction would be if they found out a snow leopard was prowling the area. Anjala had learnt from her school teacher that the snow leopard was an elusive creature and would avoid human contact at all cost, but a mother with a hungry cub may be tempted by an easy kill. The villagers' livestock would be a soft target for a powerful snow leopard like Heaven. Would Heaven attack if desperate? Most likely. This was a chance Anjala couldn't take. She understood why the locals would want to protect their animals at any cost; they were poor people living a simple life and the loss of one of their herd or flock was a loss of income they could ill afford. Both she and Rajesh knew they had to keep Heaven and her cub's whereabouts a secret.

As Anjala walked with her brother to her Aunt's flat she remembered the day they first saw Heaven and her cub; it was early October. Her father, to support the family income, helped out in the main trekking season as a Sherpa. He had heard that a small team of American climbers needed the knowledge of local Sherpas to guide them over the Annapurna Mountains but, more importantly, to assist them with climbing Machapuchare, more commonly known as Fishtail. The climbers had been given consent by the Nepalese authorities to climb the mountain with the strict instruction not to ascend the summit. Fishtail is a sacred peak in the Hindu religion associated with the God Shiva. Lord Shiva is supposed to live on the peak. The climbers would pay handsomely, but an early start the next morning was needed.

Dawn had arrived and their father shouted at them to hurry up as he needed to be down the mountainside in Pokhara to meet the American expedition team. Their father set a fast pace, too fast for them, so they let him go ahead; she and Rajesh would slowly amble down looking at their phones as they went, checking to see what messages had been left and who was on Facebook. Turning the corner, there in front of them was one of the world's most elusive big cats. A female snow leopard. Anjala recalled how Rajesh froze with fear that morning and how her heart pounded to almost breaking point. Their father had told them how to react if they came across a snow leopard: remain calm and back away slowly, for they were powerful killers who commanded respect. The likelihood of encountering such a majestic animal as the snow leopard would be extremely slim, but nevertheless treat with caution. Heaven merely stopped in her tracks. Her pale green eyes gave a fleeting glance in their direction; her light smoke-grey coat with its black open rosettes and spots made her a master of disguise, blending in beautifully with the colours of the surrounding rocks. Moments later she had vanished, melting into the natural habitat as she bounded back up the mountain.

Over the past few months, tension in the mountain villages had grown as more and more villagers reported losses and attacks on their livestock, and that snow leopard tracks had been found. Anjala kept quiet about Heaven.

In the depths of the Nepalese winter, Anjala and Rajesh had more sightings of Heaven and recently her new cub, which was now three to four months old and fresh out of the den. It was normal for snow leopards to come down from the high peaks to lower terrain in the winter months, but this brought them into contact with mankind and the inevitable tensions and conflicts that followed. Anjala had come up with the idea of leaving food out each night near the place where she and Rajesh had first encountered Heaven, the hope being if it was Heaven attacking the villagers' livestock to provide food for herself and her cub this would stop the attacks and the tensions within the villages and maybe spare her life. For a few weeks the trick worked, but stealing meat several times a week from the local meat stores in Pokhara was risky and would no doubt get her and Rajesh into trouble. The risk of getting caught increased as the weeks went by; one afternoon on the way home from school a meat store holder caught them in the act and released his dogs to give chase. They ran for their lives, but as they sprinted down the street they dropped the bag of meat and the dogs were distracted by the bag, giving her and Rajesh extra time to make their getaway. That afternoon was a narrow escape for Anjala and Rajesh and they took the decision to abandon their stealing adventures. They would have to come up with another plan.

Breakfast the next morning was a simple affair and was quickly put away. Walking to school with Rajesh a few paces behind her, being the grumpy brother as usual, Anjala spotted her father in one of the local cafés drinking tea with a small group of her village elders. She pushed the café door open, gave her father a hug and asked what the occasion was. "No occasion," her father said, but fresh tracks had been found on the edge of the village; they belonged to a female snow leopard and a cub, plus more livestock had been attacked and killed last night. Anjala's heart sank but she tried not to show it.

"What do you propose to do, father?"

"We propose to get permission to track the snow leopard down and shoot her."

Anjala's father looked at his daughter's face and read her distraught feelings.

"Sometimes, Anjala, we have to do unpleasant things, and this is one of those occasions. We must protect the village and our livestock; you know that we need to keep the animals safe so that we can sell them. I know the snow leopard is doing what she needs to do to survive for herself and her cub, but we need to survive as well. Do you see my point?"

"Yes, father."

Anjala ran out of the café, glancing up and down the street looking for Rajesh. Crossing the road, barely avoiding being run over by a school bus, she stopped to see if Rajesh was in sight. Four blocks down she caught a glimpse of her brother's blue sports bag; he had managed to meet up with some of his classmates. She pushed people out of her way as she tried to catch up with him. The traffic lights at the top of the street were green so the pedestrians had to wait. What felt like ages was only a matter of a few minutes before the lights changed in her favour. As she fidgeted around she happened to give a cursory look into the internet café; there was the Australian film crew all her friends had been talking about. Rumour had it they had come to make a documentary about snow leopards but, like most film crews, the creature had eluded them and they were going home empty-handed. She recalled her teacher one day talking about the various film crews that came to town and that their aim was to educate the world about the animals they filmed and how best to protect them from man's needs. Hastily she put two and two together. She needed their expertise in protecting Heaven and her cub, and they needed snow leopards.

Cautiously pushing the door aside she entered the internet café; the guys were busy downloading information for something she didn't understand.

"Excuse me," she spluttered.

"Yes, sweetheart?" A lady from the crew replied.

Anjala cleared her throat and started to tell the crew about her snow leopard Heaven and her cub, along with all the issues that had happened recently and what the outcome would be.

The hot chocolate drink and lemon drizzle cake she had been offered were wonderful; for a poor Nepalese mountain girl a treat of this kind was rare, and she appreciated the gesture, but there was work to be done.

The lady film director couldn't believe her luck and insisted Anjala call her Elizabeth. A plan of action had been briefly scribbled on a napkin, but Anjala was to call her father and the village elders for talks. She sent a text to her brother.

'Be here in five minutes.'

The plan was as follows:

- Anjala and Rajesh would show the film crew Heaven and her cub's hiding places; in return the film company in charge would pay the village a handsome reward for gaining access to the snow leopards.
- Anjala and Rajesh would be in the film documentary to tell their story.
- A conservation team would be set up, providing better fences to protect the villagers' livestock.
- Infrared remote cameras would be set up on all tracks/routes the snow leopards used

during darkness. The villagers could check the cameras every day and if Heaven or any other snow leopard triggered the cameras into action near the village, then the villages could take the appropriate action – mainly post lookouts to scare the cats away.

- The cameras would also allow the conservationists to study and monitor the snow leopards' activities so that more could be learnt about the habits of this great elusive cat.
- The village elders would organise official trekking expeditions so that tourists could come and learn about Heaven or other snow leopards in their natural surroundings.

Anjala thought the plan was excellent. The organised walks would bring in much needed income for the village, as foreign visitors would pay for an organised trip to see and learn more about the snow leopards. She and Rajesh could open a small café serving light refreshments; the money they made would go into the village money pot.

"Father, this is a win-win situation; the village gets more protection, a better warning system and a much needed income source. Plus Heaven and her cub will have a brighter future, as the villagers will see the snow leopards as an income source to be protected rather than as a threatening menace to their livestock."

Her father looked at her.

"Father, you know this is the right way forward."

"Anjala, we need to look at all the options and think what is right for the villagers and the snow leopards. This will take time, but we, the elders, will grant that time. For the moment make sure Heaven stays away from our livestock. But for now, both of you get to school."

"Yes, father," replied Anjala and Rajesh.

The sprint to school made them just in time for the first lesson of the day. Anjala sat at her desk and looked out of the same window she had done yesterday afternoon; the snow had started to come down again. She could see her village high up in the mountains, the peak of Fishtail in the background and somewhere, roaming the mountain slopes, was her Heaven and her cub, safe with a brighter future thanks to what she had achieved earlier.

A text appeared on her phone.

'Why do you call your snow leopard Heaven?'

It was from her father. She replied:

'Simple father, she comes down from the mountain peaks high in the heavens at dusk and goes back up to the mountain summits in the heavens at dawn, so I called her Heaven. See you soon x.'

Another text message appeared on her phone; it was from Elizabeth, the film director. They had managed to obtain some funding from the World Wildlife Fund; these funds would allow new programmes to be put in place so as to demonstrate to the world that, with careful management, wildlife and humans could exist alongside each other, bringing benefits to all concerned. For a few moments Anjala thought the message was interesting but couldn't understand the relevance to her: it wasn't until she scrolled down and she saw the invitation for herself and Rajesh to go to Australia to present the programme to schools all over Australia. Anjala's eyes lit up with the thought of going to Australia; she and her brother had never gone further than a few day trips to Kathmandu, the capital of Nepal. She had been to Tribhuvan Airport, Nepal's main international Airport on the outskirts of Kathmandu, several times as her uncle often flew out to Doha in Qatar to work on the building sites there; but she never in her wildest dreams envisaged flying out to an exotic location herself. She called her brother, but he didn't respond as usual, so she sent a message to his Facebook page; he constantly kept an eye on that. As predicted the response was immediate: *'OMG, will father let us go?'*

In her excitement Anjala had not considered that small matter; a dark horizon clouded her judgement for a few short minutes. Surely he would let them go? As she walked up the narrow mud track, a path she had trampled along hundreds of times, she pondered on how she would delicately place the proposition to her father. She looked up at the mountains that soared above her – the snow on the Annapurna peaks that dominated the skyline was being blown around high into the stratosphere, nightfall would soon descend and the street lights of Pokhara far below would soon twinkle, adding a magic charm of its own to the valley she had known as home.

The flight from Kathmandu via New Delhi in India to Perth, Australia was long and exhausting but exciting. For Anjala and her brother Rajesh every minute of this four-week adventure would be relished and remembered for years to come. Their father had reluctantly agreed, proving the strategy she had shrewdly hatched out on the trek home that late winter's afternoon had worked. Her plan was heavily weighted on emphasizing to her father that he was vital to this project and that he was included in the trip to Australia. Getting Elizabeth to visit her father and the other village elders on numerous occasions, reassuring them of her and Rajesh's safety, had also worked in tipping the balance in her favour. Stressing the trip would be a very good educational experience also added bonus points in her direction. Anjala was quite proud of her cunning prowess. Offering money to support the village funds as a little sweetener had also improved the odds. A sneaky little bribe – or so called inducement – with a nod and a wink in the right place sometimes gets the job done.

The temperature outside the main air-conditioned terminal buildings was a staggering forty degrees. As Anjala stepped out of the confines of the airport buildings the heat hit her in the face. It was winter back home but, here in Australia, it was the middle of summer. Snow leopards do not live in Australia. They belong to the mountains of the Himalayas. Australia was the land of kangaroos, wallabies, kookaburras, koala bears and other indigenous species.

The schedule was going to be busy; over twenty schools across Australia would be visited from Queensland to New South Wales to here in Western Australia. Anjala and her brother would face the students and through an interpreter explain how their snow leopard, Heaven, and her cub, who survive on the edge of life, had been saved/rescued from the hands of the village elders as a result of putting in place a more effective early warning system, notifying the villages as to Heaven's whereabouts within the vicinity. This would ensure an appropriate course of action was taken to scare her off as opposed to killing her. Better fences had been built around the villages. Anjala explained at each school that the initial money to put the necessary defences in place came from the TV company who had organised their trip here. Money to maintain the programme would come from tourists, who were eager to learn about the ways and lives of the snow leopard and prepared to pay for organised tours run by the villagers. Rajesh went on to say killing the leopards to protect the village livestock would have a knock-on effect; no snow leopards, no tourists, no income. Anjala continued the theme, saying this simple and effective programme can be adapted to protecting and rescuing other threatened wildlife in the world. To protect or rescue our wildlife from extinction you have to address the local issues that are the root causes in bringing about the decline in some of our wildlife populations. Poverty is one of the underlying factors; if your livelihood is being threatened by the natural world that exists around you, it isn't unreasonable for that community to take whatever measures it needs to protect itself, and that very often means the demise of the local wildlife. A wild animal protecting its food source would do exactly the same. There is no point tutting at the TV from the comfort of your own home condemning others who live desperate, precarious lives; you have to understand their situation and solve those issues before you can instigate a suitable programme to ensure endangered species like our snow leopard, Heaven, stand a chance of surviving this cut-throat rat race of a world we live in.

The schools Anjala and Rajesh visited were quite receptive to what they had to say; some of the schools had begun adopting their own individual projects to support the wildlife in their local area. Briefly Anjala and Rajesh had become mini celebs, as TV companies and newspapers phoned asking for interviews and inviting them into their studios. They had caught the attention of the Australian media and the short spell of being in the public limelight was powerful and exciting. The chat show hosts and the newspaper hacks were genuinely interested in their story. All the talks they had given had been well-documented and a mini TV series that tracked their every move over the last few weeks would be screened to the various world networks in a few months' time. Hopefully their story will have an impact and start to make other children around the world stop and think about the environment around them and what they could do. You never know; young teenagers from around the globe just might lift their heads from the contents of their smartphones and look to see what is happening around them. For Anjala and Rajesh, seeing new parts of the world and being newfound celebs had certainly opened their eyes and the thought of making new documentaries about the plight of the planet's wildlife in other parts of the world was enticing. Anjala could envisage herself being a social media superstar like Kim Kardashian! Wow, wouldn't she be rich! No more poverty and having to live in a tin hut with a blue corrugated roof, twelve thousand feet up a cold Himalayan mountain. But for the time being it was the long flight home.

The arrivals lounge at Tribhuvan Airport on the outskirts of Kathmandu was crowded with paparazzi. Emerging from customs via the sliding doors, Anjala and Rajesh were greeted by a wall of flashing photographers and news hacks thrusting microphones in their faces. Their story had gone viral. Rajesh was overwhelmed with all the media attention, but Anjala was only just getting started with a new life she was beginning to relish. Their mother was at the far end of the arrivals hall – the look on her face didn't exactly exude a glow of joy, quite the opposite in fact. The words back to school tomorrow for you two, uttered by her mother as they got into a waiting taxi, kind of brought Anjala back to reality; her fledgling career of being a world superstar just might have to be put on the back burner for a while. But not for long; she would work on her strategy over the next few weeks.

HAMISH

The school summer holidays in Scotland were drawing to an end; Hamish and his friends Ceardach and Niall had spent the last remaining days up in the moorlands tracking the red deer. They had built a small hideout from local stones, which they had managed to scavenge from the dry stone builders' yard at the end of the village. The hidey-hole was a perfect watchtower, particularly as they had managed to blend it into the natural surroundings by throwing purple heather and fallen tree branches from the nearby forest over the top.

Hamish had become attached to a magnificent fourteen pointer stag, which he named Rufus; this was a royal stag getting ready for probably his last autumn rut. Ceardach's mother had told them that any stag with more than twelve points on his antlers was deemed a royal stag and would be a highly prized trophy for the deer stalkers.

The late warm summer days attracted the horrible biting midges and staying in the hideout was uncomfortable, so Hamish and his friends often spent their time playing on the open moorland in full view of Rufus and his hinds. Taking turns to play Laird of the Manor was a favourite pasttime, but often ended up in a glorious fight as each vied to be the Laird and boss the others around. The great stag would watch the goings-on from a safe distance, but as the days went by he encroached ever nearer. Hamish and his friends got more excited as the big stag came closer to them. Ceardach had worked out that Rufus had become accustomed to their presence and didn't see them as a threat.

Niall's father was the estates manager for the local highland estate and on several occasions that summer he had spent the day following in his father's footsteps around the farm; he knew where the feedstock and estate machinery were kept and which drawer in his father's office the various keys to the outbuildings were kept. A thought occurred to him – putting feed out around the hideout would attract the stag, and that in turn would score him brownie points with Hamish and Ceardach, but first he needed to get his hands on the keys. He knew stealing the keys for a few hours would raise suspicion, but if he could get an imprint of the required key by pressing it into some Plasticine, that would solve the matter. All he had to do was bide his time and wait for an opportune moment. The ideal occasion arose one afternoon when the estate gillie accidentally dropped a bunch of keys on the office floor. Niall recognised the feed store key instantly; dashing across the office he grabbed the keys, turning to face the wall so nobody could see what he was up to. Taking the plasticine from his top pocket he quickly made an impression before turning to face the estate gillie and hand the keys back, making it look like he was being helpful. With the key imprint he dashed out of the office door.

"Where are you going, Niall?" shouted Miss

Turner, one of the estate office clerks.

"I'll be back shortly."

"You better, your father has asked us to look after you."

With that statement ringing in his ears, Niall was off to see the local village locksmith.

"I'm back, Miss Turner."

"Thank goodness for that, your father has told us all off for letting you go."

"Don't worry about that, Miss Turner, I'll tell him it was my fault and that I was in a rebellious mood. He'll believe that."

"What's in the bag, Niall?" enquired Hamish.

"Feedstock."

"Whatever for?" asked Ceardach.

Niall explained his reasoning and how he got access to the feed shed.

"Niall, you are a genius." screamed Hamish.

Brownie points at last, thought Niall.

"Quick march." barked Hamish and, with that order, all three headed off to the hideout.

Hamish couldn't get over Niall's ingenuity; the rutting season started in a few weeks and Rufus would need all the food source he could get to make sure he had enough energy to sustain him in the forthcoming fights he would face to protect his harem of hinds from other stags and get mating access to the hinds.

Ceardach knew that the ideal opportunity to observe the deer feeding would be early dawn. With this fact in mind, Hamish and his friends set their alarm clocks for early the next morning.

The sight that greeted them as they approached the hidey-hole was a dream to behold. There in the swirl of the morning mist, in amongst the hinds, was Rufus the royal stag. As the boys approached Rufus cautiously stepped forward, as if to protect the hinds. Hamish walked towards him. His heart was pounding; for a split second he thought his heart would burst. The great stag sniffed at the boys. Niall quietly bent down and scraped a few pellets into his hands, and with quivering arms he reached out to Rufus. To all of their amazement Rufus stepped forward and delicately nibbled at the feed in Niall's hand. Hamish could not believe his eyes; this magnificent royal stag he had named Rufus was standing directly in front of him. He stared at his antlers and counted all fourteen points. He reached out to touch Rufus and as he did so the great stag lowered his head and all three boys were able to stroke his antlers. At that moment one of the hinds gave the alarm call and within an instant the whole herd disappeared into the morning mist.

"Wow!" said Ceardach.

Hamish swiftly turned to his friends. "We must not tell anyone about this."

As they returned to the village, only Mrs Mackay, the proprietor of the village store and Post Office, spotted the boys. "Where have you three been at this hour of the morning?"

"Oh, out for a walk, Mrs Mackay," spluttered Hamish.

"A likely story indeed, Hamish McTuff. Does

your mother know that you have been out on the moor this hour of the morning?"

"Ohoooo."

"I'll take that as a no, Hamish. Well, there is fresh bread and jam on the table in the back room; go on in and have some breakfast, all of you. You look as if you've all seen a ghost. A good mug of tea will put the colour back in all of your cheeks."

Ceardach picked up the local morning paper that was on the table next to the large brown teapot. The headlines read: *'Millionaire Businessman finds Royal Stag.'* With horror he read on; an organised shoot on the nearby highland estate for corporate companies from London had attracted many wealthy clients. The shoot was starting today; many of the clients had already been out on the moors with the local gamekeepers over the past few days establishing their prime positions.

The boys looked at each other; they knew Rufus was an old stag past his best and under the culling guidelines for the stags at this time of the year he would be a prized trophy. His hinds would be safe from the stalker's guns, as it was out of season for them. They had to think fast. Niall had an idea; his father had an old quad bike that was kept in the shed at the bottom of their garden. He knew where the keys would be, plus having been taught to drive it by his older brother without his parent's knowledge at the age of ten last year just might come in useful at this precise moment. Having polished off Mrs Mackay's offered breakfast, leaving only crumbs and a thin layer of jam at the bottom of the jar, they snuck out the back door with a plan in place.

Hamish and Ceardach would head straight back to the hideout; while Niall would get his father's quad bike and meet them there shortly.

Hamish stopped halfway down the road.

"Now what are we stopping for?" asked Ceardach.

"Never mind, go to the hidey-hole," snapped Hamish as he retraced his tracks and headed home. As he sprinted up the last fifty metres of the dirt track that led to his front door, Hamish frantically tried to remember the safe combinations; he looked at the keypad on his smartphone and tried to envisage the codes he had seen on a tatty piece of paper with his father's scribbled handwriting on. Hamish had discreetly watched his father key in the new codes the other night as he placed a medium-sized dark grey plastic case in it. The safe was one of the old cast-iron affairs and sat in the corner of his father's study, which was at the far end of the outbuilding at the back of the house. The key to the study was always kept under a loose floorboard in the spare bedroom. Hamish's father had made it perfectly clear on numerous occasions to him and his mother that neither of them should go in there under any circumstances. That was his father's territory. His father was a Major in the armed services seconded to reconnaissance duties for the past twelve months; the missions he went on were top secret and, judging by the winter clothing that was piled up in the utility room,

Hamish and his mother had surmised that his last mission, which he had returned from the other night, was Russia.

At breakfast yesterday morning, his father took an urgent call; his briefcase was on the table and as he got up to take the call he closed the lid down but didn't shut the case completely. Hamish sneaked around the kitchen table and, slowly lifting the lid, peeked in to his father's briefcase. On top was a Military & Government brochure about a SkyRanger, a top of the range model. To Hamish this was a super drone or Quad copter; whatever the difference, if there was such a difference. Wow, he thought!! He'd love to have a go on that; his own Quad copter/drone his father bought him last year was a quality model but nowhere near as sophisticated as the one in his father's safe. His he operated from an app on his smartphone; tilting the phone would alter the flight path of the drone. Hamish was intrigued as to how this super drone worked; reaching across the table for his iPhone he quickly photographed the brochure. He felt like an international spy photographing top classified documents. He was careful to make sure the brochure was in exactly the same position as he placed it back in his father's briefcase as it was when he lifted it out; his father, being a military man, had an acute sense of attention to detail and would notice the brochure had been tampered with straight away and he would be severally reprimanded, punished by means of a week's grounding with no access to his laptop or phone.

Every young person's nightmare.

Hamish cast a cursory glance at the SkyRanger's specs; he was amazed to see that the flight time was up to fifty minutes and that it would stay airborne in gusty wind speeds of up to fifty miles per hour and that it could ascend up to an altitude of fifteen hundred feet with a beyond line-of-sight range of three miles. Usual facts, he thought. He looked at how easy and fast it was to assemble and was suitably impressed with its ability to take off and land vertically. Getting used to the intuitive interface pad that controlled and directed the drone would take a little time to master, but with plenty of practise he could soon overcome those issues. If only he could get his greedy, grubby little hands on it.

Hamish looked at the most recent messages on his phone; among them was a message from his mother saying that she and his father had gone to Aberdeen to do some shopping and would be back later in the afternoon. Hamish punched the air. "Yessss." He scrambled up the stairs and headed straight for the spare room; lifting the floorboard up, he lay flat on the floor and with his right arm he fumbled his way around under the floor, searching for the key. With the key in his hand and the loose floorboard put back in place he raced down the stairs, missing the odd step as he went along. Tearing across the garden he reached his father's study. Ben, the family's border collie, who was tethered to a nearby post, just looked on with amazement written in his eyes – he had never seen Hamish move with such speed and urgency. Hamish crouched down to the safe; he was reasonably confident that he knew the code to the top combination, and he knew the small keys to the combination locks were in the small red tin cashbox that sat on the top shelf, and the key to that box was at the bottom of the blue tin mug that had all his father's pens and pencils in next to the twenty seven inch screen iMac. Scrambling both combination locks, he lined the zero on both dials to the red line on the outer circumference. Working the top combination first he twisted the dial in an anticlockwise movement, stopping at the right number on the fifth turn; twisting the dial in an alternating fashion between anticlockwise and clockwise movements he stopped at the last number. If the code was right, with a further alternate twist, the dial would lock into position. With bated breath he gave a final twist of the dial, and mercifully it clicked into the locked position. Now for the bottom combination; this was going to take some huge imagination and thinking. He would have to get into his father's mind-set. The small clock that hung on the study back wall showed the time as 10am – time was against him, the others would be wondering where he was. He made several attempts but the dial was not locking into position after the last number. Ben's barking was starting to annoy him, but something jogged his memory... Ben the dog! Why did his father ask his mother the other night for Ben's full date of birth and age? Hmm... he thought. He scrambled the dial for the last time, resetting to zero, and put Ben's information in. With a huge sigh of relief the dial locked into position; turning the handle down he pulled the safe door open and there was the SkyRanger.

Ceardach's face as Hamish tipped the contents of the grey plastic case all over the place was one of utter disbelief.

"What the heck is that?"

"It's a flying saucer! What do you think it is?"

"I don't know."

"It's a drone."

"Where did you get that from?"

"It's my father's! Never mind where it came from, Ceardach."

"I take it he knows nothing about this little jaunt of yours?"

"Course he doesn't."

"What are you going to do with it, Hamish?"

"Watch."

Hamish looked down the glen as he assembled the drone, paying careful attention to the minutest detail in the instruction manual that was in a buttoned sleeve on the inside of the case's lid. Speed was vital, as he could see the cars bringing the deer stalkers winding their way up the mountainside. Soon they would be in position and the shoot would be on.

Niall quickly sped up the glen; as agreed, Hamish would stay at the watchtower with the drone scouting the area. Ceardach would ride with Niall; with one hand around Niall's waist for supposed safety and clutching a walkie-talkie in the other, the pair set off, riding roughshod across the moor, waiting for Hamish's instruction.

Hamish tapped the screen on the tablet's interface, launching the drone vertically up to a thousand feet; he anxiously scanned the glen, sending the drone in numerous directions. It wasn't long before he could see Rufus on the screen; his stag was high on the opposing ridge. Tapping the tablet, Hamish sent the SkyRanger meandering down the glen. With pinpoint accuracy he could see the deerstalkers rapidly closing in on Rufus. He screamed into the walkie-talkie Niall had thrown at him a few moments ago, with Rufus' precise coordinates. Whipping out his smartphone, he took a picture of the image that was on the tablet's interface and sent an Instragam photo to Ceardach's phone along with a text message, as the message would create a ping and just might get Ceardach's attention above the noise of the quad bike's engine. Strangely enough Ceardach felt his phone vibrate in his pocket; hanging on for dear life to Niall with his left hand he reached into his top left hand pocket with his right hand. He glimpsed at the text and the Instagram photo; yelling at Niall at the top of his voice he screamed to stop for a moment. With the quad coming to an abrupt halt Ceardach shoved his phone in Niall's face. Both of them looked at the picture and instantly recognised the ridge. Like Hamish, they knew the glen like the back of their hands, the shortcuts and the pitfalls to avoid, but so did the gamekeepers escorting the deer stalkers. Ceardach could see Rufus in the distance; he goaded Niall to push the bike to its limit, but it was no use. The deer stalkers, with the estate's faster quads, had the advantage and soon they would be in position with their high velocity rifles to take aim and claim Rufus as a prized victory. The gamekeepers and the estate would receive their money. Niall snatched Ceardach's phone and sent a text message to Hamish. *'Buzz the herd with the drone. Scare them, but make sure you send them scattering up the glen on to the next estate. If Rufus is on the next Laird's land the gamekeepers will have no authority to follow.'*

A narrow, well-trodden track that the deer used to crisscross the purple and white heather lay to Niall and Ceardach's left. It was the quickest path to the stag, but they would have to continue their venture by foot. As they raced along the beaten track they began to scream and shout, waving their arms about in the vain attempt of spooking the deer. The trick had worked but unfortunately the panicked herd, with Rufus in the fore, headed down the glen in the wrong direction. The images the SkyRanger was sending back to the tablet in Hamish's hand were not encouraging; having sent the drone down the glen tracking the deer stalkers, he could see that they were all well-camouflaged and embedded in the moorland vegetation and that the gamekeepers were clearly agitated as their game plan, that had being meticulously worked upon over the recent days, had gone seriously awry. Hamish had picked up Niall's message – sweeping the drone back towards the panicked herd that was hurtling down the glen he dropped the SkyRanger's height to five feet. Encircling Rufus with the Quad copter appeared to temporarily confuse him – it did halt him in his tracks – but that wouldn't be for long. Hamish shouted at the top of his voice for Rufus to turn and head back up the glen, not that yelling would achieve much, as they were over half a mile apart, but it made him feel better.

All three boys had been well-versed by their fathers about the hazards of the outdoor life here on the highland moors, and that being fully prepared for all eventualities was not only wise but also vital. The Scottish highland weather had many moods and some of them were not pleasant. Niall reached into his rucksack that was on Ceardach's back. At the bottom, underneath his waterproof and torch, were the two red flares he had stolen from the estate's store room. Hamish could see that Rufus was standing still, as if transfixed to the ground; this was not a good position to be in nor was it part of the intended plan, as a stationary stag was a dead stag. Looking at the tablet's screen he tapped it, sending the drone back up in to the air, as it was apparent to Hamish that the SkyRanger buzzing around Rufus's head was not having the desired effect – quite the opposite in fact. The crack of a rifle reverberated across the glen. Hamish's heart sank but as he looked up he saw, to his horror, the SkyRanger imploding into the atmosphere, sending shards of debris into the azure sky. Two flares soared high across the glen, their red vapour trails crisscrossing the distant skyline as they continued their journey to nowhere. Hamish could only assume that one of his friends must have released the flares to scare Rufus and his hinds back to the ridge and in the direction of the next estate, where they would be safe as the gamekeepers and the trophy hunters had no licence to cull there.

The three boys had accomplished what they had set out to do, but the consequences of their actions would no doubt be swift and harsh. They would have to face the wrath of the estate managers and gamekeepers, whose pay would be less than expected. The royal stag had escaped their clutches.

For Niall, he would have to face his father for stealing the flares, the quad bike and embarrassing him in front of his wealthy clients that would have paid handsomely for this day's shoot; no doubt they would be looking for some kind of compensation that would cost the estate dearly.

As for Hamish, well, he had saved his fourteen pointer royal stag that he had got to know over the last few summer months. How he was going to justify his actions to his father he had no idea, nor was he looking forward to that conversation. The SkyRanger was military property; no doubt his father would have to face his bosses to give some kind of an explanation as to how military equipment entrusted into his care was utterly destroyed. Hamish was not looking forward to the punishment his father would no doubt mete out. Nevertheless, he had achieved his goal.

CHARLIE

Charlie looked out from his small attic bedroom window; he could see all the children from the street where he lived playing in the snow. He longed to join them, but the doctors had told him that his latest operation to rid the tumour that was wrapped around the base of his spine would take months of recuperation. A small red-breasted robin crash-landed on the windowsill, scratching at the snow to get at the last remaining seeds Charlie had put out that morning. As fast as the robin had appeared from the mists of nowhere he vanished; but not without a cheeky stare at the small boy on the other side of the windowpane as if to say, *'Thanks for the food mate.'* Charlie thought to himself; wow, wouldn't it be great to fly.

A knock at the front door of the house distracted Charlie for a few seconds; he could hear the voices of his best friends Peter, Ben and Rebecca in the hallway. His crutches were propped against the small bedside locker. A small photograph sat on top of the locker was recent; his dad had taken it in the park. It was a photo of himself and his friends the day before he went into hospital. His friends had signed the back of the frame: *'To Charlie, all our love Peter, Ben and Rebecca.'*

The clattering of his friends coming up the stairs reverberated around the whole house; normally they would all sit and play computer games, but today was different. It had snowed for the first time and it was proper snow. Peter threw Charlie his crutches while Ben looked out of the attic window.

"Guys, let's go tobogganing. Look, everybody is out on the park having fun."

The prospect of playing in the snow had excited them all, but a nagging thought crossed Charlie's mind. The doctors had told his parents to keep him safe from any winter colds, as his immune system was low from the operation and the subsequent chemo treatment he had endured over the last few weeks. He was fed up with sitting at home day after day while his friends went to school; he desperately wanted to go out in the snow and have some enjoyment in his life for a change. He knew his mother and father would disapprove; their answer would be *'Another day, son.'* Looking up at the window the little red-breasted robin had returned and was hopping on and off the windowsill; each time he landed he tapped the window with his beak as if to say, *'Come on Charlie, come out to play.'*

At that precise moment Charlie had made up his mind. He was going to venture out with his friends today. He knew that the snow would only be around for a couple of days before it turned to slush, and that his friends would be extremely disappointed having missed the opportunity to have fun in the snow. They wouldn't go unless he was with them. But: how to get past Charlie's mother?

Rebecca had an idea.

"I know! I'll phone my mum and tell her that Charlie's mother wants to meet for coffee as she has had some new ideas for the nearly new clothes shop they're thinking of opening. That should distract both of them for a few hours; they won't even notice we've gone."

Great idea, thought Ben; plan A was up and running.

Peter and Ben helped Charlie down the stairs while Rebecca checked to see that her mum and Charlie's were fully engrossed in the sitting room, discussing the new shop plans over two flat white coffees. Thumbs up gave the all clear for Peter and Ben to support Charlie down the remaining steps. Charlie got a fit of the giggles; this was the most excitement he had had in days. Ben elbowed Charlie in the ribs, at the same time whispering in his right ear to shut up.

Rebecca opened the cupboard door that was under the stairs, pulling Charlie's coat and scarf off the peg; his gloves had been stuffed into his pockets. Peter got the wheelchair which the hospital had loaned the family; it was next to the French windows in the dining room. Within minutes Charlie was kitted out for a snow adventure.

Charlie's house backed on to the park. The little gate at the bottom of the garden leading to the park was a bit of a rickety affair, but there, sitting on the post, was the small red-breasted robin observing the entire goings-on. The snow covering the garden path was proving difficult for Charlie to manage in his chair. Ben remembered his dad had chopped up some bits of wood for the old kitchen

Aga; in amongst the pile there were two small planks ideal for wooden skis.

"Where are you going, Ben?" shouted Peter.

"Back in a minute," mumbled Ben as he dashed across the park to his house.

The planks of wood were propped against the garage wall. Searching around he soon found some old rope and, looking up at his dad's tools that neatly hung on the wall, he saw the hammer and next to it on a small shelf his dad's red biscuit tin full of odd screws and nails. With all the clobber neatly tucked under his arms, he raced back across the park to Charlie's.

"What are you doing, Ben?" asked Charlie.

"Watch."

Charlie got out of his chair and, within a matter of moments Ben had converted the wheelchair into a supercharged sledge with the planks of wood acting as the runners. Ben had carefully threaded the rope through the wheel spokes and around the pieces of wood before finally nailing the rope to the planks for added support.

Rebecca was impressed with Ben's masterpiece; she leant towards him and gave him a little kiss on the cheek to say well done. Ben's blush didn't go unnoticed. Charlie and Peter simply giggled as Ben tried to hide his face in his gloves.

Kitted and booted out, the gang of four headed for the park. Hours of fun followed as Peter, Ben and Rebecca took it in turn to push Charlie in his newly converted sledge up the park slopes, jumping on him as the chair freely glided down the slopes in chase of the other children's toboggans. Tumbling out of his chair with whoever was sitting on his lap as they precariously careered down the slopes was exhilarating and fun. With all the thrills and spills no one had noticed the time; even the little red robin that was flying high above them was preoccupied with all the activity that was taking place below him.

The shrill voices of Charlie and Rebecca's mothers shouting their names from the top of the hill brought the day's proceedings to an abrupt end. Charlie looked at his friends and said, "I'm in for it now. I will say it was my idea and take the blame, but thank you so much. I haven't had so much fun in a day for a long time. I miss you all when you are at school and I'm stuck at home."

The retribution was swift; once home Charlie was banished to his room. He tried explaining to his mother that it was his decision to go out and not his friends', but she was not in the mood to listen to his story. She was angry with him and he knew why. Getting a cold, for him, was a serious matter.

Charlie looked out of his small attic window; the last of the daylight was disappearing and the man in the moon was already up in the sky. Waving goodnight to the little robin, still sitting on the gatepost as if he was keeping watch, he pulled his Doctor Who curtains to shut out the rest of the world. He had enjoyed a great day with his friends. This day would stay long in his memory, be it short or long; how long? Well, that would depend on how well the cancer responded to the treatment... For a nine-year-old boy he had a positive outlook on life. He knew he was seriously ill, and that his time on this planet might be shorter than his friends. But today was a great day and had put him in a better mood; ready to face the challenges ahead.

EPHRAIM

The thin, wispy clouds that sat high above the ancient city of Jerusalem would soon dissipate as the autumn sun worked its magic, leaving a wonderful bright clear day, exceptional for this time of the year being September. For Ephraim and his Palestinian friend Ameer it would be a good business day. The early city walls that had protected the old quarter of Jerusalem for centuries against its many enemies still dominated the neighbourhood. The eight interspersed gates that allowed access to the various quarters of the old city were all aptly named, and possibly the most renowned was The Damascus Gate.

The steps down to The Damascus Gate were crowded; being Sunday it was neither the Jewish Sabbath nor the Muslim day of prayer. A young Arab woman and her daughter had commandeered some of the steps with a huge display of designer trainers; next to them was an elderly Arab gentleman selling a variety of coloured scarves all neatly displayed on a small wooden trolley. The morning was cold as Ephraim set out to the bakery to pick up his and Ameer's bread order. The warmth of the ovens and the smell of the different breads at the bakery as they came out of the fire holes, a term Ameer had given the baker's ovens, always put a smile on Ephraim's face as he entered. With the exact amount of Israeli shekels Ephraim paid for the order and asked for the delivery to be sent to his and Ameer's stall at The Damascus Gate on time and within the hour. The young lad that sat across the cash desk briefly looked up from his paperwork, and with a cursory glance of his eyes stared at Ephraim before returning back to his papers spread all over the desk.

"I'll take that look as a yes, shall I?"

"Take it whatever way you want, sir!"

Ephraim shrugged his shoulders and rolled his eyes as he left. His smartphone that was in the left inside pocket of his coat pinged; the text message was from Ameer. It simply read; '*Still waiting at the checkpoint at The Wall of Separation.*'

It was a strange friendship Ephraim and Ameer had, as it was unusual for a young Jewish boy and a Palestinian Arab boy to talk to each other, let alone become friends. They met two years ago at The Wall of Separation following Ameer's beating at the hands off Ephraim's classmates, who had picked on Ameer for being an Arab. The beating was an act of retaliation for the Jewish children that had been killed in the latest suicide bomber's attack. Their friendship developed as they had a common aim; to prove to their families and friends that a Jew and an Arab can live side by side. What they needed to do was to find common ground and work at those areas. Differences they simply needed to accept and respect.

The little bread stall that Ephraim and Ameer owned offered both Jewish and Arab breads, bagels, challah, saj and pitta breads. Their customers were the thousands of pilgrims and tourists from all differing religions coming to the old city on a daily basis to visit the holy places of Jerusalem; The Temple Mount with The Dome of the Rock and its gold roof, The Al Aqsa Mosque, The Holy Sepulchre, The Via Dolorosa and The Western Wall that was once known as The Wailing Wall. Trade was brisk that morning as the security forces would soon be closing the roads for security reasons, as world leaders gathered for the state funeral of Shimon Peres, a former President and Prime Minister of Israel, a man viewed by many as a visionary of peace. The little paper bags that they wrapped the breads in had a message on the back:

'Ephraim and Ameer are friends; we are a Jew and an Arab showing the world that Jews and Arabs can live and work side by side. www.ephraimameer.com.'

It was just before 10am when the Israeli Military started to clear the market area around The Damascus Gate in preparation for tomorrow's state funeral. As they started to pack away what was left, Ameer looked up and nudged Ephraim; in front of them stood two tall gentlemen in smart suits, highly polished shoes and dark sunglasses. They spoke with American accents. Ephraim noticed that they were armed; guns he was used to, being brought up in Jerusalem, as it was normal to see the armed military patrol the streets. It was Ameer that worked it out.

"You're The President of the USA's secret service bodyguards checking the area out for tomorrow's state funeral, aren't you?"

"Smart guy. No comment."

The two secret service guys chewed on the bagels

they had just bought as they wandered off to look at the old Arab gentleman's stall. Ephraim shouted at them before they disappeared through The Damascus Gate entering the Arab quarter.

"Get The President to contact us, all our details are on the website which is on the back of the bags."

Ameer looked at Ephraim.

"Do you seriously think The President of the USA is going to call you?"

"Who knows?"

With the market closed for the rest of the day, the two boys headed home. For Ephraim it would be a short bus ride, but for Ameer, he would have to queue again at the checkpoint at The Wall of Separation. His small hometown of Abu Dis was a Palestinian town in East Jerusalem, and for him the daily journey to school and meeting up with Ephraim meant he had to go through the wall both in the morning and in the evening with his ID papers. The wall was about eight metres in height and was constructed by the Israeli Government around 2002, with the sole purpose of protecting Israel from suicide bombers and acts of terrorism. While it had reduced the number of terror attacks on the Jewish population, it had equally made life more difficult for Ameer and his family, as their right of free movement had been restricted. Sometimes it would take Ameer and his brothers hours to cross the checkpoints depending on the time of the day. What was always interesting was to see the latest graffiti that had been daubed on the concrete wall.

The queue to get through the wall was busy, as everybody was leaving the city as the security forces took control of the area. Ameer looked at his phone as a new message appeared; *'Don't forget my Bar Mitzvah this Thursday. I know my parents won't make you welcome, but I want you there as my friend. Let's show my family not every Arab is their enemy and we can live and work together. Be at The Dung Gate at The Western Wall at 11am.'* Ameer Googled 'Bar Mitzvah'. A Jewish celebration for a thirteen-year old Jewish boy, who becomes responsible for observing the commandments. *'Wow,'* thought Ameer. Ameer replied. *'No problem see you there.'*

Ameer had barely got home when his phone rang; Ephraim was excited. He had received a reply from the American secret service guys; he needed to be along the route near Mount Herzl Cemetery early tomorrow morning. Ameer knew that the checkpoints would be closed and that he wouldn't be able to cross to west Jerusalem until Thursday, so he told Ephraim to make a placard with their names and contact details on. Having put his phone down Ameer began to have second thoughts. He was the brain, the academic out of the two of them; Ephraim was the business entrepreneur. He could envisage Ephraim scribbling a quick note down along the lines of, *'Mr Pres call us.'* The message needed to be brief and to the point. Twenty minutes later Ameer had come up with a simple effective line; he texted Ephraim *'Jew & Arab can live together. www.*

ephraimameer.com. Don't forget to take a photo!'

The following day was a beautiful autumnal day; the odd leaf or two on the trees that lined the streets of West Jerusalem had started to turn a golden brown as the trees prepared for winter. Thousands lined the cortege route; some people had camped out overnight so as to get a good vantage point. Ephraim had managed to push and bully himself to the railings, leaving those around him annoyed and extremely disgruntled, but he didn't care – he was on a mission. As the Presidential motorcade approached he bent down and picked up the rather large, crudely made placard and hoisted it up as far as he could reach. As the Presidential cavalcade passed Ephraim noticed a hand with a thumbs up gesture appear from one of the back windows that was slightly wound down; deep down he knew that President Obama had seen him. One of the secret service guys who was walking beside the car protecting the President gave a cursory glance in Ephraim's direction; a quick wink of his left eye confirmed the message had been noted.

In all the excitement Ephraim had nearly forgotten what Ameer had said about getting a photo; he dropped the placard and, scrambling around in his pockets, he grabbed his phone and got a shot of The President as he stepped out of his armour plated car. Ephraim immediately put the picture on Instagram for all his followers to see; unfortunately he was totally oblivious to the anger of the two teenage lads that were standing beside him as the jagged edges of the cheap plywood he had used to make the placard had gashed their legs. A scuffle broke out and punches were thrown. Ephraim had managed to knock one of the youths to the floor with a good right hook to the chin; within moments the military soldiers had yanked all three lads out of the crowd and thrown them in the back of a nearby police van to cool down. His mother was going to be furious with him; his Bar Mitzvah celebration was a few days away and by then all the cuts and bruises he had sustained here would be nicely matured to spoil the family pictures. His mother was going to kill him.

It was Thursday, the day of Ephraim's celebration, and Ameer was at The Dung Gate that led to The Western Wall at 11am as instructed. Ephraim in all his finery had scrubbed up quite well, despite the left black eye, nicely coloured in an array of dazzling purples, blues, yellows and greens.

"What happened to you?"

Ephraim looked at Ameer, "Don't ask."

"Have you told your parents I'm here?"

"Not quite."

"Great!"

"Well, in a roundabout way, they suspected you would show up."

"You're such a mup-head at times, Ephraim."

"Oh, take a chill pill, Ameer."

The area around The Western Wall thronged with thousands of visitors from all over the world. The queues to get through the strict airport-like security to get to the wall and The Temple Mount above it were back to the main street; those that had arrived late would be queuing for hours. Ephraim looked resplendent in his traditional Jewish attire, Kippah (skull hat), Tallit (prayer shawl) and Tefillin (small leather boxes). Ameer had taken the time to look up on the Internet to see what the significance was of the two leather boxes that the Jews strapped to their arm and heads. Ameer's understanding was that they held handwritten parchments with texts from four passages of the Torah.

Entering the men's section of the paved area that led up to the wall, Ephraim pointed to a stand that had boxes of free paper Kippahs, hinting at Ameer to put one on otherwise he would not be allowed in. Ameer discreetly placed himself apart from Ephraim and his family while the religious rituals were being carried out; he could feel his presence was creating an atmospheric tension, for not all the family were keen on Ephraim's decision to invite him. With the customs and rituals over, Ephraim glanced over his shoulder to see where Ameer was. Spotting him in the crowd sitting on a white plastic chair, he beckoned him over. Ameer hugged Ephraim and whispered congratulations in his ear; whether that was the right thing to say or not he was unsure, but that was what he had decided to say on the way here and he was going to stick with his decision. Ameer had scribbled a small prayer on a piece of paper, asking for peace throughout the world between all Jewish and Arab communities wherever they lived; Ameer had already signed it.

Ephraim read the note and, reaching for his pen that was in his inside jacket pocket, he added his signature. Together they approached the wall to which the Jewish community attached so much significance and stuffed the paper into one of the many crevices that littered the wall. As they placed the paper into the wall with their right hands, they pressed their left hands up against the wall, saying out loud the prayer that was written on the note. As both boys walked away from the wall, Ephraim's phone pinged. Ephraim looked at the message.

'The President of the United States of America would like to invite you and your friend Ameer to a private audience with himself at The White House. Please call the American Embassy in Tel Aviv on the number below to make the necessary arrangements.'

The two boys looked at the message over and over again in utter disbelief. Ephraim showed the message to his father, having explained about the secret service agents and the placard he had held aloft as the presidential motorcade swept passed him the other day. Ephraim's father was furious Ephraim had kept the last few days' activities to himself and now one of the most powerful men in the world wanted to meet his son and his best friend. What annoyed him the most was the fact his son had an appointment with The President of the United States of America and he, a senior investigative journalist for an international news corporation who travelled all over the world reporting on all kinds of global issues, had never received a request to attend The White House despite numerous requests. His own son and his Arab friend had upstaged him. Furthermore he might understand world affairs but he clearly had no idea what was going on in his own household; that he would address once Ephraim's Bar Mitzvah celebrations had finished.

Ameer sat with Ephraim's father; he opened up his laptop and went through the website that he and Ephraim had developed. All the events they had organised, like the boys' football matches after school between the local Palestinian and Jewish lads, and how he and Ephraim would go to local youth groups on both sides of The Wall of Separation talking about the small ways everyone can play their part in bringing about a safer, more peaceful neighbourhood. Ephraim showed his father the chat room site they had set up with help from friends and how hundreds of Palestinian and Jewish teenagers were talking to each other and learning how to respect their cultural differences and to take the positives from all situations.

"Why didn't you tell me about all this, Ephraim?"

"You're never here."

"What about your mother, Ephraim; did she know what you were up to?"

"No, because her attitude is we should not talk to those Arabs. They are not to be trusted."

"Ameer, what about your parents, do they…" But before Ephraim's father could finish his sentence, Ameer had cut across him. "No, is the answer to your question; they see you Jews as the problem here. You create all the divisions and make life hard for the average Arab here in Jerusalem, and you blame us for all the troubles."

Several weeks had passed and with all the preparations in place EL-AL flight LY001 from Tel Aviv touched down at New York's (JFK) International Airport. Terminal 4, as expected, was busy. American homeland security and passport control took forever. The American Embassy in Tel Aviv had taken care of all the paperwork, particularly Ameer and his father's documents, as they were Palestinians domiciled in an Arab town in East Jerusalem. Ephraim's father had worked closely with the American officials as to the timing and details of that all-important meeting. The decision to fly to New York was Ephraim's father's, as neither his son nor Ameer had left the shores of Israel before. A few days taken out of his busy work schedule to spend time with his son and Ameer, getting to know all about their aspirations, he felt was time well spent, plus a few days break relaxing and revisiting the many sights of New York would do him good. It had been a long day for Ephraim and Ameer, leaving Jerusalem last evening, checking into Ben Gurion airport and taking off just after midnight Israeli time, followed by a twelve hour flight to landing at (JFK) New York at 6am local time. Neither Ephraim nor Ameer had slept much in the last twenty-four hours, for the excitement and the adrenaline that was buzzing through their veins was enough to keep them going. They were two young teenagers both aged thirteen with the rest of their lives ahead of them; rest and sleep were well off the agenda. Ephraim's father had booked them into his usual hotel on 56th St, Manhattan, between 5th and 6th Avenues. Two rooms had been booked at the back of the hotel on the 32nd floor so that they had views of Central Park. New York in late October for Ephraim's father was New York at its best. The parks and the tree-lined avenues would be decked in autumnal colours of bright oranges, scarlets and golds. The stifling heat of summer would have passed, giving way to gentler and more acceptable temperatures.

The café on the corner of 57th St and 5th Avenue was crowded; the waiter had shown them to a small table in the corner. Ameer scanned down the breakfast menu. He had never been given so much choice as to what to have for breakfast. Ephraim leaned over and suggested the pancakes. The waiter made a suggestion that the two of them should share the breakfast. Moments later the waiter returned with a pile of thick American pancakes stacked on top of each other, with scoops of vanilla and chocolate ice cream placed around the edge of the plate. Two small jugs of hot sticky sweet maple syrup were placed next to the plate with the stacked pancakes. Both Ephraim and Ameer couldn't wait to get started. Pouring the syrup everywhere and with forks at the ready, they dived in. For the next few minutes all you good hear from the two boys was *hmm…* and *aah…* as the syrup-soaked pancakes slipped down their throats. The itinerary for the next few days was packed, taking in Central Park, Time Square, Grand Central Station, New York's underground, The Empire State Building, Ground Zero, The Brooklyn Bridge, The Bronx, Queens and other districts along with The Statue of Liberty and other amazing venues. Dinner on the last night was to be on the 67th floor of The Rockefeller Centre with the night views across Manhattan to Queens and other areas all spectacularly lit up.

The '*Big Apple*' sure lived up to its name, but shortly Ephraim and Ameer would head off to Washington D.C. Penn St. station on 8th Avenue and West 31st St was incredibly busy; the early morning train heading for Washington D.C was packed with commuters and tourists alike. The train pulled out of Penn St. station on schedule; the three and half hour journey that would take Ephraim and Ameer through the States of Pennsylvania and Maryland would give them time to get their thoughts together before they met Mr Obama. Their appointment with The President was set for 4pm that afternoon.

It was a beautiful bright, sunny day in Washington D.C. The prearranged car that would take Ephraim and Ameer along with their fathers to The White House from their hotel was five minutes early. The short drive would take them past Arlington National Cemetery, The Pentagon, over the Potomac River, past The Lincoln Memorial and onto Constitution Ave NW, turning left onto 18th St NW and then right onto Pennsylvania Ave NW and right again onto The North Lawn of The White House.

Ephraim was a little anxious and nervous, but at the same time excited. Ameer was totally cool and relaxed and was looking forward to the meeting with the most powerful man in the world. The door of the great Oval Office opened; an elegant lady in her fifties wearing a bright red suit with smart grey shoes stood in the doorway. She smiled at Ephraim and Ameer as she guided them to the nearest settee.

"The President will be along shortly. He is looking forward to meeting you; may I say how smart you guys look. Oh, the President can only spare the allotted time of twenty minutes. He has a heavy work schedule today. After your meeting I have arranged for one of the house staff to show you round. It was nice meeting you boys."

"How do we address him?" asked Ameer.

"Ah…Mr President."

"Thank you, miss."

"No problem, young man."

With that, the elegant lady disappeared through the north-east door. Ameer had looked online about the history of The Oval Office. It had four doors – the east door opened onto The Rose Garden, the west door led to The President's private office, the north-west door opened onto the main corridor in the west wing and the north-east door linked The Oval Office to The President's private secretary's office. Ameer therefore deduced, rightly or wrongly, that the tall elegant lady was

The President's private secretary.

It was a strange feeling for both of them as they sat patiently in one of the most famous rooms in the world waiting for President Obama. The west door opened and The President strode in; Ephraim couldn't remember if he was to stand or remain seated as The President approached. His half attempted fumble of getting up to shake The President's hand looked awkward and clumsy and he felt embarrassed. Ameer on the other hand, always the more confident of the two, stood up straight away, shaking The President's hand with a firm grip.

"Sit down boys, I have to admit your approach to get my attention was a little unorthodox. But you know what guys? I thought, wow! When I think back to what I was doing at your age. I was kicking a ball around the streets; I wasn't trying to build bridges between two very different communities to bring harmony to the streets I walked. I didn't have any of the foresight that you guys have. When my protection officers told me about yourselves and the message on the back of the paper bags you wrap your breads up in and to look out for a pair of teenagers, I thought OK... I spotted your placard and read the message that was scribbled across it. I looked at your website and what you two were trying to achieve and I thought to myself, these guys are succeeding where numerous peace negotiations have failed. I want to meet these guys, so I got my secretary in there to get the ball rolling, and here you are. So tell me guys."

Ephraim explained it was his idea to try and get his classmates to try and understand that not every Arab was their enemy. For a while he had been thinking that wars and battles are not won by physical violence, but they are won by changing the minds and hearts of the warring sides. A spate of Palestinian suicide bombers a few years ago had rattled the Jewish community and any Arab was eyed as a potential threat. Ephraim went on to say how he had witnessed Ameer being beaten up by several of his classmates in retaliation for the Jewish children that had died and been hurt by the suicide bombers. Ameer wasn't responsible for what had happened, but unfortunately was in the wrong place at the wrong time and got the beating. He recalled following Ameer from a distance as he walked back to The Wall of Separation, noting which checkpoint he went through. On his way home he decided enough was enough and that he should do something to stop this. For the next few days he waited at the checkpoint looking for Ameer, and it was on the fifth day that he spotted him in the queue waiting to be processed through the wall. With an air of unease he approached and spoke to Ameer and asked if they could meet up.

Ameer took over the conversation and gave the rationale behind the little meetings they had for several weeks in a small café after school. He hatched the idea of the website and put it together with help from his older brother. Ephraim came up with the idea of selling the breads and what they made would pay for hiring out the various venues for events they put together. The sports events were always well-attended and they would mix the teams so that Jews and Arabs were on the same sides, not opposing sides. The idea was to show their classmates that they could live alongside each other and become friends with our so-called enemies. The position of the stall was to attract the attention of the tourists; they would look at their website and donate funds to their cause. Those monies they put to community projects that were set up in the area to get young teenagers like themselves to play together, and most importantly respect each other's customs and learn to talk to each other about their problems rather than blowing each other up. "You see, Mr President, it is easier to influence and work on young minds; they don't carry all the baggage of what has happened in the past like the older generation do. They find it hard to move on and accept changes."

"Well guys, you have truly inspired me today. Maybe you're right, maybe we should channel more of our efforts into trying to find peace in your countries by concentrating on the younger generation and letting them develop the routes of peace for the whole region's future. I fully endorse what you are doing and will mention your names to other world leaders."

"Mr President?"

"Yes, Ephraim?"

"Can we put on our website that we have held talks with you, and that you support our work?"

"Absolutely, and thank you for coming. You have given me some fresh ideas which I will seriously consider."

"Thank you, Mr President, Have a good day." Ephraim and Ameer said in unison.

"And you guys have a safe flight home and keep doing what you do."

With the President's endorsement ringing in their ears, Ephraim and Ameer headed home to continue the work of building better relationships for young Jews and Arabs alike.

So let's keep an eye on them to see what happens next.

PRIYA

Priya was born on the outskirts of a small farming village near Khasa in the Punjab region of India. She was born blind to destitute parents that lived a hand to mouth existence. Life was harsh for the village children, as they would be expected to work to support the family. Being a girl, she held very little prestige in the community; her blindness, to some, was seen as a disgrace on the family. Her brothers and sisters were older and worked in the fields after school and integrated into the community, but Priya was very often shunned. At three she was left on the side of road with a small bundle of clothes; the family crops they had recently sown had failed due to the prolonged drought. With no work, the family were left with no choice but to up sticks. The note that was pinned to Priya's sari read: *'Take care of our daughter, whoever you are.'*

Nine years had passed since that fateful day and life for Priya had moved on. It was early in the morning and the beggars had already secured their pitches for the day. The temperature for early summer was already at thirty degrees and the streets were thronging with worshippers and tourists heading to the Temple complex. Amritsar is the centre of the Sikh religion, and at its heart lies the Harmandir Sahib, known to the world as The Golden Temple. The Temple came to the world's attention in 1984 when Indira Ghandi, the then Indian Prime Minister, gave orders for the Temple to be stormed in an attempt to control Punjabi insurgents. That decision to invade the holiest Sikh Temple resulted in her assassination on the 31st October 1984 by two of her Sikh bodyguards in the grounds of the Prime Minster's Gardens in the capital, New Delhi.

Priya never forgot the day she was left by the roadside; she often recalled the days she sat there calling out to passers-by for help, but being a blind impoverished girl from a low caste she held little value back then in Indian society. She remembered the gentle hand of a young New Zealand backpacker lady picking her up and carrying her here to Amritsar; the orphanage door being opened by a small group of children who, like herself, had been abandoned to the streets by their families. Each child had their own story to tell as to why they had been deserted; poverty and family issues were the main underlying factors in most cases.

The day was going to be busy. Her red embroidered bag was full of the tapestries she and her friends had made over the last few days; with all the worshippers and tourists out on the streets she was hoping to have a successful sales day. The door was open and most of the children from the orphanage had already left for the day. With her white stick in her right hand and her left hand on her best friend Neeta's right shoulder, she headed on her way. Priya had known Neeta for the last eight years and, being of a similar age and background, they had learnt to trust each other. They were more sisters than friends. Neeta stopped.

"Why have we stopped, Neeta?"

Standing on the step were two young ladies in their late teens, beautifully dressed in blue and purple saris. At first she didn't recognise their voices or their names, and it was only when they handed her to touch and feel a battered old rag doll with its right eye missing did she start to wonder whether the two ladies standing there were her older sisters, Wisah and Mana. Taking a small step toward them she reached to feel their faces; her hands softly followed the curves and outlines of each sister's facial features. Mana handed her a small gold bracelet that had an inscription on the outside; running her fingers over it, she immediately recognised it, as it had the names of all three sisters nicely engraved. Their grandmother, on her birth, had presented each of them with a gold bracelet bearing their names; she still had her bracelet in a drawer. The tears of emotion she had been fighting to hold back finally spilled over and poured down her cheeks; her sisters had returned.

It was mid-morning and the temperature had gone up to forty degrees. The short walk via the backstreets to The Golden Temple would take approximately twenty minutes. En route Wisah explained that they had not forgotten her and had spent years trying to find her.

"Priya, it was a friend of ours who had come to visit the temple; you sold her one of your little tapestries. She saw your bracelet with our names on, and she knew we had a blind sister called Priya whom we were desperate to find. She took a picture of you on Instagram. We immediately recognised the bracelet and have been in Amritsar for the last few days searching for you around the Temple. We showed numerous people the Instagram picture and yesterday afternoon a small group of children told us you worked as a volunteer in the soup kitchens. Last night we discreetly followed you home."

"Yes, Neeta and I go to the Langar everyday; we wash the soup bowls that are left over from the thousands of visitors that pass through the doors each day. Our pay is a free meal."

Being late today, the spot by the steps that led up to the Sikh Museum where Neeta and herself usually pitched themselves had gone. In the cut-throat business of touting your wares around the Temple complex, if you wanted the best pitch you needed to be in place early.

Nine years of street life had taught Priya to be streetwise and, despite being blind, she had learnt the hard way to be self-sufficient, a mini entrepreneur. She knew that to progress in life she would need an education, so the day a rich lady gave her a specially adapted laptop that was voice controlled and money to pay for computer classes was the day her political career started. To many that brushed by her each day she was simply a blind beggar girl; she couldn't see them but she could hear them. Listening to their conversations she knew where they had come from in the world and what they hoped to achieve. Did they stop to ask her what she wanted in life once they had purchased their little piece of tapestry bearing a sewn picture of The Golden Temple on? No. Did they care? No. Most of them were only concerned that the little tapestry piece they had bought for a couple of rupees would fit in their suitcase for the flight home.

With their main pitch taken, Priya and Neeta found an empty space outside one or the many shoe stores, where worshippers and tourists alike removed their shoes before washing their feet and entering the Temple. Neeta unfolded the yellow silk shawl, on which she and Priya placed their tapestries. The pavement was baking hot from being scorched by the overhead midday sun; Priya knelt down to feel for the edges of the shawl before tipping the contents of her red embroidered bag out. There was no point in creating a beautiful layout, as rummaging hands over the next few hours would have ruined the best of any display. The purpose was to sell the little tapestries, not show them off. The noise and the hustle and bustle from the surrounding streets was overwhelming for Wisah and Mana as they sat and watched their younger sister haggle with visitors. They were taken aback to see her fight and stand her ground amongst the scores of other children, all desperate to sell their knick-knacks for a couple of rupees. A good day in the eyes of the street children would be to have enough money for a bowl of rice and a small scrap of naan bread on the way home from the street vendors. If anything were left, those few remaining rupees would go to supporting their brothers and sisters.

Wisah was amazed by her younger sister's inner strength and ruthless determination here on the streets around the Temple; she bent down and picked up the yellow silk shawl carefully folding it before placing it in Priya's red embroidered bag. As she tied the bows securing the bag, she felt Priya's hand touch her left arm; looking up she could see Priya had something on her mind.

"Why did they leave me, Wisah?"

"Times were hard, Priya. The crops had failed, the rent hadn't been paid for months and the landlord had evicted us from the land."

"Where did you go?"

"We went to Delhi. Father got a job in a small hotel washing dishes, and Mother had several cleaning jobs."

"Where are my parents now?"

"Father died a few years ago; he had a stroke and never recovered. Mother lives with us in London."

"Hmmm…."

"Priya, we came back to look for you, but that little farming community we grew up in had gone. We asked the police and numerous nearby community elders for help. Months and years went by with no sighting of you, so after father's death we left for the UK."

"Why didn't they take me?"

"Priya, they could hardly support themselves. Father had heard that homes run by world leading charities took abandoned children with disabilities and that they were being fed and educated. He decided life for you would be better in one of those homes."

"So why didn't he and mother take me to one of those homes? They would have known where I was and how lonely and bereft I felt."

"Because, Priya, most of the homes were already overrun with orphans and would only take abandoned children. I understand how you feel...."

"You don't."

"If it's any consolation, Priya, mother has always kept a small photo of you in her purse."

"It's not! Why hasn't she come with you?"

"She doesn't know we are here. Mana and I wanted to make doubly sure that the girl in the Instagram photo was you."

"Hmmm..."

"Father did what he thought was best for you at the time, which was hard, I know."

"'You lot had value to them. You could go out to work and bring in money; pay your way. Me, I was a burden and had little value in their eyes."

"That's not true, Priya."

"Well it is to me! So you can tell your mother you have found me and I am making my own way in the world without her."

The money she and Neeta had made was tucked into a small gold silk pouch and discreetly hidden within the many folds of her sari. Her share of today's takings would pay for her computer class later that evening. The short walk to the Langar kitchens was brief, despite the streets around the Golden Temple thronging with thousands of people waiting to get into the complex. Hundreds of visiting guests were already seated, enjoying the customary lentil soup that had been prepared and was being served by numerous volunteers. For years Priya and Neeta had come in the afternoon to help wash up some of the thousands of soup bowls that were left. Their reward – a simple free meal. Some days it was the only meal they got. Mana and Wisah rolled up their sleeves to help Priya face hours of repetitive washing. Priya had the same spot every day; the layout was imprinted in her brain. Amidst all the commotion of the Langar kitchen and the noise coming from the bustling streets outside, where the rickshaws, cars and buses jostled alongside people and the sacred cows, Priya dreamed about her future and plotted a plan how she was going to achieve her goal.

The bowls kept on coming, and as they did Priya told her sisters about her dreams and aspirations to be a politician in New Delhi or an ambassador at the UN in New York, where she could become a world leader in championing the causes of disadvantaged women from developing countries, lifting them out of poverty to becoming women of influence and power. But she herself needed an education; the evening classes she attended for her computer skills she knew would not be enough, but that was all she could afford for the present time. She told Wisah and Mana about her adapted laptop a lady had given her, along with a small amount of money, but that money she had spent on surviving. She went on to tell her sisters how, at the end of her day, she would connect to the Internet back at the orphanage, lie in bed and download audio books and listen to stories. She would also get the news from around the world telling her what had happened that day. Her ultimate aim was to one day address the whole assembly at the UN and tell her story of how she rose from abject poverty to a woman of world influence, proving to mankind if you have the wish and the desire you can achieve what you set out to do.

Wisah and Mana simply listened and thought to themselves what a terrible mistake their father had made. There was nothing they could do to put that right, but they could help Priya in reaching her goals. But first they had to build back years of missing trust. That was going to take time.

The heat of the day had started to subside as evening approached. Priya asked her sisters if they would like to come with her to her evening computer classes: she would need one of them to support her as she walked to the local school. Normally one of the other children from the orphanage would accompany her there and back.

The orphanage, though busy, was considerably quieter than the Langar. The other children who lived there were eager to find out about Priya's sisters and pestered them to tell their story. Priya had taken some time out in her room to freshen up and pick up her laptop. Coming back downstairs, she could hear the commotion going on as her sisters were being bombarded with hundreds of quickfire questions. Mana accompanied Priya to the nearby school, leaving Wisah to cope with inquisitive children. Priya had changed into a different sari, the bright reds she had being wearing all day giving way to pale shades of delphinium blue and pastel pinks.

The computer class was in a small room in a nearby school. Mana noticed that none of the other students had a disability, which intrigued her as to why Priya had chosen to study with these guys. Priya had already sensed Mana's inner thoughts.

"Mana, I'm blind but I'm as good as these friends of mine on a computer. My laptop keyboard is designed to speak to me as I tap the various keys."

During a small break in the session Priya showed her friends the latest story she had written and put on Amazon for people to read or listen to. She checked her Amazon account to hear how much money she had made from the sale of her stories. Mana sat in silent awe; she and Wisah thought they had come to rescue a poor blind beggar of a girl off the streets of Amritsar who they considered to be their missing sister. This eye-opening performance from her younger sister today simply left her stunned.

With the evening class done, Priya packed her stuff away, taking Mana's right arm they walked home.

"I can sense your surprise, Mana; you thought

you and Wisah would find a pathetic blind beggar of a girl, but what you found was something else."

"Ohh... absolutely."

"Learn a lesson then. Never judge someone by what you see, judge them when you have taken the time to get to know them. Let's go to the Temple to say thank you for today and observe the procession."

"Why do you go to the Temple? You are a Hindu, not a Sikh,"

"I like to go, that is all."

The Golden Temple was beautifully lit up in the night sky; the upper half of the Temple wrapped in its gold coat shone like a beacon to the world. The waters of the sacred pool from which the Temple rose were serene and calm. Priya told Mana where to sit so she could get a good view of the procession, a nightly ritual carried out by the Temple authorities as the Guru Granth Sahib, the central holy book of Sikhism with its religious texts, is taken to the Akal Takht Sikh Parliament overnight. At precisely 4am the next morning the holy book is brought back and placed in the inner sanctum of The Harmandir Sahib, where the daily life cycle of the Sikh complex starts all over again.

For Priya, this was a life-changing day; she had found out why she was abandoned and that the only way forward was in forgiving her family by taking small steps in getting to know them but, more importantly, trust them again. Inwardly she was delighted to see her two sisters. She had shown them how resourceful and resilient she had become and what her aspirations for the future were. Deep down she knew that she would need them to achieve her goals and probably have to leave Amritsar and head for London to get the education she would need to become a world leader that straddled the world's stage. But she would only go if her friend Neeta went with her.

JUAN

Summer was Juan's favourite time of the year, and living on the outskirts of Santiago, Chile's capital city, with the Andes mountain range in the background was for this cheeky football mad twelve-year-old boy an idyllic place to grow up.

The warm evenings meant he and his friends could play football and generally make a nuisance of themselves on the streets around his house after school. Juan's house was down a narrow dirt track; the tiny abode had been the family home for the last five years. The wooden cladding that formed the main shell of the house was in a dilapidated state and the once-bright turquoise paint that adorned the house was now a washed-out pale blue. Closer inspection revealed signs of dry rot and peeling paint was pretty much in evidence. The corrugated roof fared no better and when the rains came the family would have to position buckets in various places to catch the dripping water that splattered all over the floors. The numerous phone calls to the landlord mainly went unheeded; his mother even went as far as threatening to move house, a thought that horrified Juan as all his friends lived nearby.

Juan was the youngest in the household; his brothers and sisters were considerably older than him and, like his mother, worked in the local vineyards. Being the youngest, and with his father away a lot of the time working in the copper mines around Chuquiacamata, north of Calama in the

Atacama Desert, Juan got away with things the others never did. He was the annoying cheeky chap that got under everybody's skin, but when his father was around his behaviour was almost saintly; so when his older brothers and sisters whinged about him to their father, he merely dismissed their moans. To him Juan was an exemplary young man. Their mother, on the other hand, knew where they were coming from. Often exasperated with his antics she would scold him, but to no avail; at the end of the day Juan was her lovable rogue.

It was a lovely summer's day and Juan was home early from school. It was unusual for him to be home so early in the middle of the week with everybody away at work, and having been barred from using the family computer and with his smartphone confiscated he set about the chores his mother had set him to do, ticking each job off as he completed the set tasks. Confiscating his phone along with his football generally got Juan's attention, and for all his rumbustious behaviour he was a smart cookie and knew precisely how to play his mother. Get the jobs done to her strict instructions and satisfaction and the smartphone, along with the football, would shortly be back in his possession. Tidying his room he thought could work to his advantage; he might even find some of the things he had been looking for recently. The trip to the shop to get the next few days essentials could also work in his favour. Those favourite bars of chocolate that were not on the list could just accidentally fall into the shopping basket as if by magic.

The outside yard didn't take too long to restore to its original state, having been decimated by the football game he and his friends had yesterday, which ultimately led to his detention and quarantine. The rickety old bird stand that normally stood propped up in the corner that had taken a bit of a battering as a direct result of being substituted for a goal post was easily repaired. With the shopping list firmly tucked into the back pocket of his trousers and gently pulling the yard gates to, Juan set off to the shops, running his left hand fingers along the chicken wire fence as he went.

A small gang of youths that were milling around at the bottom of his street taunted him as he approached; he knew exactly who they were and what lowlife area they had crawled out from under. With their hoodies and bikes they looked menacing and Juan could see nearby folk giving them a wide berth. Juan knew the gang leaders and what nasty pieces of work they were; no doubt they had knives hidden about their persons. One of the gang members, who was probably under instruction, mounted the pavement beside Juan.

"Going somewhere, Juan?"

"None of your business." retorted Juan.

"Whoooo…. We're a little touchy today. Mum got your phone again? Tut-tut!"

Juan felt like punching the guy's lights out, but knew that would be an unwise move; he might get up to no good himself at times but he knew when the cards were stacked against him and this was one of those occasions. Turning the corner he gave a dismissive gesture with his right hand, as if to say '*Whatever!*', but as he glanced back to see what reaction he was getting, he couldn't avoid smirking to himself as he watched the youth that had tried to intimidate him attempting a wheelie in the middle of the street in front of all his mob, only to see him completely flip off and land flat on his back with the bike crashing down on top of him. With another discreet snigger he headed off to the shop.

Over the next few days, with diplomatic relations restored to normal with his mother and his smartphone firmly back under his authority, Juan started to text all his friends to see who would be interested in playing football on the park this Sunday at 2pm. He had an idea that he wanted to run by his father; looking at his watch he realised that the call would have to wait until the evening when his father's shift at the copper mine was finished. Juan recalled sitting across from his mother at the breakfast table that morning, moaning about the fact she would be unable to speak to his father until the evening as he was on the day shift.

Arriving home from school, Juan was surprised to see the table had been set for the evening meal and that his elder brothers and sisters were back from their shifts at the vineyard. His mother on the other hand, who worked in the tourist shop, wouldn't be back until later; clearly she had given the others instructions to set the table and prepare the evening meal. Sitting at the small table with his elder brother Alejandro in the kitchen that was at the rear of the house, Juan decided to moot the idea about the charity football match he was thinking of organising on Sunday.

"What charity had you in mind, and isn't it a bit short notice Juan?" asked his brother Alejandro.

"I thought about two charities. I even thought of setting up my own."

"Tell me about the one you were thinking of setting up on your own."

"I thought about setting up a charity to raise money for disadvantaged children, Alejandro."

"To do what in particular, Juan?"

"To raise money to buy sports equipment, to pay for football training lessons, I... don't know, to get a new sports facility ground built around here, anything to give the youngsters like me something to do, something to aim for, anything to... keep them away from the street gangs and off the streets."

"Wow, Juan, that is a fantastic idea; something like that will take a lot of planning and commitment."

"Really?"

"Yes, Juan, it won't just be a couple of football games in the park on the odd Sunday afternoon when you fancy it."

"Hmm...."

"What were the other ideas you had?"

"Oh... Doesn't matter, Alejandro."

With his brother's thoughts buzzing around in his head, Juan went to his room. Sitting cross-legged on his bed, Juan opened his laptop and, scrolling down the list of topics he was studying at school, he clicked on Artificial Intelligence; opening up the page he looked at the designs of the robots he and his classmates had been working on. Juan's first dream was to be an international footballer playing in midfield for his country Chile, but he was a smart dude and knew that a footballer's career was short, and like in any sporting profession, only the few most talented players got to the very top of their game and played for their countries and overseas; he also knew that one fatal injury could cruelly end a player's career. Juan was fully aware that the world was changing rapidly and that technology was leading the way. He had taken the decision, having talked with his teachers and parents, to move school next year. He successfully applied for a scholarship to the new IT college on the other side of the city; the programme that fascinated him most was AI 'Artificial Intelligence', particularly robots. He had even gone as far as calling his robot Jorge. In his own imagination he had Jorge as a domestic robot carrying out the household chores that he hated doing. With what his brother had said downstairs in the kitchen, Juan found it difficult to concentrate on his schoolwork, so shutting the laptop down and unfurling his legs he rejoined his brother back in the kitchen.

Alejandro heard Juan coming down the stairs;

entering the kitchen Juan was slightly wrong-footed as Alejandro gently slid his smartphone across the small kitchen table. Juan picked it up, but didn't grasp the meaning of his brother's actions, nor did he comprehend the look of excitement on his face.

"What!" exclaimed Juan.

"Look at my phone."

"It's blank."

Alejandro leaned across the table, snatched the phone out of Juan's hand only to realise the interface was blank and needed reactivating with his thumbprint. Juan scrolled down the news app and as he did so he understood his brother's excitement; David Beckham was coming to Santiago to promote his new book and would be at the Estadio Monumental, the home ground of one of Chile's biggest football teams, Colo-Colo, on Av. Departmental Macul tomorrow. David Beckham, one of the world's most celebrated footballers, was in town. Juan had worshipped and followed his career path for the last several years; he even had a poster stuck on his bedroom back wall with him holding a Manchester United shirt with the number seven emblazoned on the back.

"OMG!" screamed Juan.

Juan knew exactly where the book signing venue was, for he was, like his father and brother, a huge Colo-Colo fan, but what he didn't know was the precise location of his best friend Jose's new house; it was on one of the new housing estates that had sprung up on the outskirts on the other side of the city. He phoned Jose to tell him the news and what an opportunity this was to meet the great man at last and get an autograph. Both boys were excited and agreed that they would go; they knew people would be queuing overnight outside the stadium, so they would need money, sleeping bags and food. Jose pinged his new house details across via Messenger. Juan clicked on Google Maps and opened up the app; putting Jose's new address details in he took a few moments to have a look at the picture of Jose's new house and thought to himself, '*Nice*' before saving the bus route option. His next task was to check the bus company timetable and let Jose know at what time he could be expected. Racing upstairs, Juan kicked open his bedroom door and immediately scanned the floor for his red rucksack. He checked the time on his iPhone; he had an hour before the bus passed the bottom of his street. Pulling open doors, he grabbed the necessary items of clothing he thought would be required and rammed them into his rucksack. Standing precariously on his chair he reached for his orange sleeping bag that was on top of the wardrobe; as he pulled it down a pair of old trainers he had not seen for a while came to light and tumbled to the floor. Juan looked at the trainers that were now strewn across his bedroom floor; on closer examination he discovered an old pair of socks that looked like they had been lurking in the shoes for some time. Juan picked the trainers up; the fetid smell that was wafting from them was not good. He gingerly picked the socks out and threw them into the wash basket. As for the trainers he opened his window and hurled them out into the backyard below. The only thing that he could think of at that very moment was that he had managed to track down the odious smell that had been lingering around his room for the last few weeks. With a final glance around his room and a quick check of his pockets and rucksack, Juan shut his bedroom door and headed down stairs.

Alejandro was still preparing the family meal, looking up from the kitchen table and seeing Juan in the kitchen doorway.

"I take it, Juan, you are planning or shall I say attempting to go and see Mr Beckham?"

"Absolutely!!"

"Err… have we forgotten something?"

"Nope."

"So I assume you have spoken to father or mother about this?"

"Oh gosh!"

"I'll take that as no then, Juan."

In all of his excitement and haste, Juan had not given this slight attention to detail any thought; a look of despair crossed his face. They're going to say no, they're going to say no. Placing his rucksack on the table and his sleeping bag on the floor, Juan reached into the right outside pocket of his rucksack that he had put his smartphone in. Pulling his phone out he thought '*I know, I will phone my father first; he will understand and with some reasoning he just might let me go. No point ringing mother, that would be a straight no. She hates football and no amount of rationale or magic charm is going to work there.'*

Juan scanned down his favourite contact list, hovering briefly over his father's name before tapping the screen. Juan listened intently to the ringtones on the other end of the phone; it seemed like an eternity before his father answered and, as the moments ticked by, he could feel his heart beating faster and faster in his rib cage.

Still stunned that his father completely agreed, and even asking him to get a signed book for him as well, Juan slipped his smartphone back into the outside pocket of his rucksack.

"I take it then, with the big grin all over your face, father has fallen for your sweet-talk approach?"

"He even asked me to get him a signed copy; how about that! And he's even going to clear it with mother. Yessss… get in there!"

With authorisation granted and with no time to spare, Juan hotfooted it out the door.

Walking at a brisk pace, Juan sent a text message to Jose to say he was on his way and that he was calling at the nearest ATM cash machine and local store to get money and various foodstuff and nibbles for the night ahead before getting the bus. Juan was a little taken aback when he read Jose's response *'Still negotiating with the old man and lady.'* Juan hadn't considered the fact Jose might not be allowed to go, he just assumed; well, either way, he himself was going.

The queue at the bank ATM cash machine was

long; no doubt people were withdrawing cash for the weekend. As he stood in line he suddenly realised beads of sweat had started to pour down his face; it had been an exceptionally hot day for January. He recalled his weather app showing 37^c and, even though it was early evening, the heat that had built up around Santiago throughout the day hadn't quite dissipated and the short vigorous walk had brought about a sudden sweat. Mopping his brow with a fresh wet wipe that a lady in the queue was kind enough to give him, Juan waited patiently for the cash machine. The queue soon went down and Juan withdrew what he thought was enough money for the next few days from his bank account. Standing to one side, he checked his cash before putting it in his wallet; this was something his mother had taught him, for she never trusted machines. As he put his money away, his phone pinged with a text response from Jose. It was a little emoji yellow thumbs up symbol. They were both good to go.

The bus was on time, but as Juan boarded he thought to himself, '*Why am I going from San Bernardo, a southern suburb of Santiago where I live, to Pudahuel near the international airport which is in the opposite direction of Macul, the suburb where the stadium was? Surely it makes more sense for me to go direct to the stadium and meet Jose there; I can check out Jose's new place another day.*' Juan quickly turned around, pushing past other passengers that were waiting to board the bus that went to the airport. Juan ignored the grumblings of the people he had brushed up against and sent a simple text message to Jose, '*Change of plan, see you at the stadium.*' Juan looked up at the electronic board that had been strategically placed above the bus shelter; he could see that the next bus to Macul was in five minutes time, enough time to chill out for a few moments. Looking at his phone a message from his father appeared, '*Make that two books. Oh and your mother is not a happy bunny.*'

A large crowd had already built up outside the main doors of the Estadio Monumental and the stadium security officials had started to erect crowd control barriers, no doubt to keep some form of harmony and order over the next twenty-four hours. A large banner of the man himself had been erected across the entire front of the main reception area. Juan was excited as he joined the end of the queue, but would he have the nerve and the barefaced cheek to ask David Beckham to come along to watch them play on Sunday. So far only six people had confirmed that they would be available that afternoon. How embarrassing would that be, asking David Beckham to come and watch and only six guys turned up. Juan was a bit disappointed with the response but inwardly thought, '*I bet if I told them Beckham was coming, they would all turn up.*' Jose tapped Juan on the shoulder and proceeded to give his friend a hug before putting his bags down on the floor next to Juan's; murmurings and accusations of pushing in could be heard from people further down the line. Juan turned to them and politely told them to mind their own business and that Jose was with him.

The night was going to be a long, drawn-out affair; Jose was grateful they had remembered to bring with them their warm sleeping bags as the night temperatures in Santiago could be considerably cooler than the daytime temperatures. The two boys hunkered down and started to tell each other jokes and stories; Juan started by telling Jose about his little Saturday job at his mother's place of work at the Vina Santa Rit vineyard down the road from where he lived, across the way from the Maipo River. Tourists from all over the world flocked in their thousands each week to visit the vineyard on organised tours to see how the wines are produced, and how they all ended up in the visitor centre for free wine tasting.

"So what does your mother do there?" asked Jose.

"She manages the visitor centre and makes sure the guests get plenty of free samples and spend lots of money buying the expensive bottles of wine."

"So what do you do, Juan?"

"Me! I... Well, err, I help the visitors carry their bottles to their cars or buses; sometimes I get a little tip for my transporting expertise. Get my drift."

"Yeh! And what else?"

"Well... I... Hmm, wash up all the glasses left behind by the guests, and occasionally at the end of the day when my mother isn't watching have a few cheeky little free tasters myself that have not been sampled. I can ask my mother to see if she can get you a wee Saturday job at the vineyard."

"So you're chief washer up!"

"If that's the terminology you choose to use, Jose, well then yep."

Juan went on to tell Jose about the new IT college he was going to shortly to do AI, and how he had thought about his futuristic robot Jorge and how he would programme him to do all the domestic chores he needed to do but hated doing. Juan waffled on about how he saw robots driving our cars, flying our planes, even being our friends; however Jose was getting bored listening to Juan's visual perceptions of the future and redirected the conversation back to football.

"I thought you wanted to be a major football star like me, Juan."

"I do, Jose, but you have to consider that we might not achieve that goal. Only the very few reach those echelons in the game, and you have to consider the life of a professional footballer is short and if you sustain an injury that prevents you from playing. Then what are you going to do? You need a plan B."

Considering Juan was only twelve he had a wise head on him; he wasn't always going to be the cheeky little chap that everybody saw him as or as his mother often referred to him as her lovable rogue. He had a great sense of foresight , something his friend Jose and others around him lacked. As the evening progressed and the night skies took over the two boys carried on chatting about various things. They laughed at some of the pictures their friends had posted on Facebook, Instagram and YouTube; they even put several pictures of themselves sitting outside the stadium huddled together in their sleeping bags. Finally having put the world to rights and discussing Juan's charity idea, they drifted off to sleep.

The sun rose early the next morning, as was normal for this time of the year; the weather prediction for the day was for another scorching hot day. The majestic Andes that towered over the city looked resplendent against the backdrop of a clear blue sky, and the dusting of snow that coated the highest peaks gave the finishing touches to a picture perfect postcard scene. Stirring slowly from within their sleeping bags, Juan and Jose glanced around. The decision to camp out had been the right one as the queue had stretched overnight to all around the stadium. Juan only hoped that the great man himself had plenty of patience and a good pen; he was going to need it. A couple of entrepreneurial kids had set up a temporary café selling coffees, hot chocolates and cakes at extortionate prices, but when you have a captive market directly in front of you prepared to pay any price for a warm drink Juan thought good luck to them. Hopefully by the time the security guards finally appeared on the scene they would have made some money for themselves before scarpering to avoid getting caught. Jose crawled out of his sleeping bag and raced across to the coffee lads to get two polystyrene cups of steaming hot coffee and two salted caramel muffins. The look on Jose's face as he returned with the coffees said it all. '*Yep, we have been ripped off.*' Juan didn't bother to ask Jose how much he had paid, but he did note that Jose didn't bring any loose change back. Never mind; the muffins and the hot coffee were heart warming and delicious and would sustain them both for the next few hours.

Juan and Jose's wait was short; soon after 9am the main reception doors opened and three stadium security guys ushered in the first of the waiting throng. Both boys were excited; they were going to meet their hero, and Juan was determined to ask David Beckham to come along to his charity game tomorrow. What harm could come about from asking? The man could either say yes or no; he would never know unless he asked. Shuffling their way along the queue, Juan and Jose found their way into the reception area; they were both very excited. Each of them had been instructed by their fathers to get three signed copies each. With their copies purchased, Juan and Jose went upstairs to the main foyer and joined the long line of people waiting for Mr Beckham's autograph.

As queues went, the line of people moved relatively quickly; those that had their book signed waved them around on the way out as they walked past those still waiting. Juan could feel his heart pounding away inside him; he could see the great man himself sitting at a desk only metres away from him. One of the stadium staff asked Juan if he would like a photo taken of himself as David

Beckham signed his books and as he had three books had he got the names of whom they are to be signed to ready. Of course he wanted a photo; slightly flustered, he fumbled around his pockets searching for his phone. As he did so he dropped two of the three books. Both Juan and Jose handed their phones over; Juan bent down to pick up the fallen books only to drop one of them again. In an agitated state and extremely red-faced, Juan bent down for the second time. As he stood up with all three books tightly under his control, he found himself standing directly in front of his hero. Jose stepped forward first and got his photo and books signed, while Juan took a few moments to compose himself. At last it was his turn, handing over his books and posing for his photo.

"Well young man, how are you today?"

"I'm fine, thank you."

"What is your name?"

"Juan, sir."

"Well I hope I haven't kept you waiting too long today, Juan."

"Not at all, sir."

"Do you play football?"

"Yes."

"What position do you play, Juan?"

"Oh, midfield, like yourself."

"Do you play for fun? Or are you looking to play professionally?"

"Professionally, sir."

"Are you on The Colo'Colo youth squad here?"

"Not yet, but I hope to be very shortly."

"Well I wish you all the best, Juan. Live your dream."

With that David Beckham handed Juan his autographed books, and the security protection officer guarding the great footballing hero tapped Juan on the shoulder, signalling for him to move on. As he turned away, Juan turned back and put a neatly handwritten note into David Beckham's hand.

'Sir, we are holding a charity football match tomorrow afternoon for the underprivileged kids of Chile. You would be very welcome to come; all my details and the information you need are on the note.'

David Beckham merely acknowledged the note and put it in his pocket; with that the two lads raced out of the stadium, waving their signed copies at all those that were still waiting for theirs in the queue.

Juan immediately posted his picture with David Beckham on Facebook, Instagram and other social media outlets, as did Jose. Juan even went as far as telling everybody that he had invited David Beckham to come along to his charity football match tomorrow at the Bicentenario park and thought to himself, *'Now let's see how many turn up as opposed to the paltry six that had originally volunteered.'*

Later that afternoon, Juan found himself sitting around the kitchen table, with his mother and father. His father was flicking through the book's pages and was proud that his son had plucked up the courage to go. His mother, on the other hand, was less enthusiastic; she didn't want her youngest son to follow down the volatile football route. She wanted her son to take up another profession but was unsure as to which one at present. However inwardly she was proud of Juan for taking the initiative to fulfil a dream of his, but she was not going to let her emotions show. With a comforting gentle tap on Juan's right shoulder she disappeared into the other room, where the rest of the family were sitting.

"Father!"

"Yes. Juan!"

"Can I talk to you?"

"Of course, son, you can always talk to me. What do you want to talk about?"

"I have an idea, Father, to help disadvantaged children of my age. I want to raise money by getting people to sponsor or donate money to the football matches we play on the park every Sunday afternoon, sort of '*Pay as you play.*' The money we raise would go towards buying kits and football boots for those that want to play football but can't afford to for whatever the reason. Maybe Colo-Colo might get involved, you never know. Small things can lead to big dreams for some people; you never know, Father. Oh, by the way, I've asked David Beckham to come along to the match tomorrow. I gave him my details."

"Well go for it, son, and let's hope Mr Beckham turns up."

"What time does the match start tomorrow, Juan." His father looked over the rim of his glasses and flicked through the book.

"2pm."

"Hmm…maybe I should rummage around in the shed outside to see where my old boots are?"

"Father, we don't want old codgers like you playing. Just drive me there and pay up."

Juan's father looked over the rim of his glasses for the second time, and looking directly at his son inwardly thought to himself, '*Cheeky little brat*'. But he knew in his heart Juan was right; his playing days were long over. So perhaps the boots should stay were they had been for the past few years, buried under a pile of junk in the shed at the back of the house.

"Oh by the way, Juan, your mother is booking flights down to Puntas Arena."

"Do I have to go?"

"Yes."

Puntas Arena is a small town in Chile's southern Patagonia region, and every year at this time of the year Juan's mother insisted that all the family returned to their roots to see old friends and catch up with relatives. Five years ago the decision was made to up sticks to Santiago, as job prospects and schooling opportunities were better there; with Juan's father working in the far north of the country and them living in the far south, it made sense geographically as well economically to move to Santiago. The decision was made to keep the house the family owned in Puntas Arena and rent here in Santiago.

Juan's phone kept ringing and all those that said

they couldn't make tomorrow all of a sudden had become available. '*Two faced toads*', thought Juan.

The weather for Sunday, as predicted, was another scorching hot day. Juan was up early, making sure his kit and boots were spick and span. Opening his laptop, Juan went on to Skype and waited for a few moments to see exactly how many of his friends would respond. Juan kept the conversation brief.

"This is a charity match guys, if you want to play the fee is twenty five pesos. Be at the Bicentenario Park by 1pm at the latest. The match starts at 2pm."

"What time is David Beckham getting there?" asked one of his friends.

"Wait and see, mate." replied Juan.

With that, Juan logged off his laptop and at the same time looked at the message Jose had sent to his smartphone. '*I hope he turns up, or you'll have a lot of explaining to do.*'

Juan looked at Jose's message and thought to himself, '*Me too.*' *Perhaps I should think about putting the bones to a little speech to cover myself here; keep it simple though, most of those guys are not the smartest dudes in town.*

It was midday as Juan got into his father's car and he was beginning to panic as he had received no confirmation that his hero was going to show up at the park this afternoon.

"You OK, Juan?"

"Yep," replied Juan as he turned his face to look out of the passenger front side window so that his father could not see the look of despair that was etched all over his face. He could feel his stomach churning as the car pulled into the park's main car park; he could see that lots of his friends and their fathers had turned up early and for a few split seconds he wished he was anywhere on the planet except here in Bicentenario Park.

Plucking up courage, Juan stepped out of his father's car and, as he did so, he heard his smartphone from the left outside pocket of his red rucksack ping. Scrambling to get the straps undone he could hear his phone ping for the second time. Retrieving his phone he looked at the message. *'Where in the park are you? David.'* Juan immediately replied, giving the precise location of the car park. Breathing a sigh of relief, he walked to the back of his father's car, opened the boot and took his kitbag out. As he slammed the boot lid down and looked up he could see in the near distance a cavalcade of three black cars crossing the park.

Juan's cheek had paid off; his hero had come.

The cavalcade of cars came to a halt, the doors of the third car opened first and four protection officers got out; as they walked past the second car they opened the back doors to let out The British Ambassador to Chile, who had come with her two small sons, and finally they opened the back door of the first car and Juan's hero David Beckham stepped out.

Juan's father quickly turned to Juan.

"I think you need to go and greet your guest."

Approaching David Beckham, Juan was unusually nervous.

"Hi Juan, I read your note and decided to come, but I can only spare an hour."

"That's fine." replied Juan.

"May I make a suggestion, Juan? Rather than me stand here and watch you guys play, maybe it would be better if I spent a few brief moments talking to everybody about how I started off in the game and show a few tips of how to become better players. Is that OK?"

"That's fine with me."

For those that had attended the last hour was fun, useful and over all too soon. The key message that came across was that to be successful in any profession you have to be dedicated and work hard. It was also made clear that a footballer's playing career can be short, and that any young person thinking of playing any professional sport should have a plan B option career to follow through.

Getting back into his car, David Beckham turned to Juan.

"I like your charity idea, but for it to work and benefit those that are the intended you are going to have to commit a lot of your time to it. I can support you there, but your immediate priorities are your football training and your Artificial Intelligence schooling. Call me in a couple of days' time with your future plans; perhaps you and Jose can come to London to talk more."

With those words of advice ringing in Juan's ears, the cavalcade disappeared. The thought of he and Jose going to London certainly resonated in his mind and he would definitely mull over all the things that had been said to him and call David in the next week or two.

Juan and his father were the last to leave the park; sitting in the front seat of his father's car on the way home, he quietly reflected on what had happened and been achieved over the past few days. The days had been exciting as well as inspiring, but what decisions he would make about his future we will have to wait and see.

NAEKU

The black, saturated storm clouds that had gathered over the plains of the Maasai Mara National Park for the last few hours were about to burst. A dazzling electrical storm would ensue, lighting up the African skies like a firework display. The deluge of rain that would come tumbling out of the sky would quickly turn the dried-out plains to a muddy quagmire. Riverbeds that had been dry for months would become raging torrents of cascading waters. With the fresh rains invigorating the plains, the parched lands would be transformed into a vast green carpet of vegetation. The scent of the new grasses that were carried on the wind would be picked up by the migrating herds of wildebeest, zebra and antelope already making their way north through the great Serengeti plains. This migration of hundreds of thousands of animals that followed the scents of fresh grasses was one of the world's greatest spectacles, as witnessed by overhead satellite images that were beamed into our homes via the TV, smartphones, YouTube and many other social media outlets.

The sight of the migrating herds entering their territories was good news to the resident predators, signalling the hard times of famine were over and a period of feasting was about to begin as a glut of food came their way. Lions, cheetahs, hyenas and wild dogs often timed the birth of their cubs or pups to coincide with this time of plenty, thus giving their young a fighting chance in life, but the poachers with their cunning and devious ways would be there too.

Naeku sat on the veranda that ran across the back of her house; she was grumbling to herself as the house wi-fi was playing up. The websites she was looking at were either taking forever to download or simply freezing with the buffering symbol going round and round in the middle of the screen. She was getting annoyed and starting to lose patience with her laptop. Tomorrow was going to be an important day for her; she was going to meet her grandfather for the first time and she wanted to show him that she had some knowledge of her heritage. Her grandfather was the chief village elder of a small Maasai community, living a simple life in a small kraal close to one of the seven main crossing points that the African migrating herds used to cross the mighty Mara River. She wanted to know more about the Maasai people and their customs so she could impress the man she had seen in the only photo she had of him, dressed in full Maasai warrior robes. Her father talked very little about his father; they had fallen out sometime ago about his decision to give up the pastoral, semi-nomadic ways of the traditional Maasai people, opting for a career in medicine and a more comfortable modern way of life. The wealthy suburbs of Nairobi, the capital of Kenya where she had been brought up, would be a far cry from a dusty kraal of mud huts close to the Kenyan-Tanzanian border in the Maasai Mara reserve. But she couldn't wait to go; her father was understandably a little anxious as he was going to see his father for the first time in twenty years.

The 4x4 Jeep, driven by her father, pulled off the dirt track that led to the kraal; Naeku stepped out, wearing her latest designer clothes and trainers. Her father had warned her not to expect luxury accommodation with the latest internet connections. The traditional bomba (house) that her grandfather lived in was a simple affair of timber poles fixed directly into the ground and interwoven with a lattice of branches that were covered with a mix of cow dung, mud and human urine. It was late morning when Naeku and her father finally got to meet her grandfather, as he had been out talking with other village elders about the spate of cattle rustling and recent lion and cheetah attacks on his livestock. She was slightly nervous as he approached. He was a tall elegant man dressed in the traditional Maasai red shuka with cowhide sandals on his feet. In Maasai terms he was wealthy, as he had over a hundred cattle and numerous children, but compared to her own father he was an uneducated poor man; nevertheless she had chosen to spend the next few weeks getting to know this man and his ways.

Her father and grandfather exchanged polite conversation, but it was clear for all to see that a tension existed between them and her father chose to leave by early evening. With her father gone, Naeku set about getting to know her new family.

The following morning her grandfather sat her down under a tree, the very spot where he had sat with other children he had grown up with listening to his teacher. School in his day was a few rickety desks and chairs set out under a big ash tree, providing some shade from the overhead sun; his education was limited. Nowadays the school bus picks the village children up from the end of the dirt track, taking them to the nearby government centre. From there the children progressed to the universities in Nairobi. Her grandfather suggested that she changed out of her expensive clothes and put on suitable Maasai attire, as they would be walking together all day out on the plains to see the wildlife.

Sitting to her right, propped against the bough of the big ash tree, he asked:

"Why have you come?"

"To find out more of my culture, and to see for myself the destruction mankind is bringing on the natural habitat and the wildlife. Is the plight of some of our endangered species as bad as portrayed by the TV images shown on our screens, grandfather?"

Olekina and his sister Lankenua were twins; they lived in the last bomba in the kraal near the enkang (outer fence). Olekina was intrigued as to why his grandfather was taking so much interest in this outsider. For a ten year old his curiosity often got the better of him, invariably getting him into trouble with his patriarchs. He and his grandfather often had to have words over his annoying antics and general boyish behaviour.

"I think the best way for us to talk about what

you want to know is to take a walk out onto the plains."

"Will we be safe, grandfather?"

"As long as you follow my instructions, we'll be safe. It's dangerous out there; you need to respect nature's ways. Watch and listen for the warning signs, but most importantly stick by my side."

Olekina, who had conveniently placed himself within eavesdropping distance, pretending to be busy doing nothing, scurried off to find his sister.

"Olekina!"

"Yes, Gramps."

"Grandfather to you, cheeky monkey. I suppose you've overheard that I am taking Naeku out into the bush."

"No, Grandfather."

"Hmm… One of these days, young man, your tongue and sharp wit will get you into serious trouble. Pack a rucksack, fetch your sister and be at the enkang gate in twenty minutes."

"I didn't see Olekina sneak up on us."

"You wouldn't; he's good at that. We don't call him the village gossip for nothing. If you want to spread a rumour, tell Olekina; it will be round the village and the surrounding hills within minutes. Sometimes he has his uses."

"How?"

"Oh… you know. If I want to know what's going on around here and the outlying villages there's no point asking the other elders of the village; they won't know. I ask Olekina and, if he doesn't know, he'll sure find out and get back to me. You see, Naeku, I don't need that internet and smartphone stuff; I have Olekina."

The overhead sun was powerful; most of the big cats and other predators would be sitting or sleeping under any shade they could find. Exerting energy chasing prey in full view and in the heat of the day was futile and stupid. The wildebeest, zebra and gazelles had the upper hand with their agility and speed and thousands of lookouts. By night the cats had the advantage as they generally had better night vision than the herd animals, plus it was cooler and the darkness provided the necessary cover to get up close to their target before pouncing and attacking.

Sticking to the well-trodden tracks used by the Maasai for centuries, just like their big cat neighbours do, the three children walked single file behind their grandfather. As they walked the old man began to tell them some of the stories that had been passed down from one generation to the next: how their forefathers from the Nilotic peoples had originated from the lower Nile valley, north of Lake Turkana around South Sudan and Ethiopia, how they had a fearsome reputation as warriors and cattle rustlers. He went on talking about the Maasai traditions and how those traditions were fading fast as many of the younger generation had left the family homesteads and headed for the big cities of Nairobi and Dar Es Salaam for a different life. For him, he would adhere to the Maasai ways until he died and was left out for the vultures to have their say.

Naeku spotted two young male lions perched on a small outcrop of rock no more than fifty metres away to her right; they looked nervous as they surveyed the migrating herds spread out beneath them from their vantage point. Lankenua watched them for a few minutes; they were probably two brothers who, for the first time in their young lives, had to defend and provide for themselves as a result of being kicked out of a local pride. They would have every right to be nervous, as they would be attacked and killed by the dominant male of this territory they had invaded if found; a scenario they would have to get used to until they were bigger and strong enough to fight for their own pride and patch of land.

"Grandfather."

"Yes, Lankenua, I think they are the lions that have been attacking our cattle."

The old man recalled that the villages had reported sightings of two young males new to the area that had been attacking their stock. Olekina would find out and report back.

It was nearing forty degrees and the midday sun sat high in the sky above the plains. The old man headed for the outcrop of rock that the two young male lions had temporarily claimed; he knew how to scare them off, but the view across the Mara plains would be spectacular and the shade of the four trees there would be welcome. Sitting under the shade of the trees and watching the thousands of wildebeest and zebra crisscrossing the vast plains that stretched out as far as the eye could see below them was truly amazing, Mother Nature at her best. Naeku simply sat and took in everything around her; her grandfather continued with his stories and his thoughts for the Maasai generations that would follow in his footsteps.

A small cheetah family, a young mother and her three cubs, sat aloft on a small heap of earth, most likely the remnants of an old abandoned termite mound. The old grandfather could tell she was eyeing up a small zebra calf or gazelle and was getting ready for her next kill; she had three small cubs to feed so there was no midday snooze for her, not like the lazy lion prides that camped in her territory. They would be sprawled out flat on their backs, legs in the air, still digesting last night's meal with not a care in the world.

The three children sat transfixed as the thrill of the hunt was on; the mother cheetah slipped off the mound, snarling at her cubs to do the same and hide themselves in the long grass until she returned. The mother cheetah had positioned herself downwind of her victim, a zebra calf, slowly stalking forward inch by inch, blade by blade of grass. Crouching down, eyes locked on the calf, she sprang. The calf, crying for its mother's protection, ran for its life. Naeku had her hands over her mouth, screaming to herself, desperately hoping that the little calf would outpace the mother cheetah with its zigzagging, twisting, turning, ducking and diving. It was all over within minutes. A cloud of dust that was thrown up into the air was the signal the chase was over; the little cheetah cubs would be having lunch shortly. The old grandfather turned to his grandchildren:

"One animal's loss is another animal's gain; that's Mother Nature's rules here on the great African plains."

Naeku looked at her grandfather with teary eyes; she knew the ways of life here in the bush, but it was still hard to see a little life snuffed out so violently.

Nightfall was close at hand; their grandfather, once a proud fighting warrior, knew it wasn't safe out on the plains at night because the big cats and other predators would be stirring themselves for the nightly business of hunting prey. The night's cast of characters would soon be emerging from their burrows to face whatever the night threw at them, and those animals that had endured the punishing heat and dust of the day would be looking for a safe place to rest. With a bit of luck they might see the morning again.

Walking back the track they had come, Naeku heard a commotion from behind a clump of bushes; a group of youths had gathered, sitting on quad bikes smoking whatever. Naeku and her cousins knew exactly what these yobs were up to. They were the unscrupulous poachers, who didn't care about the animals they harmed as long as the illegal traffickers paid them. They killed or stole to order; their ill-gotten gains they would spend buying flash bikes or the latest designer gear from the posh shops in Nairobi.

The old grandfather whispered to Olekina:

"Take your sister and Naeku back to the kraal. Get a message to the park rangers and tip them off as to my whereabouts and don't come back. Do you hear me?"

"Yes grandfather, whatever."

The old grandfather knew in his heart Olekina would be back and that he would probably be sweet talking Naeku and his sister to do likewise at this precise moment. He shrugged his shoulders in utter despair; he loved Olekina but knew one day he'd come a cropper. The old warrior nudged his way through the bushes so as to get a closer look at the yobs; he recognised some of them and would be talking to the elders of their villages. As far as he could ascertain there weren't many rifles. Only one of them was armed; he would be the lookout, so he assumed they were not on a mission to kill the rhinos or elephants for their horns and tusks tonight. The cloth bags that were scattered on the ground hinted they were after cubs, mainly cheetah cubs, as they fetched a good price on the black market. The cubs' destination? Rich Arabs in the Gulf states, where the cheetah was a highly prized fashion symbol, a must-have object prowling the immaculately manicured gardens of the wealthy or in the front seats of their BMWs and Mercs.

Olekina had done his job; the park rangers had arrived at the kraal within the hour, anxious to get going and catch the poachers red-handed. The head ranger turned to Naeku: "Send a text to your grandfather. Tell him we're on our way and to text back with his location."

Before Naeku could open her mouth, Olekina butted in: "You're having a laugh! 'Texting!' That old man wouldn't know how to switch a phone on! We'd better show you the way."

With a cheeky right-eyed wink at Naeku and his sister, it was mission accomplished! They were off for some action.

The blazing heat of the day had given way to a chilly night; the overhead moon gave some light to what could only be described as a pitch-black sky. Naeku was amazed at the thousands of stars that glittered high up in the night's stratosphere; yes, she could see the stars from her bedroom window back at home, but the city lights would dim the view; here on the great African plains of the Maasai Mara, away from the big city, the night sky was stunning. Naeku was walking behind the head ranger, keeping her torch directed at the ground as instructed; the decision had been taken not to take the park jeeps, as the lights and the noise of the engines would spook the poachers, giving them time to escape into the night on their bikes. The walk to the edge of the Mara River from the kraal was dangerous. The nightly sounds of the plains sent a shiver down Naeku's spine; she wished she was tucked up in her own bed Facebooking her friends. A nearby pride of lions roared into the night, letting everybody know of their presence; in the distance the low rumblings of a herd of elephants could be heard as they called out messages of reassurance to each other.

Naeku's grandfather was sitting in a tree as they

approached; scrambling down, he greeted the park rangers, informing them that the poachers had gone off into the bush. He had heard the young lads discussing their tactics; it was the three cheetah cubs they had spotted earlier that afternoon they had in mind as their next target.

One of the rangers asked how far ahead the poachers were. Naeku's old warrior grandfather speculated that the men were probably a few hundred metres ahead.

"How many are we talking about? Are they armed?" asked the head ranger.

"Four, and I recognise the stickers on the bikes; they come from a neighbouring village. I think one or two at the most are armed," replied Olekina.

Olekina's grandfather simply nodded.

"Naeku, Olekina, do you know where the mother cheetah and the cubs are?" asked one of the rangers.

"Yes, under the small outcrop we sat on earlier."

A single gunshot rang out across the night plain. The park rangers raced towards where the shot had come from; the six rangers fired in the air as they charged forward, surrounding the gang of four. Having been taken completely by surprise, the poachers dropped the tied sacks that had the three cubs in and headed towards the river, but quickly ran into a wall of angry hippos that were emerging from the river for their nightly feed on the nearby grassy plain. Trapped by a wall of hippos, notorious for being the most dangerous animal in Africa, the poaching gang dropped their weapons and surrendered. Three of the rangers fired flares to head off the startled hippos, sending them scurrying back to the river.

Standing on the outcrop of rock, the old grandfather explained to Naeku and the twins the gang would have waited for the mother cheetah to head off hunting before approaching the cubs. The cubs' instinct would be to lie perfectly still in the face of danger. The net that was thrown over them would have prevented them from escaping the gang's clutches. The mother must have heard their cries for help, abandoned her hunt and headed back to protect her cubs. The gang heard her coming and, once she was in range, shot her. That was the gunshot they heard.

The park rangers acted quickly, cuffing all four of the poachers; the commotion would have attracted the attention of numerous predators who would soon be on the scene to investigate the goings-on, placing everybody in danger. Olekina shouted at Naeku and his sister to run and pick up the sacks with the cubs in. The cubs were heavy, and their wriggling around made it really difficult to get a firm grip of the sacks.

Naeku struggled with her cheetah cub, but she was determined to walk back to the kraal. She was angry with the poachers; they didn't care about what they had done tonight, they were simply annoyed with themselves for getting caught, which meant they would not be paid for their ill-gotten deeds and furthermore would be looking at a custodial sentence of several years in a Nairobi jail.

As for the three cheetah cubs; well, if left out on the plains without their mother's protection they would be dead within days, either killed by the lions or hyenas or simply dying from starvation. The loss of their mother would be devastating to these eight-week-old cubs; normally in the wild they would stay with their mother for up to eighteen months, learning all the necessary skills in life to become successful wild cheetahs. The rangers, like on so many occasions these days, were left with no option but to take the cubs to a specialised rescue centre for cheetahs; there they would be looked after and lovingly cared for by the staff. A training programme would be put in place over the next few years with the ultimate aim of releasing them back into the wild when the time was right. At least they had escaped the clutches of being some rich or famous person's pet trophy.

The last few weeks Naeku had spent with her grandfather learning about the Maasai ways and what was happening on the open plains had been an eye-opening experience, but now back in her bedroom, Naeku was looking on the internet as to find out what to do about the desperate plight of Africa's declining wildlife. Her father had said to her there was no point in being angry about what had happened; she needed to come up with a plan, something that would prick the conscience of world leaders as well as the rich and famous who saw the cubs as must-have accessories. Equally she would have to understand the mindset of the poachers and what led them to do the things they do, challenge and work with them. Invariably poverty was the driving force behind the poachers' actions and she would need to look at a programme of how to support them to get a better education and way of life. These challenges would be taxing, but if she really wanted to stop the mass destruction of the African wildlife she would have to work hard over the next few years.

A simpler challenge, though, was to work on her father, to start building a fresh relation with his father before it was too late.

That she would start tomorrow.

DUSCHA

Yakutia Airlines flight R3477 from Moscow's Vnukovo International Airport touched down at Yakutsk airport twenty-four hours late, having been delayed as a direct result of adverse weather conditions. The normal night flight time for the 757-200 was around seven hours, with a bit of give and take for unseen circumstances. The blizzards that had been raging across the Central Siberian Plateau over the last few days had finally blown themselves out. Duscha, standing in the middle of the arrivals hall with her older brother Mikhail, who had driven them the short distance to the airport that stood on the northern perimeter of the city, looked at the weather app on her phone. It was showing minus seventeen. Spring was just around the corner but winter hadn't quite finished sweeping the area; she had one last trick up her sleeve. The snowstorm that was spreading south from the Arctic Circle would arrive later that night, bringing with it more snow to the city that was already buried deep in it. Yakutsh is the capital city of the Russian Republic of Sakha, sitting on the Lena River approximately four hundred and fifty kilometres south of the Arctic Circle. With a population fast approaching three hundred thousand, Yakutsh had been home to Duscha for the past eleven years.

Duscha's father appeared tired as he emerged into the arrivals hall. Tucked neatly about his person was a collection of carefully wrapped parcels from the famous kyrishko store on Tverskaya St. in Moscow. Her father often flew to Moscow to lecture young medical students studying at Moscow's universities and carry out complex brain surgery on Moscow's rich and famous. As a practising neurosurgeon for the past twenty years, he had acquired quite a respectful reputation amongst Russia's elite medical professionals. Duscha couldn't wait to get home and unwrap the contents of her parcels, try them on and post pictures of herself posing to all her friends on Facebook, Instagram and Pinterest. The thought had even crossed her mind to get her closest friend Boris to video her and post on YouTube to see if she could go viral and be seen by millions of viewers across the planet. *'Hmmm'*.... now that was a thought!

Still in her own little world of fantasy Duscha was soon brought back to reality as the automatic doors that led to the car parks swished open, sweeping in a blast of ice-laden biting Siberian air. Walking to the car with her father and brother was fun; the airport authorities had only bothered to clear the snow away from certain areas around the terminal buildings. The rest was still covered with deep, crisp, hard, glistening snow, which made a sharp crunching noise underfoot. She was taken by surprise to see her father and brother embroiled in a snowball fight; clearly this was a father and son moment, taking time out to enjoy the snow. The speed and ferocity with which the snow fight was being undertaken was an irresistible challenge to her. With her precious cargo safely secured in the boot of the family car, she threw herself into the snow battle, pitting herself against her father and brother. The family snowball fight was brought to an abrupt end by the sound of two Russian Su-34 fighter jets buzzing the airport as they circled round in preparation to land. Rumours abounded that President Putin was to make a brief appearance at the nearby diamond mine in the next twenty-four hours, and these fighter jets were no doubt part of the advance presidential protection squad.

The world of ballet was Duscha's world. Her dream of becoming a principal dancer to Russia's most famous of ballet companies, The Bolshoi Ballet Company, founded in 1776 by Prince Pyotr Urusov and Michael Maddox, would be the pinnacle in her dancing career. To travel the world and dance in front of millions of people was her ultimate aspiration, but those days at present were nothing but imaginary thoughts buried deep in her brain matter; years of toil and exhaustive training lay ahead of her.

It had been a long day. Duscha headed to her room, pulling shut her bedroom curtains, but not before taking one fleeting glance down the street she lived on. The view from her front bedroom window looked out across the city skyline; one advantage of living in the house at the top of the hill. The snowstorm that had been predicted had arrived with a vengeance. The fresh snowflakes hardly had time to settle before the angry winds picked them back up again, scattering them far and wide across the deserted city streets. Only the odd howls of foolhardy dogs still prowling the streets looking for the last scraps of food from unprotected bins could be heard; soon even they would be heading home to their owner's houses, if they had any sense.

Sitting cross-legged on her blush pink and aqua striped duvet that was covered in beautiful hand stitched Babushka Russian dolls of varying sizes and colours, painstakingly done by her mother last year as part of her birthday present, Duscha leaned forward to reach for the elegantly wrapped parcels her father had brought back with him earlier on. Tearing at the paper and removing the lid from the box to the first parcel and carefully peeling away the silver grey tissue paper, Duscha gently lifted the cerise tutu out of the box. Holding it up to get a better look, she examined the intricate gold embroidered fleur-de-lys pattern she had specifically asked to be placed around the edge of the skirt section. The matching deep crimson under layers added to the overall effect. Duscha quickly opened the other boxes and was delighted with their contents; rummaging through the piles of boxes, tissue and wrapping paper she started to panic. Where were her ballet pointe shoes? She looked under her bed, and around her room; finally flinging open her bedroom door she dashed downstairs and stood in front of her father.

"Papa, where are my ballet shoes? They're not here; you must have left them behind somewhere."

Her father calmly looked up from reading one of

his medical journals; sitting quietly, he asked her:

"Are you sure you have looked everywhere?"

"Of course I'm sure I have looked everywhere, papa"

"Well what is that parcel next to the front door in the hallway?"

Duscha swivelled her head in the direction her father's eyes were pointing. For a twelve-year-old girl going on sixteen, at times she could behave like a demonstrative little super brat with a temper to match. Rather ashamedly and slightly red-faced, she opened the box that was in the hallway and there were her size three red satin ballet pointe shoes with red silk laces to match. Humiliated, she tried to sneak up the stairs. Halfway up she could hear her father.

"I take it you found your shoes then?"

"Err, yes papa?"

"Did I hear the words *sorry, papa*."

"Sorry, papa."

Tossing the box aside and discarding the tissue paper haphazardly, she quickly laced her pointe shoes. She had specifically asked for red satin as opposed to the normal traditional pasty pink. Duscha had recently read an old children's story, '*The Red Shoes*' by the Danish Author Hans Christian Andersen, where the rich shoemaker had made a pair of red shoes for a Count's daughter, but they didn't fit so he sold them to a little orphaned girl called Karen who lived with a wealthy old lady. The red shoes would dance of their own accord, and whenever she wore the shoes the little girl would attract a lot of attention as she danced. With that inspired thought buried deep in her illogical mind she envisaged herself being a prima ballerina dancing all over the world, in front of Kings, Queens and Presidents.

It was bitterly cold the next morning as Duscha and her brother waited at the bus stop. As the next bus arrived, a small crowd of people emerged from the café across the way, holding in their hands polystyrene mugs of steaming hot coffee and tea. They had clearly taken the choice to wait in the warm café as opposed to standing in the freezing Arctic conditions. The small group of people quickly boarded the bus and took their seats. Duscha and her brother sat at the front. The short ride into the city centre would be a matter of minutes; removing her fur gloves, she tapped the messenger app on her phone and sent a message to her friend Boris to meet her outside the dance school on ul. Kulakovskogo behind the Mammoth Museum; with it being Saturday the morning's ballet class would be a rigorous session, with there being no day school. Earlier in the week Duscha had arranged to meet up with some of her friends after her dancing session, at the cinema centre just off ul. Kirova. The distinctive blue glass pyramid roof of the centre, along with its modern design, was in stark contrast to the austere buildings that dated back to the old Soviet Union days. Lunch would be a quick snack from one of the fast food outlets that crowded the main foyers before darting into one of the many auditoriums to see La La Land. Her brother Mikhail was heading off to his Saturday job at one of the main department stores in the city centre and, like Duscha, he had made arrangements to meet up with some of his friends after work at the local sports centre to play five-a-side football.

Boris was sitting on the steps outside the dance school well wrapped up against the cold; the weather app on his phone was showing minus twenty-six. Duscha sprinted up the steps; she was anxious to get out of the cold, but more importantly she was eager to show off her new outfit to the other girls in the dance school. Boris had only sat on the step for a few short minutes while he waited for Duscha, but that was enough to give him two frozen buttocks. As he got up to give Duscha a hug he quickly put his hands behind his back in an attempt to restore life to his nether regions.

"What are you doing, Boris?"

"I'm warming my bum cheeks, is that OK with you?"

"Whatever."

Boris lent forward to give Duscha a peck on the cheek, but Duscha merely swept past him; she had other important matters to attend to. Boris, feeling slightly embarrassed in front of his friends who were watching from an upstairs window, bent down to pick up his grey rucksack and raced after Duscha. Reaching the top of the steps Duscha pushed the swing doors open that led to a slightly dilapidated foyer, off which to the right were the stairs leading to the main dance hall on the first floor. In its heyday this little back street theatre would have been rather grand, but neglect and lack of state investment left the place feeling tired. The beautiful crystal chandeliers that would have once hung majestically from the ornate ceiling had long gone, most likely stolen to order on the black market. Cheap, bare florescent tubes now provided the light and even they didn't cover the holes left behind where the chandeliers had once shone. Even the internal plaster work, that had been there for decades, was now crumbling and peeling off, revealing the bullet holes that had left their deep scars in the walls from numerous skirmishes from WW2.

Not many of the ballet students had arrived; normally Duscha was one of the last to turn up and she would walk into a scene of dancers getting changed with their earpieces glued into their ears, listening to free downloaded music on their smart phones, but for once she had made the effort to be early as she had something in mind and Boris was key to that plan. Her strategy was simple; to quickly get changed into her ballet outfit with her red satin pointe shoes, take to the virtually empty hall and go through her basic routine with Boris videoing all her moves.

"So this is why you got me here so early in the morning? For me to video you and no doubt work my magic and put it on YouTube so that you can see how many hits you can get from around the world. Hmm… ."

"Oooh… No comment Mr Boris. Well…you are supposed to be the class IT whizz and what's a girl supposed to do these days to draw the world's attention? I'm… merely tapping into local resources for one's own purpose. "

"That's what's called taking advantage, Miss Duscha!"

"I'd prefer to say 'working smart', Mr Boris."

"How stupid of me, I thought for one brief moment you wanted to meet up and spend time with me before your so-called hectic day started!"

With a gleeful glint in her right eye she cast Boris a discreet little wink.

The three young boys that were secretly hiding behind the old grand piano in the far corner of the hall, having watched Boris and Duscha's rather simple approach to flirting, could no longer control their inward sniggers and broke out into complete raucous hysterics. Having brought attention to themselves, Boris sent them one of his stern, wry faces and, coupled with veiled threats to rearrange certain parts of their anatomy, the giggling trio departed with haste.

Boris put the video on YouTube, but as he did so a Facebook message flashed across the face of Duscha's smartphone. '*I agree The Elbphilharmonie in Hamburg Germany is an amazing building.*' Boris was intrigued as to why Duscha had shared an image of a stunning building. For a split second he thought about tapping into Duscha's Facebook page, but his conscience was telling him that was the wrong thing to do. He wouldn't like people accessing what was on his phone. Hurriedly he finished uploading Duscha's video to YouTube. Rummaging through his bag, he pulled out his phone. Gently tapping the Wikipedia app he searched '*Elbphilharmonie*'. Boris quickly scrolled down the image page; it was a newly constructed concert hall/hotel with luxury apartments for wealthy Germans. The building itself was in the HafenCity quarter of Hamburg down by the Elbe River, a converted old warehouse crowned with a glassy construction that resembled a hoisted sail or water wave. It looked magnificent at night, all lit up, dominating Hamburg's city skyline. What was Duscha's fascination with this breathtaking building? Did she think that one day she would be able to dance there? Boris, still mystified, closed down the app and threw his phone into his bag. Slinging his sports bag over his right shoulder he left the dance hall for his football training. Before he left he posted a message on her messenger page, '*Call me this afternoon.*' With that, he handed her phone to one of the male dancers who had just started his warm-up routine.

The morning class had been vigorous and relentless. Duscha was exhausted; the tutors had set a punishing schedule and were looking for perfection as well as stamina; all the students felt an air of tension had prevailed around the place, which was unusual. What the reason was nobody amongst the students quite knew.

However, rumours had started to circulate that a talent scout from Russia's most renowned ballet company, The Bolshoi Ballet, based at The Bolshoi Theatre, Theatre Square, 1, Moscow, was within the vicinity and was looking for new young blood for future performances. The professional life span of a modern ballerina could be short if unforeseen injuries forced them into unexpected retirement. With that nagging fear always looming in the background, the company was always on the lookout for fresh talent that could be trained and nurtured, ready to step up when required, thus ensuring the company continued to flourish in an ever-demanding world.

The film had finished; Duscha sent a text message to her father to say that she was waiting outside the cinema centre; daylight hours in Siberia in winter were short, so it was dark when she emerged from the cinema. To her surprise Boris was waiting for her, so she waved her friends off.

"Text me when you get home, girls!"

"Well I wasn't expecting to see you; how did your football training go? My father's on his way to pick me up, do you want a lift home as well?"

"Yeah, that would be good. How was your day?"

"Hhmm…interesting, the tutors really put us through our paces today. They were demanding and shouting for perfection and the atmosphere was intense and horrible."

"Why?"

"Not sure. There was a very distinctive elegant lady sitting up in the gallery; she was wearing a white ermine fur coat with a matching fur cloud hat. She appeared on occasions to be tapping furiously on a laptop."

"Did you recognise her?"

"No, but my friend Olga seems to think she is from St Petersburg from the label on her suitcase that was left unattended for hours outside the hall doors."

Duscha's father pulled up in his new BMW7; she climbed into the front seat while Boris scrambled in the back having slung his bag in first. Before she had even managed to fasten her seatbelt, her father inquired as to how she had gotten on today at her ballet. He wanted the best for her and to be a successful person and he had heard from one of the tutors that they had received an unannounced visit from a highly influential person from The Bolshoi Ballet Company observing the students. Duscha listened intently to her father's comments; the woman in the white fur coat who had sat rather po-faced in the gallery must have been Moscow's spy in the camp. Her imagination was fired up and, deep in her own thoughts, she barely recalled Boris getting out off the car. Anxious to get home and log on to her laptop, as the little charge indicator on her smartphone was showing red at one per cent meant she had insufficient power to access YouTube; she was eager to see how many hits her video had had and the overall reaction on Facebook from all her ballet friends, who by now must have heard that the mystery woman sitting in the gods was Moscow's scout.

Several days had passed; Duscha was slightly disappointed with the numbers that had watched her video. Her father had got the impression that she expected it to go viral overnight and reminded her that to be a successful dancer was going to take years of arduous work. With her father's words resonating deep in her thoughts, she headed off to school. The recent blizzards had given way to a period of tranquillity and calm, but the snow and ice that remained underfoot gave a crisp crunching noise as her feet made contact with the ground as she walked along the wide pavements. Temporarily distracted by the crushing sound of the snow and ice as she marched along, she almost missed the pinging noise coming from her phone. Briefly stopping, she reached into her outside pocket; pulling out her phone she saw the little red dot in the top right hand corner of her mail app icon, which indicated she had a new email message. Tapping the blue app with the envelope image clearly emblazoned on, she opened up the message; momentarily transfixed to the ground she gently brushed her right mid-finger across the screen and, as she scrolled down the displayed text, her heart began to pound harder and harder in her ribcage. The email was from The Bolshoi Ballet Company's official email address. *'Having watched your performance the other day, and taking into consideration the comments of your tutors, we would like you to attend trial auditions here in Moscow later this month. Would you please confirm your acceptance by replying to this email within the next two days.*

If you don't reply within the timescale specified, we will assume that you are not interested in taking this offer up. I'm sure you realise an offer of this nature is very rare and that places to attend an audition of this nature are highly sought after.'

An old lady passerby stopped, tapped her on the shoulder and enquired if she was alright. Glancing up from her phone Duscha stared momentarily into the weather-beaten face of the old lady before replying:

"I'm fine; thank you."

Still slightly taken aback by the message, she turned her head back towards the old lady, who by now was halfway down the street; for a split second she thought about running after the lady to share her news, but then thought perhaps not. Duscha's mind was preoccupied for most of the day; she had decided not to tell anybody her news until she had spoken with her father later that night. It was mid afternoon and it was times like these that she wished her mother was close at hand to talk to, but she and her father had split up and divorced several years ago. She had now remarried and lived with her new husband on the outskirts of Rome in Italy.

As a family that followed the teachings of the Russian Orthodox Church, Duscha was always quizzical when it came to her mother's business affairs; she had started off as a prison guard at the local jail house, but had worked her way into the Russian diplomatic protection service. Her last posting was part of the team that protected the former Italian Ambassador to Moscow, whom she had recently married. Now working at the Vatican, she protects Pope Francis; a Russian Orthodox worshipper guarding the life of the head of the Roman Catholic faith. How ironic. Duscha could only imagine the responsibility of having to protect such a high-risk public person; but today she just wanted her mother to be here and be her mum. She sent her mother a text message with her news, but before she sent it she wondered what time was it in Rome. It was 2pm in the afternoon here so it would be... It was far too complex to work that out. She abandoned that thought and sent the text regardless.

The school bell rang, indicating the end of the day; going through the daily ritual of layering up, with coats, gloves, scarves and throwing her blue rucksack over her right shoulder, she headed off home. As she pushed opened the school doors a blast of icy cold wind hit her in the face. She tightened the straps of her wool lined hat, thinking that an extra tug would at least keep her ears warm. She wondered what was for tea.

Walking up the drive to the front door, Duscha could see the figure of her father sitting at his desk through the window of his downstairs study; as she walked by the window she tapped on the glass. Her father was on the phone, no doubt to a rich client; looking up he gave a brief wave and mouthed something to her through the glass as if to say the front door was open. The smell of home cooking wafted around the house. Duscha dumped her stuff in the middle of the hall and headed straight for the kitchen. She was starving. Her father, despite being a clever brain surgeon, was also an exceptional cook. Clearly he had been working from home today and had taken time to do some baking, evidenced by the fresh breads and cakes piled high on cooling trays on the big kitchen table. Duscha lifted the lid of a large pot that was sitting in the middle of the big Aga stove. Looking into the pot, Duscha could see that her father had made a hearty winter stew that was slowly simmering away. Turning back to face the table with all the fresh baking on, she caught the outline of her father and brother standing in the kitchen doorway; reading the look on their faces she knew they knew, but still Mikhail asked the question:

"Well, have you got something to tell us?"

"Might have."

"Well!" her father exclaimed.

"Well what! You both know already; don't you? I take it, papa, that you were copied in by email this morning?"

"Yes, and I've just got off the phone with your mother, to whom you sent a text message this afternoon."

"Ahh. I thought I would…"

"That's not a problem, sweetheart, she's your mother. She might live in another country, but we do occasionally talk to each other about you two if a joint decision about your futures is required."

"Can I email the ballet company academy, papa,

to say that I will be attending the auditions?"

"You can; but there is no need. I've already...."

"Papa! That wasn't your call."

Mikhail looked at his father as if to say well that's you told off.

"Err... tea anyone? The stew smells good, papa," muttered Mikhail.

Mikhail's meek attempt to deflect a family row appeared to have temporarily worked as all three of them sat down around the kitchen table to steaming bowls of hot stew and fresh homemade sweet bread rolls that had cranberries, raisins and cashew nuts in.

Duscha and her father, having put their little disagreement to one side for the time being, sat together for a while in the study. Most family decisions, for some bizarre reason, took place in their father's study. Mikhail could hear the discussion taking place behind the closed door; clearly his father had been busy today phoning his friends in Moscow putting arrangements in place for Duscha's visit, but what he wasn't prepared for was his father's insistence that he was to accompany his sister. The look on his sister's face as she flung open the study door and stomping off to her room left Mikhail with the impression that she had evidently not succeeded in getting all her own way with her ideas of going to Moscow. The words *'Your brother is going with you, or you're not going at all'* resonated in his ears as his sister brushed past him with a scowl etched firmly on her face. Mikhail had never been to Moscow and now he was rather looking forward to going; his father had long described Moscow as a city steeped in history but also a dangerous place.

Duscha's father had relented over his children's choice of transport; for him the direct seven-hour flight to Moscow's Vnukovo International Airport made far better sense, but Duscha and her brother Mikhail opted for the much longer Trans Siberian Railway. For them this was an adventure as well, as Duscha's future and the eight days it would take as opposed to a seven-hour flight was far more of interest in their eyes. It also meant they got an extra week off school, something their father was not happy with. But they did agree to fly back.

The bus ride south from Yakutsk to the small town of Amur close to the Chinese border was an arduous one, but the breathtaking mountain scenery of the Yablonovy and Stanovoy Mountain Ranges made up for the cold rickety ride on the old bus. From there Duscha and her brother boarded a train to Chita. Chita was one of the many towns and cities that lay on the infamous Trans Siberian Railway Line. Built between 1891 and 1916, the line linked Moscow to Vladivostok. Vladivostok was one of Russia's most eastern cities, being closer to Japan than Moscow itself. Duscha's father had paid for a bunk-bed compartment for two; the two of them would have to share for the entire duration of the journey. The three thousand nine hundred mile journey to platform three at Moscow's Yaroslaskaya terminal would take the two of them right across the heart of Russia, passing well known cities such as Irkutsk on the Mongolian border, Taishet, Novosibirsk, Omsk, Tyumen, Perm, Kirov and finally Moscow.

As journeys went the great train ride held its points of interest as well as its periods of boredom, but for Duscha and her brother this was a journey of nostalgia as well as a mode of transport, for both of them recalled their grandmother's story of how their great-great grandparents fled St Petersburg to Moscow in the late winter/early spring of 1917 to escape the clutches of the Bolsheviks' Red Army. It was widely rumoured that their great-great grandparents worked in the kitchens of Tsar Nicholas II's Winter Palace in St Petersburg as bakers and that Tsarina Alexandria would often come down to the kitchens and request that more breads be baked and distributed to the peasants who would queue daily outside the palace walls for scraps of food. When the Tsar and his family were overthrown and forced into exile, a lot of the domestic staff fled, fearing for their lives. Family rumours over the decades strongly believed that great-great grandmother stole a Faberge ruby and diamond encrusted pendant from Grand Duchess Anastasia, the Tsar's youngest daughter, before she left, stitching it into the lining of her undergarments. She clearly knew how important the pendant was and that it would be extremely valuable and no doubt come in useful one day. Following the assassination of the Tsar and his family at Ipatiev House at Yekaterinburg in July 1918, the family fled again, fearing that their neighbours had started to suspect that they had close links to the deposed royal family and could lose their own lives. This time they fled to the wilds of Siberia, taking the Trans Siberian Railway to Chita, and headed for the diamond mines nearby. Their grandfather refused to serve in the army in WW2 and for that he was sent to one of the Gulags around Yakutsk. With the war over and their grandfather surviving the hard labour camp, the family settled in Yakutsk working in the diamond mines. After the war their grandmother wanted to move to Moscow where she had been a ballet dancer herself in The Bolshoi Ballet, but their grandfather refused to go for some reason. Duscha was always grateful her grandmother introduced her to ballet and she would often enjoy watching her grandmother dance. Duscha often wondered why her mother's side of the family had so little to do with them and that it was her father's family that dominated the scene. Maybe one day she would ask her father about that.

Duscha and Mikhail had always found the story of how the family had come to live in Yakutsk fascinating, so the journey for them was kind of a trip down memory lane, except they were travelling in relative comfort and security; not like that of their great-great grandparents, who would have had to endure utter hardship as poor peasants trying to survive the last few months of WW1. Plus they would have to endure the intense summer heat of central Russia. The story of the Imperial Pendant; was it true? Only their grandmother knew that; but their father did say his mother had sold some jewellery on the black market and that the money raised was enough to put him through medical school. Was their father's education funded by a piece of jewellery strongly rumoured to be connected to The Grand Duchess Anastasia, the youngest daughter of Tsar Nicholas II? Wow, that would be a good story to put out on her social media outlets, hmm... how many hits would she get? Mikhail could see what she was thinking and simply retorted:

"Don't bother."

Platform three at Moscow's Yaroslaskaya station was crowded with excited tourists eager to board the train that would take them into the inner sanctum of Russia. Squeezing their way through the hordes of people, Duscha and her brother Mikhail emerged from the terminal buildings onto Komsomolskaya Square. Duscha was anxious to get going; a whole week cooped up on a train with very little room to practise her daily floor routine and exercises every modern dancer needed to carry out had driven her mad. A text message appeared on her phone, '*I'm by the newspaper stand across the square. I'm holding a purple umbrella aloft in my right hand.*' Looking up from her phone she scanned her eyes up and down the square searching for a newspaper stand; she spotted the lady waving the umbrella and was shocked to see that the lady was actually her mother. Duscha shouted at Mikhail:

"It's mother!"

"Where?" snapped Mikhail.

"Over there, you numphead."

"Excuse me! How was I supposed to know our mother was here?" protested Mikhail.

"Oh shut up, for goodness sake."

"Oh… charming!" uttered Mikhail.

Mikhail was about to continue when his phone went off in his left outside pocket. Grabbing the phone he looked at the screen. It was his father.

"Hello son, so you have arrived."

"How…"

"Your mother has just sent me a text message."

"Oh! I take it that you planned for mother to be here then? And it was her you were talking to the other day in the study about our arrangements and not one of your rich clients?"

"Yep, have a great few days with your mother. She has the keys to the apartment. Ring me when you are about to leave Moscow."

"Apparently father had arranged for mother to be here, some so-called mother time."

"Oh wow! Well don't just stand there, Mikhail, pick all our stuff up. Places to go, people to see, things to do."

With those parting words ringing in his ears, he watched Duscha dash across the street, weaving herself around the traffic. For a few brief moments he thought to himself, *'What did her last slave die of?'*

Komsomolskaya metro station was only a short distance. Duscha descended down the steps into the bowels of Moscow's intricate underground system; as she did so she clutched the bag that had her expensive designer ballet costume in tightly to her chest. She had been warned about the pick-pocket gangs that operated here under Moscow's busy streets. Mikhail had no concerns for his safety in amongst the heaving masses that thronged the station; he did have one of the world's most experienced bodyguards behind him – his mother. If she could protect The Pope, then keeping a watchful eye on him and his sister should be a relatively easy task for her. As Duscha jostled her way in the crowd, she looked up to the ornate ceiling; the dazzling chandeliers and beautiful artwork was mesmerising. Her father had told her to look at the ceilings if they went on the underground metro, for Moscow's metro stations were world renowned for their stunning architecture.

Kropotkinskaya station was only a few stops along the line. It was hot and stuffy on the underground and Duscha was pleased when she was back up to street level. Gogolevsky Boulevard was an expensive part of Moscow; the two bedroom small apartment their father owned was only a short walk along the boulevard from the metro station. The apartment was on the third floor and looked across to Moscow's Museum of Modern Art. Down from the museum was the Cathedral of Christ the Saviour, one of the most significant buildings in Moscow, apart from The Kremlin, which was close by. Duscha's father always stayed at the apartment when he visited Moscow on business; his mother had purchased the apartment when he came to Moscow to study. The family assumed the money to buy the apartment came from the black market sale of the Faberge ruby and diamond pendant. Did the secret buyer or buyers know about the pendant's historical background? They probably did; they would have had their own experts to establish the piece's authenticity.

The little apartment was a simple affair; functional but basic. Her father really never talked about it. Nevertheless, rightly or wrongly, Duscha assumed the place would have had a little more opulence about it. Still, it was a pleasant surprise as she and Mikhail had expected to be staying with some of her father's posh clients. Her father had quite a fun sneaky side to him at times and enjoyed springing the odd surprise on them. However she wasn't here for the views. She had several auditions to attend over the next two days.

Mikhail, now free of escort duties, planned what sights he was going to visit, starting off with Red Square and The Kremlin; sitting through numerous dance routines was not really his thing. The following morning, as his mother and Duscha left for the auditions, he wished his sister good luck and quietly slipped down the stairs and out the door. Duscha carefully checked that she had everything. Today was an important day and she didn't want to mess up. She had the place and the times firmly imprinted in her head.

The queue at the audition hall to the academy started at the doors and trailed around the corner and down the street. Duscha's heart sank; she hadn't expected to see so many applicants all vying for a place at the famous Bolshoi Ballet Academy. The doors opened and all the girls flooded in, found a changing spot and headed to the backstage rehearsal area. Duscha, like all the other girls, had her brief with what dance moves the judges were looking for and in what sequence. They had the next hour to warm up and practise before the auditions would start. Duscha was nervous; she had the basic abilities to be a successful ballerina but at times her nerves got the better of her. She hoped her little red satin pointe shoes would work their magic. Her mother gave her a reassuring hug and reminded her she would face countless auditions in her career and she was just going to have to conquer her nerves, but that would come with experience.

It was a long wait for Duscha's five minutes in front of the panel of academy judges; as she walked out onto the stage she could see the three stern faces of the people that could possibly change the outcome of her life sitting at a table a short distance away. Giving her name and number, she nodded at the lady who was standing at the side of the stage with her finger hovering over the button that would start the music to her routine. Lifted by the feel of the music, she could feel her red satin pointe shoes glide across the stage floor. As she danced she began to relax and enjoy herself, but the brief routine was soon over as someone shouted.

"Thank you! Next."

Over the next few days further auditions followed, with no hint as to how well she was doing, but both she and her mother noticed that the number of girls showing up for each session had diminished quite substantially. Clearly the panel of judges had been whittling the contestants down until they got what they were looking for.

It was late on Sunday evening when Duscha and three other girls got a message asking them to return to the auditions. Standing on the stage with her mother and brother beside her, Duscha watched as the three judges came onto the stage. It was only now that she recognised the judge on the end was the tall elegant lady that wore the white fur ermine coat up in the gallery. The small man that sat in the middle of the table throughout the auditions smiled for the first time.

"Congratulations, girls. In these four letters are each of your confirmation documents offering you places at The Bolshoi Ballet Academy. Please read the paperwork carefully and get your parents to sign giving their permission for you to join us here in Moscow. Oh, in the other set of envelopes are tickets for tomorrow night's performance of Swan Lake and an invitation to meet the cast afterwards. See you tomorrow night. Goodnight." The small man looked quite pleased with himself having delivered his little speech just then. With this done, he smartly left the stage with the other judges.

The look of astonishment written across Duscha's face was clear to see; she turned to a member of the stage crew and asked them quite politely to take a photo of her, her mother and brother while she held her letter of offer. The whole world would shortly know about her achievement. But before she left she called her father with the news. She couldn't wait to see the reaction of her friends on Facebook and Instagram.

A night at Russia's most prestigious ballet was not to be attended in jeans and T-shirts. Rising early next morning, the order of the day set by their mother was to get Duscha and Mikhail suitably attired for tonight's performance. For Duscha an elegant evening gown and for Mikhail a white jacket, bow tie, studded shirt, black trousers, cummerbund that matched the colour of Duscha's dress and of course new shoes. If time allowed, some lunch at a posh café and maybe a little sightseeing.

Duscha enjoyed her day spending time with her mother and of course getting to try on lots of different dresses. The final choice was a pale powder blue long evening gown with a white chiffon shawl that had a silver thread fleck running through it. She looked amazing, as did Mikhail in his white taffeta dinner jacket and pale blue bow tie with matching cummerbund.

The Bolshoi theatre looked spectacular all lit up against the backdrop of Moscow's night sky; the flakes of snow that had started to float down and settle on the pavements underfoot gave the scene a touch of mystical magic. Small crowds had started to mill around the theatre's main door; they, like

Duscha, were excited at the thought of attending tonight's performance. For many it would be an experience of a lifetime.

The theatre staff were busy in the white foyer, and for some reason temporary walk through security stands had been erected like at the airport; people were asked to pass under the stands and remove any metal objects and place them in the plastic boxes provided so that they could be separately scanned again, just like at the airport. Duscha turned to her mother.

"What's all this about?"

Her mother replied, "Maybe somebody of importance is coming tonight."

'Ooooh...' thought Mikhail, 'I wonder who.'

As Mikhail stepped through the security ring, he asked one of the guys who had in his hand a mini metal detector who was coming this evening. The tall well-built man merely smiled and pointed Mikhail in the direction of the ornate stairs that led up to the main auditorium.

Walking into the main auditorium, Duscha was taken aback with its lavish, stunning décor. The six layers of circles with their individual boxes all decked out in brilliant crimson curtains with white and gold balcony fronts looked impressive and the centre box where the Tsars and Presidents sat looked particularly regal. The red carpet and the individual red chairs that made up the stalls added to the overall effect. Duscha's seat with that of her mother's, brother's and the families of the other three girls that had been successful in getting into the school were at the back on the left side of the main aisle on a raised platform.

The performance was about to start, but before it did a spontaneous clap went around the theatre; Duscha, leaning forward and turning her head slightly to the right and upwards towards the centre box, saw President Vladimir Putin take his seat. Mikhail immediately turned to his mother.

"So that's why all the security was put in place, for the President! Wow."

Duscha was completely overawed by the night's production of Swan Lake, and couldn't wait to meet the cast. The cast gathered in The Choral Hall; everybody was asked to line up against the walls, as The President would shortly come along to meet the staff and the performers. Duscha felt a bit of a fraud; she had had no input with tonight's arrangements, yet here she was about to meet The President, Vladimir Putin. Gently shaking her hand, he asked her name and commented with a smile on his face that her evening attire was not quite a tutu. Duscha very briefly explained how she had come to be standing here in front of him. He merely replied rather gently.

"Well, young lady, you have your work cut out over the next few years. I wish you well."

With that, he continued down the long line of people before leaving the theatre and returning to The Kremlin.

The excitement and thrills of the last few days would live long in her memory, but tomorrow she and Mikhail had a long flight back to Yakutsk and their mother would return to Rome. Her schooling to become a world class prima ballerina dancing all over the world would start in a couple of months, maybe not at the Elbphilharmonie in Hamburg, as she had finally accepted that it was a concert hall more than a theatre for dance. Nevertheless she still admired the pictures of the building itself. Maybe she would dance in London's West End or on Broadway, New York. Who knows, let's just wait and see! But she had got into The Bolshoi Ballet Academy and that was an achievement in its own right.

ANARU

Anaru was born in Dunedin, a city known for its Scottish and Maori heritage, on the east coast of South Island, New Zealand. His father's side of the family originated from Aberdeen in Scotland, arriving in New Zealand close to forty years ago. His mother's descendants could be traced back to one of the local Maori tribes around Rotorua on North Island. When he was born, his father had insisted in keeping the Scottish family traditional name of Andrew, but his mother wanted a Maori connection; hence the compromise. Anaru, the Maori for Andrew.

Queenstown, where Anaru grew up, was a small resort town that sat on the shore of Lake Wakatipu in Otago, a region in the south-west corner of South Island, New Zealand. The town itself was renowned for its sporting excellence; in winter the Southern Alps, the backbone of South Island that surrounded Queenstown, attracted thousands of skiers from around the world. In summer, G-force paragliding, trekking, hang gliding, water paragliding, jet skiing, parasailing and numerous other water sports attracted people in their thousands to the town and the lake. But for Anaru rugby was his sport; he passionately followed the Otago Highlanders, the area super rugby team based in Dunedin, going with his father to all the home games. The All Blacks Rugby Union team were not only the most dominant force in the southern hemisphere, but they held the number one slot in the world rankings. Anybody that followed rugby, be that Union or League, knew about The All Blacks. He would sit with his father and friends in the bars of Queenstown in his All Black T-shirt, glued to the TV screens watching the international games. His idol was Dan Carter, fly-half, the position he loved to play.

His mother was getting concerned about him and, having spoken with his father, an appointment was made for Anaru to attend the local doctor's surgery. She explained the changes in Anaru's general behaviour, how he was exhausted coming home from school, the bruises on his body, lack of appetite, the numerous coughs and sore throats, the recent bout of pneumonia, that he was complaining his knee joints hurt. Her instincts were telling her that something more sinister was lurking in the background. She was right.

It had been nearly three years since he was diagnosed with leukaemia; he recalled the day that he sat in the consultant's room with the doctor confirming to his parents that all the tests they had run concluded he had leukaemia, specifically (A.L.L) Acute Lymphoblastic Leukaemia. A blood cancer. He distinctly remembered looking at his parents and watching the blood drain from their faces; he could even call to mind his father, who was sitting on his left, slumping in his seat and burying his head in his hands, his mother simply staring out of the window with a vacant look as if she had seen a ghost. He was nine years old at the time, a little boy who didn't fully understand what was happening to him or what was coming his way. Dr Smith, the consultant from Southlands Hospital in Invercargill, had suggested they make another appointment to discuss the options available, but more importantly to take time out for all of them to absorb the devastating news.

Dr Smith had said right from the start the treatment was going to be long and difficult. There would be good days and dark days, numerous trips back and forward from Queenstown to Southlands Hospital in Invercargill. The treatment would be varied, possibly ranging from chemotherapy and radiotherapy to a variety of drugs. All would depend on how Anaru reacted to the different treatments as to what the next course of action would be. The good news was that the leukaemia had been caught in its early stages and that the prognosis outcome was very good, eighty to ninety percent. However Anaru would be under Dr Smith's team for the next two to three years.

Sitting opposite his mother at the breakfast table in the large farmhouse kitchen, Anaru reached for the envelope his mother had slipped across the table. They both knew what the letter was about. The stamp had Invercargill branded all over it. It was from the hospital. It was hard to believe that three years had passed since that fateful day, but it had.

The letter was brief; Dr Smith had personally signed it. It was the letter he and his parents had been longing for; he had been given the all-clear, and Dr Smith didn't want to see him any more and that he would look out for his name on the team sheets of the Otago Highlanders matches and hopefully as an All Black, straddling the world stage representing New Zealand like his hero Dan Carter.

The farmhands were busy, as the sheep farm that had been in the family for decades was preparing for the summer shearing. Anaru's mother had organised the hired contractors that were due in the next few days to shear the six thousand Merino sheep. It would take the contractors the best part of two weeks working from dawn to dusk to accomplish the enormous task.

Anaru raced down the track down to Walter Peak, the sheep station on the lakeshore that was set up for the summer tourists to experience life on a sheep farm, plus get a posh meal in the fancy restaurant there at rip-off prices. If rich Americans and Europeans wanted to pay those prices, well, let them pay, thought Anaru. As he neared Walter Peak he could see the TSS Earnslaw, the old coal-fired steamship that criss crossed Lake Wakapitu several times a day bringing the tourists back and forth between here and Queenstown. The old steamship was some way out on the lake; on board were the sheep contractors that would spend the next few weeks on their farm. No shearing for Anaru this year; he had other plans now that he had been given the all-clear.

Anaru had texted his mates his wonderful news; he had taken a selfie of himself and his mother at the breakfast table holding up that letter and posted it on Facebook and Instagram. As he reached the small wooden jetty on the tiny shingle beach at Walter Peak his mobile phone kept pinging as the messages of '*Congratulations*' appeared on his screen.

Looking through his contact list on his phone, he came to Mr O'Connell; gently touching the screen over the number, the call was placed.

"Hello, who is it?"

"Mr O'Connell, it's Anaru."

"Hello son, what can I do for you?"

"I got the all clear from Dr Smith today. I know yesterday was the 16th of January and that was the last day of registering for the U14 team for 2016, but could you please make an exception? I have the fifty-five dollars subs and a letter of consent from my mother and father. I'm on my way now. Please Mr O'Connell; I won't let you down."

"Anaru, that is fantastic news. Meet me after lunch at the school gates."

"Thanks, Mr O'Connell."

As he put his phone down a message flashed across its screen.

"Welcome to Wakatipu High School U14 rugby season 2016. Training is every Tuesday and Thursday at 4pm, don't be late."

"Yesss," shouted Anaru to himself as he punched the air.

The mist that had cloaked the entire area, hiding the mountain peaks of the Southern Alps from view earlier, had evaporated as the summer sun had melted the mist away, giving rise to what promised to be another beautiful summer's day. A few bees were frantically buzzing around a small clump of late flowering Lupins down by the water's edge, collecting the last of the nectar. Their bright vivid colours of deep purple, pale pinks, blues, creams and yellows blended in nicely against the strong turquoise blue of the sky and the dark blue waters of the lake as they gently swayed in the light breeze blowing on the shore.

The tranquillity of Lake Wakatipu was shattered as the powerful outboard motors of the thunder jet ripped their way across the water's surface, sending wash hither and thither as the speed jet zigzagged its way to the wooden jetty at Walter Peak, where Anaru was standing. His eldest sister, who with her partner owned and ran the thunder jet business. Anaru appreciated the time his sister had taken out of her busy schedule to pick him up; he'd initially planned on taking the ninety minute ferry crossing on the TSS Earnslaw like he normally did, spending the time reading the latest book he had ordered off the internet about the most recent laws the rugby authorities had introduced this season. But clearly his sister had other ideas. Pulling alongside the jetty, his sister shouted at him to jump in and throw the red life jacket on.

Gently pulling back on the throttle and turning the wheel, Anaru, with his sister positioned directly behind him, steered the powerboat away from the jetty and headed out to the deeper waters of the lake, where he was able to bring the boat to almost full power. The boat ate up the water as it skimmed and bounced at great speed across the lake surface. His sister could see the smile on his face but she quickly grabbed his hand to ease back on the throttle as a thunder jet, like a big beast, could easily flip over in inexperienced hands. Anaru was enjoying the ride of his life; all he could think about was the faces of his friends as he came into the small harbour at Queenstown. Quad biking he was used too, as he would often go with his father and the farm hands on his better days rounding up the sheep on the steep hillsides. Rightly or wrongly he assumed that steering the speed boat would be similar to riding the quad bike; like any twelve-year old lad, the dangers of flipping never entered his head. He just wanted the thrill of the ride.

All his friends had gathered at the café that fronted the shingle beach; cool milkshakes, french fries and different burgers all smothered in disgusting varieties of sauces were the order of the day. His friends had come to share his celebration. With the selfies posted on to Facebook, Instagram and any other social media outlets he and his friends had registered for done, he headed off for his appointment with Mr O'Connell. Anaru checked the time on his phone; he realised he was going to be late and, remembering the text he had received that morning about punctuality, he raced through the town streets, shouting at people to get out of his way. Fryer St was directly ahead; with moments to spare, having sprinted the entire length of the street, he reached the school gates in the nick of time.

"Hmm… maybe I should put you on the wing, Anaru, following that impressive spurt!"

Anaru hadn't got the energy to reply, huffing and puffing to catch his breath; he was out of condition. All the chemo, radiotherapy and drugs over the last few years had taken it out of him, leaving him physically weak. Some serious training would be required; no doubt Mr O'Connell had that firmly in hand. Rummaging around the bottom of his rucksack, Anaru pulled out the plastic bag he had his fifty-five New Zealand dollars in, along with the letter from his parents.

"So, Anaru, you want to be the next Dan Carter? Fly-half for The All Blacks…"

"Yes, sir."

"Well, training starts tomorrow, 4pm sharp, on those fields across there where you played your Rippa Rugby four years ago."

"I know, sir, but that was the non-contact days. I'm going to get my head kicked in now. I need to toughen up."

"Yep… Oh, Anaru."

"Yes."

"Don't turn up to training at the last moment. That's rude. OK?"

With that veiled threat, Anaru shuffled off at a leisurely pace back into town. He looked at his registration form. An elderly man walking his dog was heading in his direction. Anaru stopped him and asked if he would mind taking a photo of him holding his registration form. The elderly man obliged.

"I'll take a few, just to make sure. Now what button do I press on this smartphone of yours?"

Anaru selected the picture that he thought would best reflect his good side; not that he was a poser in any way, but one had to think of image. The other snapshots he deleted; he had enough photos blocking up his phone. Clicking on Dr Smith's team's email address, he sent the image of himself holding his registration documents. He tagged a message to the picture:

'To Dr Smith. Today is a new day in my new life, the life you and your team gave back to me; the last three years have been so challenging. I wanted to personally thank you for what you all did for me; you have no idea what it means to me to be able to play my rugby. I want to thank you from the bottom of my heart and thought the best way to do this was by sending you a photo of myself and to let you know my training to become New Zealand's fly-half in years to come starts tomorrow. Oh, by the way, you can see that my hair has started to come back. I'll need a haircut soon. Can't wait to go to the barbers and get my haircut. Thank you love Anaru.'

It was a glorious summer's day as he ambled his way back to the café on the lakeside where all his friends were still sitting. His sister had promised him and his friend Pete a parasailing lesson and that was an offer he was taking up. As he neared the café he could see that his friend Pete was already togged up and that his wetsuit was folded across the yellow plastic chair next to the bins. The two of them were so excited; they had seen many visitors come to Queenstown and enjoy the thrill of the ride. Today was their turn. Fully kitted and harnessed in, the speed jet slipped its mooring and headed for the open water of the lake. With full throttle on and the bright orange and blue canopy with a smiley face on fully open, Anaru and his friend Pete were lifted off the jet, high in to the air. It was exhilarating as the wind tore at their faces, the speedboat below them zigzagging and swivelling in all directions, adding to the fun. But like most things in life the ride came to an end; Anaru and his friend Pete disrobed and returned to the party.

Anaru looked at the messages on his phone; his father had texted to say that he had booked a table at the Sky Gondola restaurant for all the family and for him to be at the cable car terminal at 7pm for the ride up to the restaurant. His mother would bring a change of clothes.

That's cool, he loved going up there for dinner. The view across the mountains and the lake were spectacular.

Two messages appeared; they were from the former All Black Players Dan Carter and Richie McCaw.

'Well done mate, brill news, I've got two tickets for you and your dad to watch The All Blacks v Wales at the Westpac Stadium, Wellington on 18th July 2016. Don't forget to sing the National Anthem. God defend New Zealand. Oh if you want to sing the Welsh National Anthem, Land of my Fathers, then you had better download it from the Internet. Dan C.'

'Wow, what fantastic news son!!!. Well done. I've arranged for the latest All Black kit to be sent to your school with your name on the back. Wear it with pride mate!! Richie.'

How did they know, pondered Anaru? I bet my father had something to do with this, he thought.

Mark O'Connell sent a group text out to all the guys, *'Just to let you all know, some of the Otago Highlander players are at the school tomorrow and the talent scouts will be looking for new recruits for the future. So be on time, especially you Anaru.'*

Summer holidays Anaru loved, but this had been a very special and emotional day for him. Three years of battling leukaemia had come to an end and he could now face a new future; a future playing rugby, with the aspiration of one day playing fly-half for New Zealand.

DANTEL

The orphanage in Arequipa was situated in the back streets. El Misti, the dormant volcano that dominated the skyline of Peru's second city, was visible from Dantel's room. The white, snow-capped peak dazzled against the clear azure blue sky, a normal summer's day for a city high in the Peruvian Andes.

Dantel knocked on Emilio's door; he was surprised when his brother didn't answer and merely assumed that he had left early to play football, as there was no school today with it being Saturday. The two brothers were very different in character; Dantel was the academic while Emilio was more of a sporty nature. The orphanage was unusually quiet for this time of the morning and Dantel couldn't understand why; nevertheless, he went back to his room to continue with his reading. He glanced at the photograph of his parents, which he kept on top of a small locker in the corner of his room. He distinctly remembered the day five years ago, when two heavily-armed men in full riot gear from the local Policia banged on their front door. With them was a small figure of a lady dressed as a nun; this was the first time he and Emilio met Mother Anastasia, whom they always referred to as Mother A from that day onwards. She sat them down and explained that their parents were involved with one of the street drug cartels and that there had been a skirmish in a nearby village with the Drug Enforcement Agency from Lima. The outcome was that their parents had been shot and had died of their injuries. They had been left as orphans. The orphanage, run by Mother A, had twelve children in it, all there as a result of the impact of parents or close relatives losing their lives as a result of drug-related issues.

Dantel texted his brother, *'Where are you? Did you feel that tremor?'*

'Stop worrying Dantel, we often get the shakes, we live in an earthquake zone man. See you back at lunch, better still come down to watch me play, usual place, get some money from Mother A, then we can go to the café down by the monastery for lunch. Emilio.'

Dantel knew precisely which café Emilio was referring to; they often went there after school to catch up with friends. The café was next to the Santa Catalina Monastery on Ugarte. If he ran he would be there in twenty minutes; cutting through the back streets and along the Rio Chili would shorten the journey. As he ran towards the Puente Bajo Grau Bridge that spanned the Rio Chili, the main river that flowed through Arequipa, his phone rang. It was Mayu, one of the older children from the home.

"Where are you, Dantel? Mother A is panicking; the social media websites and the local radio stations are warning people to leave the city because the tremors the city has experienced over the past few days are getting stronger. Where is Emilio?"

"He is with his football friends in the derelict yard next to the petrol station on Av La Marina."

"Mother A says for both of you to get back here now; she is packing the minibus in readiness to evacuate."

"Okay Mayu, we will be there shortly."

Dantel knew the drill as to what to do when an earthquake struck – head to a door or dash under the table or bed, whatever would break the fall of tumbling masonry. He also knew Emilio knew the procedure. The school and Mother A had taught them that the newly-constructed buildings were safer, as they had been designed to withstand the forces of a major earthquake, but the older, more traditional properties would collapse. Both of them knew the earthquake itself was not the main killer, but being crushed to death by old, poorly-built houses was.

The earthquake struck at 11.01am. Dantel reached for the street lamp and clung to it with all his physical strength; the ground to his left opened up and the noise of the land splitting apart was deafening. He could hear people screaming. Glass was showering down from upstairs windows, underground water pipes cracked, spilling water and sewage everywhere, gas pipes exploded; he watched the bridge that he was about to cross bend and twist until it finally snapped, sending cars and people downriver. The old buildings crumpled with ease, spilling their contents onto the surrounding streets; he could see people being buried alive under the falling brick and stonework that tumbled from the heavens. The street lamp he so desperately hung on to swayed violently as the ground continued ripping itself apart. An old wooden window frame struck him on the back of his head. The bang on the head caused Dantel to black out. He felt himself falling; as he fell he must have hit his head on hard stone, for when he woke up slightly dazed moments later he saw blood on his jacket sleeve where his head had come to rest. Dantel fumbled around the pavement looking for his phone. Still feeling light-headed, he got to his feet and saw his phone a few paces ahead. He reached down to pick it up, amazed it still worked. The time was 11.07am.

Looking around, the level of destruction was beyond belief. Six minutes ago everything was in perfect working order, but now all he could see was carnage. The last six minutes felt like an eternity but the ground had, for now, fallen silent. The aftershocks would come shortly, as they always did, and they would be as strong as the original quake. For now Dantel had to somehow find his ten-year-old brother in all this chaos.

The bridge had sustained quite a lot of damage; he needed to cross it to get to Emilio. For several minutes he stared across, mapping out the best route; people were screaming for help all around him, but he shut them out of his thoughts. Still slightly dazed, he picked his way through the strewn debris of twisted concrete; the iron rods that had been embedded into the concrete to strengthen it were sticking up all over the place. Their snapped, sharp edges would easily gash his legs; an injury was the last thing he wanted at this precise moment. The railing was surprisingly intact; using that as support, he managed to get three-quarters of the way across. The earthquake had sent the rest of the bridge tumbling into the river below. A small builders' merchants van abandoned by its owner was precariously balancing on the edge. Dantel carefully reached across; opening the back doors he saw a length of rope and, fastening one end to the railings, he shouted at a group of people that were standing at the far end of the bridge. "Catch." Moments later he had managed to scramble to the other side, thanking the people who had helped him as he raced off to where Emilio and his friends would be.

The city emergency services had started to respond to the situation; sirens could be heard going off throughout the streets. Reaching the old derelict yard next to the petrol station, Dantel could see that the old block of flats that had stood empty for years on the other side of the yard had collapsed, covering Emilio's football spot. Dantel stopped in his tracks; leaning against a wall he looked at the pile of rubble. Deep within his heart he knew Emilio and his friends were buried deep. Was Emilio dead, alive, hurt? He couldn't imagine, but he knew one thing; he had to get help.

Racing across the street, he ignored the man shouting at him from the petrol station. The man was trying to tell him and others that the petrol storage tanks underneath the pumps had been ruptured by the earthquake and were leaking. Dantel could smell the fumes; the spillage was clearly visible flowing down the street, but what Dantel had forgotten in his panic was the risk of a fireball explosion if the petrol ignited. Further along Av La Marina a small group of people had already flagged down a passing fire engine. Dantel saw them and sprinted; as he reached them he could feel his heart and lungs giving out with complete exhaustion. Collapsing at the feet of the firemen, he screamed for help. Within a few minutes he had regained his breath; apologising for his rudeness to the bystanders he promptly guided everybody to the collapsed building that had engulfed Emilio and his friends.

A spotty teenager who was standing by the Chief Fire Officer was surprised to get a text from one of his friends asking if he was alright; everybody assumed that the phone networks would have been put out of action, but apparently not. Dantel sent a message to Emilio, hoping and praying he would get a response. Everybody knew how to conduct a search; it had been drilled into them from their schooldays. The first few hours were vital. You worked in an organised manner, being careful as you lifted the rubble away. You worked as a team and you worked in silence so that you could listen out for voices calling out for help from below.

Dantel stood in line as the adults and fire crew had started to clear a small area directly in front of them. The Chief Fire Officer had taken charge of the site and made sure that as the fallen concrete and bricks were picked up and passed down the line of helpers their actions were not causing the collapsed building to collapse even further and potentially put lives at risk. Dantel was the youngest in the group, being twelve years of age, and as such was placed at the end of the line. It was his job to throw the rubble down the street out of harm's way. He was looking up the line when the phone in his trouser pocket pinged; reaching for his phone he quickly read the message that was on the screen.

'Dantel I'm alive. I think I have broken my left leg, it is trapped under a big block of concrete. I cannot feel my foot. I can see blood around my ankle from my torch on the phone. All of us are trapped under a large block of concrete. Get us out of here.'

'Where were you Emilio in the yard when the earthquake stuck?'

'We were at the far end furthest form the petrol station, near where all the graffiti is.'

'Emilio can you see any of the graffiti?'

'Yes.'

'Send me a snapshot of it.'

Dantel looked at the snapshot image; he knew exactly where that was.

'I know where that filthy graffiti is. I'm coming to get you. I have a rescue team on site now. I'm coming to get you bruv. X'

Dantel shouted at the others and showed the messages to the Chief Fire Officer.

The temperature in Arequipa had increased as the day progressed. The rescue team had put out requests for any construction companies that had diggers or drills to bring them to the site on Av La

Marina. Local TV companies had got hold of the story and had turned up. Reporters with camera crews were sending out up-to date live coverage of the rescue.

Dantel texted Emilio to tell him he and his friends were on national TV.

It was early evening before a digger was found; by now the heat of the day was starting to cool and the onset of the night sky meant that the floodlights, that had been given with a small generator, needed to be switched on. The earthquake had damaged the power lines to the city and, as night approached, Arequipa was plunged into darkness, making rescue operations difficult and dangerous. Aftershocks still shook the area, causing disruption to the search team as they would have to stop and take cover. Seven hours had passed and Emilio and his friends were still trapped underground. Dantel kept sending messages of hope; Emilio replied several times, but the last response Dantel had received from his brother was over an hour ago. He was beginning to get anxious; the rescue team assumed Emilio's phone had died and reassured Dantel they would get his brother out.

The digger had carefully removed layers of rubble. Dantel could see the top of the graffiti; he knew they were only feet away. The Chief Fire Officer ordered the digger to stop; from now on they would use their hands to dig the boys out. Every five minutes Dantel shouted Emilio, followed by a moment of silence by everybody as they listened for a response. Dantel was getting tired and distraught; the day's events had exhausted him and Emilio wasn't responding. He kept on calling his brother and finally, twenty minutes later, a faint voice could be heard. Frantic hands kept tearing away at the earth. Dantel had all of a sudden found a new wave of energy; he tore at the ground and, a few minutes later, a small opening emerged. Through it a hand appeared, Dantel recognising it as Emilio's, for on the thumb was their father's wedding ring.

Dantel had done his work; he had found his brother and now it was up to the rescue team to finish the job off. The reporters and camera crews crowded around, one by one; as the small opening had been enlarged the boys emerged to cheers of jubilation from the waiting onlookers. Miraculously the boys escaped relatively unscathed, with only minor cuts and bruises to show for their ordeal. Dantel peered into the hole and he could see Emilio still trapped, his left leg caught under a large concrete block. The Chief Fire Officer took one look at Emilio's position; he had seen situations like this on several occasions and from the amount of blood Emilio was sitting in it did not look good. They would need to get a paramedic to Emilio to administer painkillers; once they started working around him to remove the concrete block the pain would become unbearable. All Dantel could do was talk to his brother as the rescue team worked through the rest of the night to free him.

In the early hours of morning Emilio was freed;

as his head appeared above the ground for the first time in eighteen hours, the large crowd that had spent the night sleeping in the open in fear of further aftershocks applauded. Mother A was there at the site, as she had been all night. Emilio was ushered into a nearby ambulance and while sitting in the back as the ambulance crew prepared Emilio for the short trip to the hospital, a message appeared on Dantel's phone. It was from the Peruvian President.

'I am so glad to see that both of you have survived this terrible earthquake. I cannot begin to imagine what you have been through. I was out of the country on a business trip when the earthquake struck our land. I am flying down this afternoon to Arequipa to see the damage for myself and what we need to do to repair your city. I have asked if I could come to visit you both in hospital. See you this afternoon.'

"How did the President get your number, Dantel?"

"No idea, bruv."

For Dantel the fact the President was coming to see them was exciting, but more importantly he still had his brother and both of them were alive. The brothers would never forget this day, but like most people they would learn to live with the occasional disasters; equally they would go on to enjoy the rest of their lives celebrating each other's achievements.

Dantel was grateful for the slight gap in the rubble that allowed his and Emilio's phone signals to connect that ultimately saved Emilio's life.

GUIA

It was 4am; the reminder call on her mobile phone had gone off. With bleary eyes she quietly rolled herself out of bed, tossing the duvet aside. Two messages and one Facebook notification showed on the phone; her Twitter account had been extraordinarily quiet throughout the night, much to her dismay. Kaahi was already up and sitting at the family table, fitting his prosthetic leg to his stump. He had come to Brazil from Somalia three years ago as an illegal immigrant. The war that had been raging there for several years had not only destroyed his homeland, but also left him orphaned; homeless and without his left leg beneath his kneecap. The mine he had stood on had totally destroyed all the bone and tissues. The decision to amputate was taken by one of the top surgeons at the main hospital in Mogadishu, Somalia's capital city.

Guia had first noticed Kaahi sitting amongst the down-and-outs in one of the narrow alleyways where she and her father delivered soup to the homeless in the nearby favela. What struck her most about Kaahi was how polite, clean and well-spoken he was; the normal response from the street people was aggression and foul language, often caused by the side-effects of alcohol and drugs. For weeks she and her father would do the evening soup run, and every night Kaahi would wait in the same place for his soup and whatever Guia and her father had managed to scrounge from the local shops and cafes. He was in pain from the infection that had infiltrated his stump; Guia could see the pain etched on his face. One night, walking home, she told her father about the young Somali boy and his desperate plight; she explained to her father how she had taken the time to get to know Kaahi, that his dream was to take part in the 2016 Paralympics there in Rio De Janeiro, a city known to the world as simply Rio.

The following morning Guia's father had made a decision; they would trawl the favela back streets looking for Kaahi. Her father knew that if gangrene had taken hold Kaahi wouldn't survive much longer. It was late afternoon when Guia spotted a bundle of rags, propped up against the sides of a dilapidated wooden hut whose orange faded sides had been heavily daubed with honour badges from one of the local gangs. It was the green stick wedged between the window and the doorframe that Guia instantly recognised; carefully pulling back the tattered rags two frightened dark eyes stared back at her; it was Kaahi, the young, twelve-year-old emaciated black boy. Guia tapped him gently on the shoulder; looking slightly dazed and shielding his eyes from the bright afternoon sun he smiled at Guia, exposing a wonderful set of white African teeth.

"Kaahi, you are coming to live with us. End of."
"Why, Guia?"
"You just are."

The small shanty house she shared with her father and three sisters consisted of a small kitchen to the front, along with a moderately sized living room that led onto a small terrace that was littered with small model houses made out of breeze block or milk crates painted in bright pinks, yellows, greens and purples. It was a hobby her mother had until she passed away two years ago. The three small bedrooms that sat directly above the living room were accessed by a hole in the ceiling through which a ladder was placed. For the toilet and washing facilities; well, that was a trip to their aunt's four doors down.

It was clear for all to see that Kaahi's leg was badly infected and that he needed urgent medical treatment. The look on her father's face said it all; getting treatment at the local hospitals would be difficult, as Kaahi had no identification papers or money.

It was early evening and the storms that had been promised had arrived. Guia went to her room; the noise the rain made as it pelted down on the corrugated roof was deafening. Her bed was the bottom bunk and under it was a gold box; in it was a blue bank passbook. Pulling it out and scrambling down the ladder she showed her father how much was in her account. Her father was astonished; he had an inkling that she had an account but how much was in the account shocked him.

"How... have you managed to accumulate all this money?"

"Father! I have been writing short stories and putting them on Amazon. What I make from the stories goes to my business bank account each month, so you see I have enough money to pay for a private doctor at one of the smart clinics near the beach at Copacabana."

"But you don't have a computer, so how…?"

"I go to an internet café after school each day down by the beach. The money I have made was to go towards a laptop and a mobile phone, so I could write my stories from home."

"We'll talk about this later, but for now you need to go and get an appointment for Kaahi."

With the threat of further discussions with her father re the money in her bank account, she left for the smart part of Copacabana. She knew how the conversation with her father would go, but she would stand her ground, for this money was hers, her future and escape from the poverty-stricken violent favela she lived in.

The appointment with the consultant next morning was brief; Kaahi was given a course of antibiotics to clear up the infection, with a further appointment made for two weeks time to see what further treatments would be required, if necessary of course.

Guia knew about Kaahi's dream to become a gold medal winner in the Rio 2016 Paralympics; she also knew that to run for Brazil, Kaahi would have to become a Brazilian citizen. How to register for citizenship and what procedures to follow she had no idea, but the government website on Brazilian Citizenship would be a good place to start.

"Where're we going, Guia?"

"To the internet café."

"Why?"

"Firstly to look up and print off the guidelines of how to make you a Brazilian, and secondly to see who are the best trainers/coaches to help you get your gold medal."

"Why are you doing this for me? Nobody has cared about me, here or back in Somalia."

"I may only be nine years old, but I have ambitions. My sisters might want to stay in the slums and drag up their children here, but I don't. I want to make something of my life, challenge the world, be someone. I saw something in you that I haven't seen on the streets around here; someone with a dream, a goal in life. I want to help you achieve that gold medal dream, challenge, whatever."

"Wow, you're one gutsy lady."

"Yep, I'm going places. You never know – by drawing attention to your running abilities, someone might take notice of me one day and coach me to be an Olympic gold medallist in the Tokyo Games 2020."

"Cool."

"Plus, I looked up on the Internet, the world's greatest runners come from Somalia, Ethiopia, Kenya and that part of East Africa."

"What if the Brazilian authorities reject my application?"

"Then we will challenge them; if necessary you'll have to run as an independent athlete and compete under the Olympic Flag."

"How do you know that?"

"I've done my research."

The Internet café was busy. Sitting in her favourite spot Guia logged on to her account; she hated that little circle that appeared in the middle of the screen, as if buffering round and round. Frustrated while waiting for the wi-fi connection to kick in, she turned to Kaahi.

"How did you get to Brazil from Somalia?"

"Long story."

"Well?"

"A friend's father worked at the airport on the freight side; for the right money I was smuggled onto the cargo deck in a crate. The flight was to Rio. I was discovered by the custom officials at the airport and handed over to the local authorities. They placed me in a children's home; it was an awful place, so I ran away."

The three years Kaahi had lived in the household had seen many achievements, along with numerous drawbacks from the various government departments. Getting Kaahi into schools and finding the right coaches with suitable training programmes adapted to Kaahi's needs had been tough going at times. With each challenge faced and overcome, Guia found herself sitting across the breakfast table at 4am on this wet, miserable, damp and dark morning. The trophies that were scattered around the room highlighted Kaahi's success in the two hundred and four hundred metre sprint track events he had run in over the last few years, both in Brazil and overseas. With his citizenship granted and all his accomplishments in sprinting, he had drawn the attention of the various Brazilian sporting organisations and was shortlisted to represent Brazil in the Rio games in the T44 two hundred and four hundred metre track events. Guia's money from the sale of her books on Amazon had gone some way to supporting the gold medal dream. Small sponsorships along with donations from friends kept Kaahi's hopes and aspirations of being an Paralympic champion alive.

The games were three months away, but the punishing training programme still had to be maintained on a daily basis. The city of Rio was abuzz with excitement as the opening ceremony loomed ever nearer. Guia opened the door; she was not looking forward to her run alongside Kaahi and the others. Taking a brief moment she looked down out across the city that lay sprawled beneath her and across the harbour; the two most famous landmarks known to the entire world that gave Rio its identity dominated the skyline. On her left was the illuminated statue of Christ the Redeemer, standing thirty metres in height and perched seven hundred metres up on the Corcovado Mountain. To her right was Sugarloaf Mountain, a block of granite rising from the sea to a height of approximately four hundred metres. In a few hours time, when the rain clouds had evaporated and the sun had positioned itself high in the sky, thousands of tourists would flock to these iconic symbols, have their photos taken and immediately download them on to Facebook and other various social media sites for all their friends to see. Would these tourists come and visit her shack of a home high on the hillside of one of the poorest favelas that surrounded the city? She doubted it very much. The tour operators and the police would have advised them to stay well away for fear of being shot.

Kaahi had sprinted off down the narrow streets; his new prosthetic leg with the carbon fibre blade had been specially adapted for him. His last prosthetic leg had taken several weeks to get used to. This one he needed to get used to sharpish; any adjustments that were needed would have to be sorted out quickly as the Paralympics were just around the corner. Two legs had been ordered; the second was for emergencies in case of unforeseen circumstances, mainly to cover theft. The legs were expensive, costing over eight thousand US Dollars for two; the gangs that prowled the streets could easily get a fair price on the black market and with the money buy more drugs to feed the habit of the rich that lived in the skyscrapers down near the harbour.

Guia looked on with pride as she watched Kaahi and his running mates disappear from her view; she was no match for her so-called adopted brother. The emaciated figure she and her father brought home three years ago had turned into the highly toned body of a future Paralympic champion. The lads that ran with Kaahi were from the same running club, but didn't have the same desires or ambitions in life. They knew what the training plan was for the morning; normally Guia ran with Kaahi, but today was one of her off days. She had told him at breakfast if she wasn't able to keep up with him he was to wait at the lower end of Copacabana beach. Kaahi's running mates also acted as bodyguards, fending off any unwanted paparazzi that lurked around the many hidden alleyways and street corners. As the games neared, the media intrusion on potential athletes increased; some attention was welcome, some was not.

Many of Guia's friends saw her as a determined young lady; despite her young age of twelve she had an astute business brain. She texted a few of her friends, explaining she was running on her own as Kaahi had gone ahead. She knew which mates would have their mobiles switched on and that the phone would be on the pillow or within arm's reach. Within minutes two boys who sat behind her in school were by her side, dishevelled and grumpy, there to protect her from any undesirable characters roaming the streets at this early hour of the day. Her phone pinged and she stopped to read a text from Kaahi.

'*TV crews out at beach.*'

Copacabana beach was quiet at this time of the morning, for the party revellers from last night had gone home by now and the tourists and locals that would later flock in their hundreds to soak up the sun and ride the waves were still in their beds. Guia spotted the TV vans parked up; she knew Kaahi and the others ahead would have brushed them off. What was important to Kaahi was getting the attention of the Paralympic committee and winning his races over the next few meets, not chatting to TV presenters looking for stories to put on their live breakfast shows that morning. Guia understood the power of the media; she knew the more media coverage an athlete got, the better the sponsorship deals from the big corporate companies would be, but that athlete would need to ensure the gold medals would go round their necks and not their rivals'. Guia crossed over the road and knocked on the doors of several of the TV vans. A few of the TV crews politely told her to go away, but those that expressed an interest she happily gave interviews, telling them how Kaahi arrived in Brazil and how he had got to where he was now.

Over the next few weeks the daily routine continued. Kaahi stuck to the rigorous training plan put in place by his coaching team and won all his races, putting him in a strong position with the Paralympic committee. Guia went on various TV shows talking about Kaahi; she also took advantage of the social media avenues that were freely available, posting several videos of Kaahi training on YouTube. She even went as far as writing a short story about him and downloaded that on to Amazon for all her readers that had bought her stories over the years to read about.

It was mid-July, the day that the Paralympic select committees would make their decisions as to who would be in the squad to represent Brazil at the Rio Paralympic games 2016. It was a long day; friends kept texting both Guia and Kaahi asking whether they had heard anything from the committee. The tension around the living room was mounting as the day went on. The table that Guia and Kaahi had chatted over and eaten around for the last three years was getting crowded as friends and family gathered throughout the day. Finally the call they had been waiting for came through at 3pm. Kaahi recognised the number on the screen; taking a deep breath he pressed the accept button, stood up and walked outside onto the terrace that had all Guia's late mother's brightly coloured model houses on. The room went silent. Guia hovered by the back door, anxious to see the look on Kaahi's face as he carefully listened to the voice on the other end. A smile steadily crept across Kaahi's face, showing those beautiful white African teeth of his. Putting the phone down on a plant pot he turned to Guia:

"T44 two hundred and four hundred metres Rio 2016 HERE I COME!!!."

Guia took a step back and leant against the wall. He had done it, she had done it, they had done it; a poor black boy from East Africa was going to represent Brazil on the world stage at the Rio 2016 Paralympic Games. At the age of fifteen Kaahi was off to the greatest games of his life. Tomorrow he and Guia would head off to Sao Paulo, where the Brazilian Paralympic Committee was going to announce to the public who had been selected and for what event.

Two months had almost passed from the day

Kaahi had been officially told he had been selected. Training had been rigorous but today, the 7th September 2016, he would walk into the Maracana stadium behind the Brazilian flag. Being the host nation, the Brazilian team would be the last team to enter the world famous stadium in the Parade of Nations. This year approximately one hundred and sixty countries were being represented, roughly four thousand four hundred athletes. This was going to be a wonderful spectacle.

Kaahi's moment had come, dressed like most of the other Brazilian athletes in his green suit with splashes of yellow and blue on his jacket. The long wait was worth it as he entered the tunnel. He could hear the roar of the dignitaries, overseas spectators and of course the Brazilian supporters who had packed the seventy-eight thousand-seater stadium to the rafters. The noise was electrifying as the crowd spotted the green, yellow and blue of the Brazilian flag entering the stadium.

Guia and her father had taken up their seats; this was a moment Guia had dreamed of for years. She could see Kaahi taking pictures on his phone. Pride swelled up inside her and a little tear rolled down her cheek. Her father gently turned to her and, with a large finger, delicately wiped the tear away. With all the athletes in place the ceremony continued, a large image of a pulsating heart attracting everybody's attention. it was supposed to represent the life, passion and spirit of each Paralympic athlete. Tomorrow the games would start.

The Olympic Stadium was in the Maracana zone, a short distance from the Olympic Village where most of the Brazilian team had based themselves. Kaahi's coach and mentor had always told him that on the big occasions race tactics and mental attitude were as important as timing. Guia and the team that had been put in place to support him knew that Kaafi's youthful inexperience was a weak point and that the other athletes racing against him today would exploit that, as they were more experienced runners. It was a well-known fact that an athlete could be the best in his field, but on the day what counted most was the athlete's mental attitude and belief in him or herself. Tactics and frame of mind was a discussion Guia and Kaahi often had around the breakfast table at 4am in the morning as they prepared for the first of the daily runs. Kaahi was aware of what the people around him were saying and he felt confident that his head was in the right place for next few days.

Storm clouds had gathered over the Olympic Stadium; Guia looked up from her place at trackside and, seeing the deep black threatening clouds hovering above, quietly prayed to herself that the clouds would hang on to their watery contents for a few more minutes. The first of the T44 200 metre qualifying races was about to start. The names of the competitors and the countries they represented were read out over the stadium speakers. Kaahi was in lane three, a good lane to have. As his name was read out a large cheer went up in the stadium, Kaahi waved at the crowd, acknowledging their support before settling down and waiting for the starter's pistol to go off. They were off; the roar of the crowd filled Kaahi's head as he sprinted round the bend. He could feel and see the other athletes around him but as long as he stayed within spitting distance of his main rival from the USA, he stood a good chance of getting to the final. Guia jumped up and down in her seat, shouting her head off as Kaahi entered the back straight, but something wasn't right. Kaahi stumbled. He appeared to lose control of his blade and became unbalanced; face down on the track and not finishing meant Kaahi's medal hopes for the two hundred metres were gone. Guia saw the look of frustration and disappointment written all over his face and wondered how they would begin to put the sparkle back into his confidence to face the T44 400 challenge tomorrow. A despondent Kaahi sat down at the side of the track; the support team, still in shock at what had happened, came alongside him. All Guia could do was watch from her seat. Kaahi explained what he thought had gone wrong; the fitting of his prosthetic leg around his stump for some reason didn't feel right and had become loose going round the bend. Closer examination by the team proved that the issue was not the prosthetic leg but Kaahi's inexperience on the day. In all of his excitement he had simply not ensured his stump was properly secured in the socket. Lesson learnt.

Kaahi was angry with himself for making such a stupid mistake, a mistake he was never going to repeat. Today he had another opportunity to prove himself; with his prosthetic leg properly fitted and checked by Guia and his coach, he walked out onto the track with more determination than ever to qualify for the 400 metre final on Friday afternoon. This time running in lane two, he lined up on the starting blocks. The strategy was firmly in his head, where to be at the various stages of the race and which rivals to keep an eye on. The pistol had gone off, the roar of the crowd he'd completely blocked out; he was on track, the plan was working and his main rivals where were they should be. All he needed to do was maintain his position, stay upright and focus on the finish line. He was delighted he had come first, which went against the advice from the team and Guia, but for him it was the right decision. With the race over he gathered up his things and left the stadium knowing in his heart he had qualified and headed for the training grounds. For the next few days of his life he would live, sleep and breathe the T44 400 metre final.

Guia was angry; she had texted Kaahi several times over the last two days but he had returned none of her messages. Clearly he had taken the decision to shut himself off from the world and focus on the race of his life. The moment had come; it was Friday afternoon and the final of the T44 400 metres was ten minutes away. Guia and her father had taken their usual seats. She was nervous, tense and still angry with Kaahi, but that anger she would have to put aside as she watched

Kaahi emerge onto the track. In her right hand was the Brazilian flag, which she would hand to Kaahi for his lap of honour; this was a prearranged agreement they had discussed several weeks ago.

The stadium was full. Kaahi was in lane four, a really good lane; his main rival from the USA was in lane three. The other athletes taking part were from Canada, China, New Zealand, Ukraine, South Africa and oddly enough a young guy from Somalia. The crowd cheered as the stadium announcer read out the names of the athletes and where they originated from; a huge cheer erupted as Kaahi's name was mentioned, and he reacted to the crowd by waving his right hand, at the same time smiling revealing his beautiful African teeth. A hush descended across the stadium as the starter raised his hand with the pistol in. The athletes steadied themselves, waiting anxiously for the click of the gun. The pistol was fired and they were off. The New Zealand and South African contenders were off to a good start; so were the Canadian and the Somalia guy. Kaahi and his American rival were in fifth and sixth place. The strategy was going to plan; everybody knew the last sixty metres were the most important. Kaahi could hear the roar of the crowd urging him on and two hundred metres in he and the American had moved up to third and fourth places respectively; at this stage of the race he was in the right position. The early leaders had started to wane a bit. Thirty-three seconds in and approaching the third bend Kaahi and his American rival had manoeuvred themselves into second and third positions, The Chinese guy had started to apply some pressure and was sitting comfortably on their shoulders; as the homestretch approached the Brazilians in the crowd could sense a medal coming on and Kaahi could feel the excitement and tension of the stadium as the crowd screamed at him to keep going. Guia was exhausted with the excitement, jumping up and down, flapping her arms all over the place, goading Kaahi across the winning line. Kaahi could feel the presence of the American and Chinese athletes bearing down on him. His heart was pounding out of his chest, ready to burst, his lungs were on fire and every muscle fibre in his body was stretched to its full potential. He could see the finishing line, his rivals were by his side; somehow he had to find that extra bit of energy from somewhere. Ten metres out and his American contender had taken the edge and was in first place; he prayed for extra energy and from nowhere a surge of power swelled in his aching limbs. He had crossed the line. He knew he had got a medal; what colour it was he didn't know.

Exhausted and mentally spent, he collapsed on the track. Guia had jumped over the security barrier, much to the annoyance of the track officials, not that she cared. She ran to Kaahi, who was still on the ground. The crowd were ecstatic but it was too close to call. Kaahi's coach and team remained calm, daring not to dream what the outcome was going to be. They stared at the scoreboard for what seemed like an eternity; with bated breath they waited and waited. The tension was almost unbearable and then the results came through. The stadium exploded with delight; Brazil had its first gold medal of the games, Kaahi had done it. He had won the gold medal. Brazil took the gold; it was silver for the USA and bronze for China. Kaahi picked himself of the floor, dusted himself down and grabbed the flag from Guia. Draping the flag around himself he headed off on his lap of honour. As he sauntered around the stadium waving at the crowd all he could see was a sea of green, yellow and blue as thousands of flags were being waved about all over the place.

Guia took a few moments to reflect on what had happened. Three years ago this gold medal Paralympic champion was an emaciated African boy that she and her father had scraped off an alleyway in one of the poorest favelas of Rio. All the short stories she had toiled over and sold on Amazon to support Kaahi to achieve his dream, along with the arduous training at all unearthly hours of the day, had paid off. She knew what she wanted from the next four years; a gold medal herself from the Tokyo games 2020.

All that remained was for Kaahi to attend the medal ceremony that night and get his gold medal. The ceremony was brief; Kaahi had got his gold medal. Guia could see the tears of joy flowing down Kaahi's face as he stood on the podium, watching his flag being raised on the stand as the Brazilian national anthem was being played.

Holding his gold medal aloft for the world's

media to photograph him was a proud moment for Kaahi. The press would be anxious to get his story. He caught Guia's eye and, walking across to her, took his medal off and said;

"This is for you, for without you I couldn't have achieved what I have done today. Thank you from the bottom of my heart. Shall we both go to Tokyo 2020 and get you a gold medal as well? Maybe I'll get one for the 200 metres? What do you say?"

"Absolutely."

EMERITA

The small Swiss Alpine city of Davos lies near the southern German border. For Emerita and her three-year-old St Bernard rescue dog, Gretel, it was home. Mid-winter in the Alps meant deep snow and with that came the reality of avalanches, as layers of snow that had built up on the mountains over the harsh winter months became unstable, threatening to engulf everything that lay in their paths.

Emerita's house overlooked Davos; from her bedroom balcony she could see right across the valley that was spread out beneath her. The rooftops of the hotels, cafés, shops and churches that made up the small city were clothed in beautiful, soft glistening snow. The mountains in their splendid white winter coats looked majestic, but Emerita, like many of her friends, knew the hidden dangers that lay behind this picturesque setting.

Davos in the main was a quiet, backwater place, but for three days every year in late January, world political and business leaders from over a hundred countries came to discuss world issues. Emerita watched from her high vantage point as helicopters carrying world dignitaries landed at the various temporary heliports that had sprung up overnight. Her mother had told her what this year's theme was, but that was several days ago and, like any other twelve-year old girl, what her mother said normally went in one ear and straight out the other. Emerita looked around her room to see where she had put her laptop; clothes and shoes lay strewn all over the place. On the back of the door was a pinned message on bright yellow paper; the blue writing that had been hastily scribbled on it simply read:

'Tidy your room.'

Ignoring the message, she continued to scour her room. Gretel had taken her usual position on the bed. Emerita quickly realised that her laptop was embedded under Gretel, evidenced clearly by a white cable protruding from beneath her enormous head. She smartly pushed Gretel off her bed and, having retrieved the laptop, she logged on to the Internet with the aid of the house wi-fi, googling World Economic Forum Davos Switzerland. The Fourth Industrial Revolution meant nothing to her, but she did recall her brother Heinrich last night at dinner saying that this year's talks were all about building a better world for all. How? He wasn't sure, but it would involve improving technology and getting more people, particularly from poor countries, to use the internet. No doubt Heinrich would tell her more later, as he was working at the conference centre where the talks were being held.

Emerita continued to lie on her bed; logging on to her Facebook page she looked to see what her friends were up to. Gretel made herself known by placing a large paw gently on the duvet. Emerita looked at her best friend, whom she loved and adored; she could see from the look in Gretel's eyes the unceremonious way she had been dumped off the bed did not meet with approval. Standing a little less than a metre high, with one blue eye and one brown eye, she attempted to get back on the bed only to be rebuffed by Emerita. Her thick white coat with its deep chestnut-red patches was well suited to her surroundings, keeping her well insulated against the biting cold and making her visible in the snow blizzards that often raged for days on end in the high Alps in this mountainous region of Switzerland.

The cars bringing the delegates to the economic summit were lined up outside the conference centre, patiently waiting their turn to discharge the various world leaders. From her bedroom balcony vantage point Emerita could see the entire goings-on. The world's press were out in force, taking pictures of the rich and famous. The television on her bedroom wall had started to report that there had been an avalanche in the Davos Jacobshorn ski resort area and that a small group of cross-country skiers had been caught in the path of the avalanche and had been reported missing. A local TV company had managed to get footage of the avalanche as it happened from a skier who had videoed the event from her phone. Rumours had started to circulate that the wife of the French Ambassador to Germany was one of the skiers trapped.

Emerita's father flung open the door to her room. "We need to go."

He was reading a text message he had received

from the nearby mountain rescue team.

'All team members please report to the station immediately, we have received an urgent call requesting help to rescue a small party of cross-country skiers trapped by recent avalanche in the Davos Jacobshorn area.'

The rescue team managed by her father was often called out in the winter months to rescue skiers that had got into trouble; the call could come at any time and the team would have to be ready at a moment's notice. Having watched her father train and manage the team over the years, she opted to follow in his footsteps and had started her training last year. Her brother Heinrich had already started to train Gretel right from her early days as a fluffy young pup.

Gretel instinctively knew the call had come and was already outside pawing at the back of the four-wheel drive Jeep; en route she had picked up the traditional small wooden oak barrel that would hang round her neck, containing the all-important brandy synonymous with her breed and role in rescue. Emerita's father had already given instructions to a small helicopter crew. Within minutes the red helicopter of the rescue team had been scrambled and was airborne. On board, a doctor from the local hospital, along with two very experienced members of the team, were looking at their brief. Their job – explore the accident site, assess the situation and report back to Emerita's father.

The radio conversation with the pilot was short;

they had found the avalanche, the position was extremely dangerous and he would not be able to land the helicopter, so the rescue would have to be done on foot. The doctor and the other two members of the team were being winched down as they were speaking. The order was given by Emerita's father that the doctor and the other two were not to start the rescue mission until the full squad was assembled at the site.

Five minutes from receiving the call, the full team had assembled at the rescue station. Heinrich had already downloaded to everybody's phone maps of the area and made sure a paper version was in their rucksacks. With the team being fully briefed and everybody understanding their job, Emerita's father gave the go ahead to start the rescue. Emerita herself would take charge of Gretel, as Gretel was her dog.

The cable car station was only two blocks away on Bramabuelstrasse; Emerita had phoned the station warning them that they were on the way and to have a cable car available. The team loaded the cable car with all the equipment; Emerita sat quietly in the corner, keeping a watchful eye on Gretel and making sure she didn't jump up and down all over the place breaking the medical boxes or the important climbing gear. The Jacobshornbahn cable ride was split in two; at the halfway point at Ischalp they would have to switch cars, relocating all their stuff. As they ascended to the top, the cable car swayed as the wind buffeted it from all sides. The weather conditions had improved as the day went on; the snow blizzards that ushered in the day had given way to beautiful clear blue skies, creating the ideal setting for a good day's skiing. The avalanche unfortunately had put paid to that as the ski resorts suspended all activities. Emerita could see all the skiers heading back down the mountain to Davos, no doubt to the cafés and bars.

Gretel was getting excited; she could smell the snow and knew she was on an adventure. The doors of the cable car opened and a blast of ice-laced wind hit them all in the face. Emerita knew the first rules of any rescue; listen to the person in charge and follow instructions to the letter. Confirmation had filtered through that the cross-country skiers were a party of three, and that the French Ambassador to Germany had confirmed that his wife was in that small party, along with two members of his staff. The team got their apparatus ready; Emerita's father had taken the decision to rope Emerita to himself, as she was an inexperienced climber. Word had got around as to what had happened and that a rescue team was on its way. A rather large gentleman approached the squad and briefly explained who he was and that the cross-country party had only ventured out for a brief few hours' exercise and that they were experienced mountaineers. They were travelling light but had taken the minimal necessary essentials. "We have some clothing items in the rucksacks over there belonging to our friends; perhaps the dog could get scent markings?" Emerita dashed to the rucksacks and rummaged around, pulling out various designer T-shirts; she whistled to Gretel and wrapped the T-shirts around her nose, taking care to make sure Gretel got a good sniff of each item. The perfume on the French Ambassador's wife's clothes was very distinctive and no doubt expensive. Emerita knew how many hours of training her brother Heinrich had put into training Gretel for an event like this, particularly around looking for hidden objects by following the scent trail. St Bernards had been known to sniff bodies out that had been buried under three metres of snow.

Gretel's tail was up; she was raring to go. Despite being Emerita's dog, Heinrich had done all the training, so he rightly took the lead with Gretel close to his side. Eight members of the team followed, Emerita still roped to her father. The narrow track that led them to the avalanche site was treacherous. The whole team walked in silence so as to hear the slightest call for help. All eyes were peeled to the snowy slopes looking for any visible signs that could possibly indicate a fresh avalanche was imminent.

Forty minutes had passed since they had left the cable car; Heinrich spotted the other members of the rescue team who had been winched down by the helicopter over an hour ago, their bright orange coats plain to see. Emerita could see the extent of the avalanche and for a few seconds thought to herself, the cross-country skiers must be dead. She had never experienced the full force of an avalanche, but she had listened to people's personal ordeals and the stories they told about the velocity of the cascading snow and ice with all the debris trapped within, the deafening noise as thousands of tonnes of white stuff hurled down the mountainside and the swirling winds that sucked up everything in its path. She had seen the body bags that contained the corpses of those who hadn't survived past avalanches laid out on the floor of the rescue station. She had also seen the broken bodies of survivors taking months to heal. She knew the dangers that confronted her as she stood patiently waiting for her father's orders.

Emerita's father had listened to his team and had decided that the best course of action was to let Gretel do what she was trained to do. Freed to do her job, Gretel set to work sniffing the freshly-strewn snow. Hours passed, and with nightfall fast approaching the pressures were mounting to find the skiers, as fading light and falling temperatures would add further difficulties to an already challenging rescue. Heinrich kept close to Gretel as she scoured up and down the mountainside.

Nightfall took hold and the team switched on their powerful torches, scanning the slopes as they tracked Gretel's movements. Emerita's father had started to discuss with the team the possibility of calling off the search, as the weather forecast had predicted snowstorms for the next few hours, and resuming in the morning. The consequences on taking that decision would be three dead bodies. He could see the reports in all the papers and social media sources. *'Swiss search team fail to rescue French Ambassador's wife.'* The general consensus among the team was to hang on for another hour; the blizzard that was blowing up from Italy was not due for another hour or two.

Emerita nudged her father in the back. "Father, look." Gretel had stopped meandering all over the place and was actually circling around a small patch of snow fifty metres below where they stood; her tail was up, her nose buried in the snow, and she had started to paw at the ground. Gretel sat back and began barking, indicating to all she had found the cross-country skiers. For Gretel her job was done, but for everybody else theirs had just started.

The whole group slowly descended the mountain to where Heinrich and Gretel were stationed. The lighting equipment was set up, the helicopter that had returned to base had been recalled and instructed to land at the ski resort. Emerita shouted to the team to be silent. Her father looked at her in surprise, but ignoring his facial expressions she laid herself flat on the ground; she took a deep breath before yelling at the top of her voice, "Can you hear me?" She repeated the message several times, remembering to listen for a reply. Moments later the tip of a ski pole broke the surface of the snow. Heinrich quickly realised that the cross-country skiers were probably no more than a metre down. Emerita grabbed a spade; she was not going to be outdone by her brother and the other men around her. She knew that when you dig people out it was done in an orderly manner so as to ensure your actions did not cause further destruction of the scene, thus putting the lives of those being rescued and those doing the rescuing at greater risk.

Snow had started to fall and the wind was picking up speed; the storm was early. The team continued digging as this was going to be a race against time. At last they had broken through; the skiers where buried a little deeper than originally thought. Heinrich could see that two ski poles had been tied together to form a long pole that eventually ruptured the surface. The French party of skiers had been lucky, as they had managed to make it into a small cave before the wall of snow hit them; all three ladies appeared to be in good health apart from cuts and bruises and the onset of hypothermia. The French Ambassador's wife had sprained her ankle badly and was in considerable discomfort. The first two ladies were helped out and immediately wrapped in silver foil blankets for warmth. Emerita put her hands on two small plastic beakers, carefully pouring the brandy that was around Gretel's neck to warm the ladies up.

Further examination of the French Ambassador's wife by the team doctor revealed the damage was possibly more than a nasty sprain; he suspected she had a serious fracture. Carefully strapping her right leg and administering a small amount of morphine to ease the pain, he gave the all clear to go. Other members of the team climbed down to assist and, as gently as they could, they lifted the French Ambassador's wife to the surface; the pain was clearly visible on her face, yet she kept a dignified silence. The whole team had taken the decision that this lady should be flown direct to the nearest local hospital. With the helicopter hovering high above them and the stretcher securely harnessed to the winch, the doctor and his patient were hauled up to the helicopter. As they ascended the winds from the storm combined with the downdraft from the helicopter's blades caused the stretcher to swing violently around. The pilot had to draw on all his skills and expertise to keep the helicopter airborne and was relieved when the doctor and the French Ambassador's wife were securely on board. With the door firmly shut the helicopter departed down the valley.

The rescue team, delighted with the outcome, gathered their equipment with a sense of urgency, for the snow was now falling heavily and visibility was deteriorating fast. Emerita's father knew the mountain like the back of his hand and it was going to take all his experience to guide the team off the mountain and back to base. The two remaining survivors were roped to two members of the team for safety and support. Emerita had attached herself to her father. She was feeling very insecure at this precise moment.

The cable car ride back down the mountain was swift; the car itself was warm, which was welcome. Emerita looked at her phone; there was a message from her mother. *Tell your father that I'm extremely annoyed with him for taking you up on a dangerous rescue, and I will be having words with him.* Emerita tapped her father on the shoulder and showed him the message. He looked at her, shrugged his shoulders and simply said to her, "You have made me a very proud man. Don't worry about your mother, I'll get your brother to calm her down."

This had been an adventurous day for Emerita, from watching world dignitaries arriving at The World Economic Forum to rescuing a French Ambassador's wife trapped in an avalanche.

"What do you think caused the avalanche, Father?"

"Who knows, sweetheart."

"Is mother going to kill you?"

"Probably."

SAIF AND ZAHID

Saif sat alongside his brother Zahid; the once small back street café in Aleppo had been the life and soul of the neighbourhood, but all that remained now was a bombed-out shell, much like all the buildings that once stood proudly on that street. A layer of dust covered the red plastic tablecloth and the purple chairs. Last night's air raids had been particularly bad; the Russian fighter jets tore up the night sky, dropping their bombs indiscriminately. The devastation was clear to see as great plumes of smoke still billowed high above the city. Saif could hear the ambulance sirens still wailing in the background, no doubt taking people to what remained of the various city hospitals.

The Syrian war was now in its fifth year and, like many children of his and Zahid's age, the conflict had left its mark. Their parents had been killed years ago, leaving the two brothers to survive on the streets of Aleppo amidst the bombs and the bullets. Saif, being the elder of the two, now twelve, had always felt responsible for his younger brother who, from the age of two, had developed Muscular Dystrophy and was now wheelchair bound. The street shelter they had lived in for the last few months with other abandoned street kids had taken a direct hit the other night. The shelter that was home for himself and Zahid was ruined beyond recognition. Many of his friends had died that night. He and Zahid only survived by sleeping in their usual place, under the old concrete block supported by stones that acted as legs, creating a kind of table. The table took the brunt of the falling masonry. Dazed and badly wounded, the emergency services managed to pull him and Zahid out alive.

Saif remembered sitting in the back of the ambulance, covered in blood and debris, looking at the large gash in his brother's right leg; he equally called to mind the screaming of other children everywhere in the hospital corridors waiting for attention. He recalled running around desperately, trying to get the nurse's attention, begging, screaming at them to look at Zahid's leg. He knew without immediate help Zahid would have bled to death in hours. Two things street life had taught Saif; look after number one and fight hard to protect what little you had.

The little bombed out café had been home for the last two days, having been patched up by the medical staff at the hospital and turfed out back onto the streets. For Zahid, being eight, life was extremely challenging living in a war torn country and having to cope with his condition, which now confined him to a wheelchair. Life was tough but, like Saif, he too had learnt the art of surviving the streets of Aleppo; he knew living off people's sympathy alone would get him nowhere in life. Drawing on his wits, he spotted the other night in the hospital a battered old wheelchair that an old lady had got out off to go to the toilet. Scraping himself along the floor and dragging himself into the chair he shouted at Saif and, within minutes, the two brothers had scarpered out of the hospital, vanishing down the back streets into thin air.

Zahid looked up to see what was making the loud rumbling noise that was also shaking the buildings along the street; to his astonishment it was a Syrian armoured tank. The tank he was used to seeing prowling round the streets of his city Aleppo, but what surprised him was the fact it was being driven and controlled by a group of teenage youths. It rumbled past the two brothers and the three heavily-armed, spotty-faced boys that sat on top of the tank waved as if acknowledging Saif and Zahid. Within minutes the armoured tank came to an abrupt stop. The youths jumped down from the tank and two more crawled out from the tank's inner belly. Zahid shouted at Saif to push him down the street to where the tank had stopped; to both brothers' shock they watched the lads strip off and jump into what appeared to be a small crater filled with fresh water. Saif acknowledged the look on Zahid's face; both of them knew the streets around here like the back of their hands and couldn't recall seeing this pool before. Instantaneously Saif jumped into the water crater, having carefully removed his bandages. Zahid simply sat and watched all the frolickings of enjoyment. It was good to see Saif having a few moments of fun, plus like himself Saif was beginning to stink and a good wash wouldn't go amiss; he only wished he could join them. Zahid was amazed to see the guys had brought along their own shower gel. A couple of the lads had clambered out of the small crater and started to remove the scraps of clothes he was wearing, gently picking him up and lowering him to the others, taking care to ensure his heavily bandaged right leg was held high to ensure it was kept dry. The so-called bath was a welcome relief, but as the others drove off in the armoured tank Saif had worked out that the hole must have been created by one of last night's bombs that hit the city and that the explosion had ruptured a main water pipe, filling the hole nicely and creating the small public swimming bath.

The day was hotting up; both Saif and Zahid knew their wet bodies would soon dry out with the day's heat, so quickly threw on the rags they had for clothes. Saif noticed a piece of paper tucked under the cushion of Zahid's newly acquired chair; pulling it from under his brother, Saif quickly read the message.

'Payment received! Al-Otrosh Mosque front steps Friday.'

Saif knew exactly what this message meant and so did Zahid. The old lady whose chair they had cunningly stolen the other night had been in touch with underground organisations to get herself, and no doubt some of her family, out of Syria, the most likely destination being somewhere in Europe. The world had come to know these organisations as unscrupulous people traffickers. Do they care who they rip off? No. Would they check the identification of those they were moving around! Probably not. The thought crossed both brothers' minds: could this be an unexpected escape plan? A route to a better, safer, life? Where would they go? The UK, Sweden, Germany possibly? With these thoughts racing through their minds they headed to the mosque. Today was Friday, the day of prayer for those that followed the Muslim faith.

Saif had broken into a sweat as he pushed his brother through the war torn streets of Aleppo. For Zahid the ride was bumpy and rough, but he had become accustomed to this mode of transport; he knew that the long road to Europe would be extremely challenging. He had seen the pictures from the TV; the images that were beamed around the world showing children like him dying from starvation and exhaustion or drowning in the Mediterranean Sea. For him and Saif this was a risk worth taking, as there was nothing for them here in Aleppo. Tomorrow a barrel bomb or a sniper's bullet could kill both of them.

The blue ribbon that had been tied to the left handle of the wheelchair had perplexed Saif. Now he was beginning to think it was some kind of code. Would the people traffickers be looking for a wheelchair with a blue ribbon? Curiosity had got the better of him.

Friday being the day of prayer meant the area around the Mosque was predictably busy. The brothers waited patiently by the steps, as the message hadn't given a specific time. It was late evening when a man and a woman, heavily disguised by red keffiyehs across their faces, pulled up in an battered old green van. The woman wound down the window and shouted a couple of names. Saif assumed that these names were something to do with the old lady. With nothing to lose, Saif pushed Zahid towards the van, but as he did so he felt a sharp cosh on the head; as he fell to the ground he could faintly hear a groan from Zahid. Rightly or wrongly he assumed Zahid had been knocked unconscious like himself. Clearly the traffickers were taking no chances with being identified and had taken the necessary precautions.

As Saif came round, he started to realise that he was blindfolded and that his arms and feet had been tied together with what he could only assume was some kind of tape. An instant panic flashed across his mind; where was Zahid? He moved slightly to his right and, as he did so, he could feel the spokes of a wheel brushing against his right arm; shuffling forward he could feel the warmth of a leg and, with a huge sigh of relief, he quietly whispered his brother's name. Moments later a muffled voice responded. 'Saif, you there bro?' The rocking motion of the van started to make Saif sick, but he restrained himself from throwing up as he didn't want to draw attention to himself. The two brothers kept whispering messages of comfort to each other. How long they had been travelling for and where were they neither of them had any idea.

What felt like an eternity came to an abrupt end. The van screeched to a halt. Zahid could hear the van's front doors being opened and slammed shut; he could also hear raised voices outside. All of a sudden the back doors opened and a sharp blast of cold air swept its way in, giving a welcome breath of freshness. The night air swiftly brought both brothers to their full senses. Saif could feel a sharp knife tugging at the tape that had bound his arms and legs; a note was thrust into his trouser pocket but what was on it would have to wait for a few minutes. Still blindfolded, Saif could hear the van disappear into the middle of the night. Who brought himself and Zahid to this precise spot he would never know, nor did he care.

Saif and Zahid had no idea how long they were unconscious for; had they been drugged? All they knew was they were confused, exhausted and starving. The only possessions they owned in the world were the tattered rags of clothes they had on. Saif quietly turned to a small group of women and children. He asked a young mother who was breastfeeding a small baby, where were they?

"You're on a beach, sweetheart."

"Which beach?"

"A small beach just up from Dikili on the Turkish coastline."

Saif stared at Zahid; he could see the terror in his brother's eyes. Both of them had seen the TV images of small inflatable boats battling against the elements of the cruel Aegean sea, boats capsizing, the lucky ones picked up by the rescue boats and the rest taken by the sea never to be seen or heard again. Zahid took Saif's right hand.

"We have no choice, Saif; nothing to go back to."

"I know."

The crossing to the Greek Island of Lesbos was going to be perilous, even if the waters were calm. Still holding his brother's hand, Zahid looked into his brother's eyes.

"If the boat sinks, let me go and save yourself."

No more words were needed; they both knew, living with Muscular Dystrophy, Zahid would struggle to swim.

All of a sudden a great commotion welled up amongst the crowd as the noise of two outboard motors could be heard tearing up the waters of the small bay. Two bright orange inflatable boats came into sight. The crowd surged forward, surrounding the boats, women screaming at their children to stay close. A rather rude big man yelled at the top of his voice.

"We're not taking that wheelchair. Get him out of it."

It was every man for himself as the crowds waded out to the boats, children clambering aboard, shouting at their friends to hurry up. Saif, from nowhere, found the strength to lift Zahid out of his wheelchair and place him over his right shoulder. Struggling, he managed to wade into the water and, on reaching the first boat, two women hauled Zahid on to the boat. Saif heaved himself on board; Zahid had wriggled his way into the centre, thinking that this would be the safest place. Life jackets were handed around, but there weren't enough for everybody. Zahid turned to Saif.

"You wear it."

The body of the inflatable moulded itself to

the gentle up and down swells of the sea, but that didn't last for long. Dawn had broken, revealing a dullish grey day; as the morning progressed the gentle swells intensified as the waters around them became choppy. Saif could see the other inflatable boat ahead of them, bobbing up and down with the strengthening waves. The wind had picked up and people started to become agitated; the panic on a few faces started to show as the boat began taking on water. The water was sloshing around people's feet; several youngsters had started to bale out the water with various plastic containers that were to hand. Saif seized a large plastic tub that a young family had brought with them; grabbing it he frantically started to bale out some of the water swishing around his feet. The situation was getting desperate; more water was being taken on board than could be baled out; the outcome would be inevitable, but how long had they got before the vessel sank? A powerful speedboat appeared from nowhere, pulling alongside both inflatables; the people traffickers clearly didn't want to be caught by the Greek Authorities so abandoned ship, leaving the innocent people in the boats to the mercy of the sea. As fast as the powerboat arrived it disappeared.

The inflatable only lasted another hour. The attempt to keep the boat afloat, at least until the Greek coastline was in sight, failed. Squeals of panic could be heard everywhere as mothers tried desperately to cling to their children. The waters were bitterly cold; those that had life jackets clung to others to give what little support they could. Saif had managed to set the two flares off; a young girl had noticed them when she got on the boat and had passed them to Saif for safekeeping. Zahid prayed that the red vapour trail given off by the flares that soared into the sky would attract the attention of any ships within the immediate vicinity. The coldness of the water was the biggest killer and both brothers knew that. Saif hung on to Zahid, but as time slipped by he found it increasingly difficult to keep hold of the brother who meant so much to him. At times Zahid would slip under the water as the swell of the sea engulfed them; Saif would redouble his effort and manage to retrieve Zahid, but for how long he could do this? He knew in his heart the answer was not for much longer. Zahid had said when the moment came to let him go and save himself.

Saif, exhausted, wet, hungry and in the depths of despair, must have passed out temporarily for he did not see or hear the Greek rescue boat that had come alongside him. Looking frantically around him he couldn't see Zahid. A large hand grabbed him by the scruff of his neck and plucked him out of the sea. A silver foil sheet was draped around him; looking at the man straight in the face he whispered, 'My brother.' The Greek man placed his large hands around Saif's face, gently turning Saif's head to see a small body wrapped in tin foil being gently warmed by two women. It was Zahid. They had survived, and they were alive.

The port of Mytilini, the main town on the

Greek Island of Lesbos, was thriving with the daily hustle and bustle of life. Sitting huddled together in their tin foil blankets aboard the rescue boat, Saif and Zahid watched with trepidation as the boat pulled alongside the harbour walls. Cruise ships and the island ferry boats filled the small port, as well as little fishing boats belonging to the locals bobbing up and down in the water. On the quayside was a well-drilled team of volunteers used to the sight of the rescue boats bringing desperate refugee children from war torn Syria. The two brothers sat quietly on a little bench. Saif had already had a quiet word with one of the volunteer workers, who wore a bright yellow T-shirt with the letters UNHCR printed on the front in blue. Moments later the young girl came back with a small wheelchair. Zahid, still traumatised, asked the young lady, "Do you work for the United Nations?"

"No, I'm a volunteer."

"Where do you come from?"

"France."

"Whereabouts?"

"Paris."

"Oh! Perhaps Saif and myself will go there."

"Wow, but let's get you and your brother sorted out first, OK?"

"Cool."

Saif spotted the big Greek gentleman that had plucked him out of the sea; gently getting up he walked along the quayside. With a slight tap on the shoulder the big man turned around and Saif held out his hand.

"I want to thank you for pulling me out of the sea." The tears flowed down his cheeks as he asked, "What happened to the other women and children in the boat?"

The tall Greek man knelt down, took Saif's small frail hands into his own huge hands and looked Saif in the eye.

"I'm so sorry, young man, but we were too late; a lot of the children drowned along with their mothers."

Saif slumped to the ground and completely broke down in tears. The big Greek man scooped him up in his arms and held him tight. This moment of tenderness from someone Saif had never met before was the most comforting feeling he had known in a long time.

A small room at the back of the rescue centre was Saif and Zahid's next port of call; thousands of migrants and refugees had started the process here to enter the EU for a better life. Saif wheeled his brother in; both of them told the story of what had happened to them and where they wanted to go. The look of astonishment from the team of people that sat on the other side of the table, hearing what plans the brothers had, was a picture to behold. It was agreed that the normal camp designated for orphaned child refugees would be too dangerous for Zahid with his physical disabilities. Reports had started to emerge over the last few days of infighting and assaults on Syrian child refugees from Afghan and Iraqi children; refugees themselves having being forced to leave their own countries due to violence and persecution. Drug gangs had infiltrated the camp, spreading their evil ways; bullying and blackmail was rife. The police had been called into deal with the matter. The perimeter fence, on numerous occasions, had been knocked down and those children that escaped were still at large, probably in another country by now.

The Polka camp, with its wooden buildings and tents shaded from the sun by the surrounding pine trees, would be a better choice; there the two boys could rest from their ordeal for a while, have their needs assessed and supported. By registering with the Greek Authorities they could get the ferry to Athens and from there to the destination of their dreams. For Saif and Zahid that would be Sweden.

All the best lads.

MALAINA

The Fall was Malaina's favourite time of the year. She loved to see the trees that lined the avenues and parks around her home of Quebec City put on their autumnal colours of golds, coppers and scarlets. This splash of colour that decked the city would be short-lived, as the heavy snows of winter would shortly put in an appearance. She loved the Fall as that meant Halloween, for all the neighbours' houses would be decorated with goblins, trolls, scarecrows and wizards along with other spooky stuff. Shop windows would be adorned with carved-out pumpkins and the candles or little lights that were placed inside them would light up their scary faces in the night. But more importantly she loved the Fall as it meant the ice hockey season started.

Quebec City sits on the St Lawrence River in Canada's mostly French-speaking Quebec Province; one of its main parks is the Plaines d'Abraham, and it was here Malaina found herself sitting on a park bench with her sister next to a cannon that had been mounted on a small plinth. The building behind them on Avenue George VI was the Fondation du Musee National des Beaux-Arts-Du Quebec, a well-known city landmark. Every Saturday morning the two sisters would come to this park bench and wait patiently for their mother to turn up. Some Saturdays their mother would turn up; if she did, she was invariably late and always weighed down by the plastic bags that contained her worldly possessions. Other Saturdays she simply didn't show; on those occasions the sisters would phone their father and if he was not available to escort them they would resort to phoning a few of the lads from the boys' school ice hockey squad for protection. It was too dangerous for Malaina and her sister to go on their own, searching the streets amongst the homeless, the down and outs, the dropouts, the mentally disturbed and the drug addicts. For years their mother had suffered from bouts of depression, alcohol and drug addiction. Ever since her own mother died as a result of overdosing on cocaine. The depression and the addictions appeared to be hereditary on their mother's side, as the family tree exposed several family members having suffered or died from related mental illness problems.

A cold chill from the Northern Tundra suddenly swept across the park, reminding Malaina that winter, with its freezing temperatures of anything down to minus twenty degrees celsius and snowdrifts of up to two metres, was just around the corner. Even large parts of the mighty St Lawrence River itself froze over in the deepest depths of Canada's bleak winter months. Malaina and all her high school friends often went skating on the river; they had great fun and would spend hours messing around until the port authorities shouted at them to get off. Quebec City in winter was no place for those that lived their lives on the streets. They would be dead from hypothermia within days.

At last their mother turned up, and for once

she was sober, lucid and amiable. Malaina gave her mother a large hug; she didn't kiss her as she had no idea where her mother had been or what company she had kept. Their father still loved their mother and every Saturday morning made sure that Malaina and her sister had enough money to buy shoes, clothes and food. Whatever their mother needed, money was no object. He made it clear, though, that they were not to give the money to their mother, as she would simply spend it on alcohol and drugs. Every week Malaina's father, who ran the family's highly profitable winery business that had been owned by the family for decades, would go to the local charities that provided clean needles for homeless drug addicts and collect fresh supplies along with empty boxes to dispose of the used needles. If their mother remembered to bring her used box back, which invariably she didn't, he would take the box back to the places that sterilised them and leave money for the charity to carry out its mission. The staff at the various centres knew him well; he hated going to those places. He went more out of compassion than desire, but it was still a place he dreaded going to. Many people criticised him for doing this, as they saw it as a means of temptation, for providing the clean needles was only fuelling the issue. But what else could their father do? He had spent a vast amount of money paying for rehab programmes, along with various treatments, and while they temporally helped, inevitably their mother would return to her addictive ways. Malaina and her sister supported their father on this matter, as they couldn't stop their mother from abusing drugs, so at least she had clean needles.

Today's top priority for Malaina was to take her mother to see some of the new charity centres that were opening up across the city that would provide warmth and shelter over the winter months; her father had given her a list of the places he had visited and made enquiries over the last few days. Whichever one her mother chose, she would let her father know so that he could at least make a financial contribution to the shelter and make sure their heating bill was covered. It was difficult for Malaina and her sister having to do this every week; she was fifteen and her younger sister was twelve, and very often she resented the fact that she had been placed in this position through no fault of her own. She was a stroppy teenager who wanted to go out shopping with her friends on a Saturday and not have to be dealing with an alcoholic, drug addict mother. Her father understood how she and her sister felt; they had talked about the situation on numerous occasions. He still loved his wife, but she would have nothing to do with him and would only talk to her daughters and that was on a good day.

Last year their father had bought a caravan for their mother to stay in on the edge of the vineyard, but she rarely came, and when she did she brought with her hordes of her so called *druggie friends* who raided the vineyard stocks and caused mayhem amongst the island neighbours, who had to put up with abuse and needles scattered everywhere. After several run-ins and confrontations with the police for public disorder offences, their mother and friends were arrested and spent several months in prison. Their father couldn't risk a similar situation happening again on their doorstep, hence he looked for suitable sheltered accommodation in the city this year. The family lawyer had obtained an order through the courts banning their mother from coming near the family vineyard, which was also their home. Their father's thinking behind this decision was simply an attempt to protect Malaina and her sister from unpredictable vagrant attacks close to where they lived.

Home for Malaina was the top floor of an old converted barn on the midstream river island of Ile-d'Orleans. From her bedroom window, where she sat to do her schoolwork, she could see across the vineyard with its rows of vines all neatly set out in straight lines. Beyond the vineyard was the mighty St Lawrence River, and beyond that was Quebec City itself. At night-time she would stare at the city streetlights on the other side of the river and often wondered what street and shop doorway her mother was in, or what park bench she was on. Downstairs was the shop and café where the tourists and visitors would come after having had a guided tour from her grandfather, who would have meticulously explained the whole wine making process from picking the grapes through to fermentation and eventually bottling. Malaina very often helped out in the café at busy times; she was not allowed in the shop as she was too young to advise and sell the wines. Of the two sisters Malaina was the sporty one, whereas her younger sister was more the academic.

It was Monday morning, and Malaina could hear her father shouting at her and her sister to get their skinny butts out of bed, the school bus would be at the top of the narrow gravel track in forty minutes. Malaina begrudgingly rolled herself out from underneath her duvet, and as she slouched back from the bathroom she all of a sudden remembered she had the second ice hockey training session of the season after school. Where was her kit? She stomped around the house, kicking and tossing things around. Where had she put it?

"What are you looking for?" asked her father.

"My ice hockey kit."

"I told you to get all your stuff ready for school last night before you went to bed."

'Yeah, yeah!....' thought Malaina to herself as she half-heartedly listened to her father muttering in the background about not being prepared as usual.

Her sister, *'Miss all organised'*, called: "It's in the utility room across the yard where you last left it on Friday night."

'Oh great!' thought Malaina, one sweaty, crumpled, smelly kit. Wow! The rest of the squad are going to love me. Her father had made porridge. She hated it; why couldn't they have pancakes or French toast like the rest of her friends had for breakfast? No, her father insisted on them

having porridge as it was healthier; blah! blah!...
Malaina had just started her porridge when
the school bus horn went, signalling its arrival.
Grabbing her packed lunch, she hurled herself out
the kitchen door and down the steps, remembering
to cross the yard and pick up her dirty kit. She
dashed to the top of the track where her sister was
patiently waiting for her. In a fluster she threw
herself on the bus, grateful it had arrived early as
it spared her having to force the rest of that awful
porridge down her throat.

It was still dark as they drove along Chemin
Royal, the main road that circumvented the small
island. A small queue of early commuters had
started to build up at the entrance to the only
suspension bridge that connected the island to the
mainland. It would be another hour by the time
the bus had completed all its pick ups and arrive
at the school gates on Rue de Maisonneuve. The
banter on the bus was lively for an early Monday
morning, as everybody was discussing what they
had got up to over the weekend and looking at
the latest photos on their Facebook and Instagram
accounts. Malaina knew nobody would be
interested in what she had done over the weekend
so she sat quietly looking out the bus window. Her
best friend tapped her on the shoulder as they got
off.

"How's your mum?"

"She was sober for once; sober enough to refuse
even contemplating sorting a shelter out for the
winter."

"Oh…"

"Yeah! Oh indeed. So we'll have to try again next Saturday, another waste of time and trip. I told my father he will have to come with us next time and the two of them will have to row over the matter, that is if mother turns up, and if she does what state she is in."

"Hey! Have you heard The Prime Minister is coming to Quebec City in two weeks time?"

"No… Why?" said Malaina.

"Apparently he wants to see for himself how the city authorities are spending the sport grants they received from the government and what they are doing about the city's homeless situation." Malaina was intrigued as to how her best friend knew about this.

Malaina handed in her ice hockey registration form to Mrs Xavier, the head of school sports for the year. The deadline was last week; it had been at the bottom of her bag for the last ten days. Mrs Xavier muttered some inaudible words of disapproval as she tucked the form into that morning's call register folder. Her father had signed the form giving his consent for her to play in this year's ice hockey season. Training started that afternoon at the old ice rink down the road that the school, along with other schools in Quebec City, used for training purposes. The squad of twenty needed to be kitted out and ready to start at 4pm. It would be a tight schedule to be there on time, as most of them had a history tutorial that didn't finish until 3.30pm. Malaina and her friends wanted to be in the squad, so this was something they were going to have to manage on a regular basis. The squad was made up of twelve forwards that were divided into four groups of three; each group was known as a line, consisting of a centre and two wings, along with six in defence again made up of three pairs of two and finally two goalies. At any one moment on the rink, the team consisted of six players, three forwards, two in defence and a goalie. The first game was in a fortnight's time and as Malania's best friend had already hinted at, it was strongly rumoured that The Prime Minister might be there.

The school training centre that was down the road was, as expected, extremely cold; Malaina shoved the changing room door open as she charged in. The poor unsuspecting girl that was immediately behind the door was unimpressed with Malaina's bullish entry as she dusted herself down and picked her stuff off the floor with a smug smile on her face; revenge would be sweet out on the rink. Malaina, oblivious to her actions, tipped the contents of her heavy sports bag on the floor. A quick glance revealed that everything was in order. Hockey stick, skates, helmet with cage and mouth guard, neck protector, protector combo comprising of shin, shoulder and elbow pad; jill, padded shorts, protective gloves and most importantly this year's school jersey. Mrs Xavier was already on the rink waiting as St Pat's junior girls team spilled out of the changing room. Malaina was hoping for right wing in one of the forward lines; she wasn't bothered which one of the four lines as long as she was on the right wing. Sitting on the bench Mrs Xavier went through her trial team positions, as she wanted to see for herself who would be in all the positions and what pairings worked best.

The last few weeks' training had, as expected, been tough, but Malaina had secured left wing in the second forward line; she would have preferred being on the right, but as the coach pointed out, a strong team needs interchangeable players and individuals need to understand the school team comes first. It had been confirmed that morning that the Canadian Prime Minister, Mr Justin Trudeau, would be visiting the school in the afternoon; for security reasons the precise time was on a need to know basis and his itinerary would be disclosed nearer the time. A comment appeared on the school website, '*Anybody wishing to ask the Prime Minister a serious question please post it on the website by 10am. Two sensible questions will be chosen by the school council; the two successful students will be notified by lunchtime.*' Malaina thought for a few moments would she or would she not like to meet the Prime Minister, hmm…? She posted a question around mental health issues and how it affects the homeless and how was his government going to resolve the issue?

For years Malaina had watched her mother's decline as the effects of the drug and alcohol addiction took an ever firmer hold; she was angry at how easy it was to obtain the drugs despite the

Drug Enforcement Agency's best efforts to stem the supplies flowing into Canada from countries like Colombia, Mexico and Peru. She was appalled to see the street drug sellers sitting in their blacked-out Mercs outside school gates approaching the students, despite the police department's numerous attempts to catch them red-handed. Her father had warned her to never approach the drug traffickers under any circumstances as they were unpredictable, dangerous people who could well be armed. To the students that fell foul of the traffickers she would track down and show them photographs of her mother of how she looked years ago and how she appeared now, telling them how it had impacted her life.

The Prime Minister's entourage entered the school grounds shortly before 4pm. Malaina had already been notified that she would be addressing Mr Trudeau and to be in the school reception by 4.30pm. For a usually confident person, Malaina was feeling slightly apprehensive and began to wish she had never posted that reply on the school website. She stood patiently at the end of the queue as the Prime Minister worked his way along the long line of people wishing to shake his hand; next to her were two chairs and a small table that had been hastily arranged creating a small reception area. On the table a large floral display gave a splash of colour to what was normally a drab area where most of the students threw their bags as they waited to speak to whoever in the school administration team was reluctantly on duty that day. Mr Trudeau had finally got to her. Shaking her hand he pointed to the chairs; he had been clearly briefed by his officious-looking aide in the smart red dress suit who was engrossed in her iPad, no doubt making sure that Mr Trudeau stuck to his itinerary.

As she sat down the Prime Minister asked what position she played in the school ice hockey team.

"Right wing, second forward line."

Extremely embarrassed, she corrected herself, "Sorry, left wing."

"Don't be embarrassed, I hear from my aides that you are playing Bec High this afternoon, May I come and watch? I used to play centre forward line two. Do you enjoy getting battered to death on the ice rink?"

"Sometimes, particularly when you have to dig deep to win. If we win the bruises are worth it."

Malaina briefly explained her mother's background and what had led up to her question. She had rehearsed what she was going to say with her friends at lunchtime at the little café across the road.

The Prime Minister was impressed with the level of knowledge and understanding she had for a fifteen year old.

"You know, Malaina, being Prime Minister you have to take tough and very often unpopular decisions. You have to balance out what you think is fair for the country. Those decisions you take affect everybody in different ways; some benefit, some lose. Making cuts to services hurts, but if we haven't got the money to spend then we need to cut back. I don't have all the answers to our country's issues; it's up to all Canadians to pull together. So my question to you is, what can you do to get round the problems that people like your mother face everyday on the streets of Quebec City?"

"I don't know."

"OK, let me tell you about how I overcame an issue I had at senior school; it wasn't drugs related or to do with homelessness, but the same principles can be applied to yourself here. My quandary was the level of bullying I witnessed in the school I went to. One of my friends was being bullied as he was into dance, drama and music; he wasn't interested like most of us in the rough bruising game of ice hockey. In fact a lot of my classmates thought he was effeminate and possibly gay. He was stigmatised and bullied to such an extent that he confided in me that he had contemplated committing suicide. "

"So what did you do, Mr Trudeau?"

"I spoke to my late father, who at the time just happened to be the then Prime Minister; he didn't give me the answer, like I'm not giving you the answer here. But he pointed me in the direction of a small group of people that met in a small backroom of a local community centre every Monday night. I went along to their meetings and got to know the people and their stories and how their lives had been destroyed by bullies. I took my friends along who were doing the bullying."

"How did you get them to go?"

"Aah! That was easy, I told them we were going to an ice hockey meet and that some of the girls from the school across the way would be there."

"You lied to them."

"Well, not quite; I had arranged for the ladies to meet us in a local coffee shop afterwards, but first I made my friends sit through the whole meeting so that they could see and listen for themselves to see what victims of bullying go through. I told them how my friend had confided in me, and that as a result of their actions he had contemplated taking his life. I asked them in front of the girls in the café how they felt about that and what were they going to do to resolve the matter. They hadn't got a clue as to what damage they had inflicted on my friend; to them, looking good in front of their mates was all about acting tough. I learnt from those meetings that being tough is not simply about being physically strong, but putting your inner strengths to the challenge and learning to apply those strengths at the right time. At times in life physical strength is required, as in ice hockey, but other times a gentler inner strength is required. We blokes are not as good as you ladies are in this field of diplomacy. So what did I achieve by dragging my friends along to those meetings, apart from embarrassing them in front of the girls they were trying to impress and score brownie points in front of?"

"Yes! What did you achieve?"

"Well, two of them kept going back to those

meetings and now run global international charities for people whose lives have been destroyed by conflicts of war, in particular those soldiers that have witnessed horrendous scenes of killing and destruction and have not been able to cope with civilian life. You see them sitting on the streets of some of the world's biggest cities, including here in Canada. Those two guys channel all their efforts and strengths into raising money to provide shelter and accommodation for those vulnerable men and women, people we walk by and look away from every day.

"They had seen the error of their ways and being the big boys and facing other school bullies earned them brownie points with the ladies. Win, win yeah! But the first thing they did was to go and talk to my friend and learn from him that different people bring different talents to the world and, while we might not care for differing values, we need to respect them."

"Wow."

"But, like me, they started to change things gradually. Firstly they talked to the school council, they identified other school bullies and got them into the ice hockey teams. Every game they played they got the school students to make a donation to the local charity that had been chosen for that game. As I said, I don't have all the answers. Think about what I said. Let me know how you get on." With that Mr Trudeau stood up, tapped Malaina on the shoulder and, with a well-rehearsed political smile, shuffled off down the corridor with the

Head Teacher and the lady in the red suit still furiously tapping on the iPad interface.

The ice hockey game against Bec City was extremely physical, and sure enough the girl she had slammed the door into in the changing room got her revenge; the brutal shove had been meticulously timed and when the moment presented itself sent Malaina crashing into the barriers. The bruised ribs she would feel for weeks.

The beating Bec City had inflicted on St Pat's hurt; in the changing rooms afterwards the coach merely implied in her brusque team talk that they were not good enough, and needed to focus on what they were doing, plus practise more, learn from their mistakes and move on. With the ticking off over, Malaina and her friends showered and headed off to the new cinema complex to watch the latest Tom Hanks movie, where he plays the airline pilot that successfully lands a passenger jet on the Potomac River in Washington DC.

It was dark when Malaina and her friends came out of the cinema complex; as agreed her father was waiting in the car park. All her other friends had made their own arrangements getting home. Throwing her ice hockey bag with all its smelly kit onto the back seat, she clambered into the passenger seat beside her father. Closing the door and belting up she slumped into the seat; it had been a long day. Her father turned to her.

"Shame about the match, can't win them all."

It had been snowing for the best part of an hour. Malaina stared at the windscreen wipers that swished backwards and forwards, clearing the wet splodges of fluffy snow that landed on the car's windscreen.

"Yeah... tell that to Mrs Xavier, the coach."

"So you all got a telling off?"

"Yep."

"Shall I take you to the doctor tomorrow to get those ribs looked at?"

"Nah... he'll only say there is nothing he can do, so go away."

"Did you get to meet the Prime Minster?"

"Yes."

"So what did he have to say?"

"He was... actually, father, can we talk about this in the morning? I'm really tired."

"Sure."

The car turned onto the narrow track that led down to the vineyard. Malaina loved to hear the crunching noise the car's tyres made as they drove over the gravel. Getting out of the car, she walked a few paces beyond the outbuildings; turning back to her right, she could see her sister's bedroom light spilling out from an upstairs window. She never pulled her curtains at night, something Malaina never understood. Holding her right side as if giving some protection from the pain, Malaina gently twisted her body to the left, and between the heavy snowflakes she could just about make out Quebec's city street lights on the other side of the St Lawrence River. Reaching gingerly into her coat's top inside left pocket, she pulled her phone out and sent a quick text message to her mother,

'*Hope you found somewhere warm and safe tonight x*'. She put her phone away; she knew her mother wouldn't reply, but it made her feel better within herself for sending it.

Malaina couldn't sleep. Every time she attempted to turn over in bed the searing pain from her bruised ribs kicked in; she coughed a couple of times in the night and honestly thought she was going to die. That girl from school was a marked person. Drawing back the curtains she could see that the snow was still falling; the weather app on her phone was indicating heavy snow for the next few days. Lying still, gazing at the sky, Malaina reflected on what Prime Minister Justin Trudeau had said to her the previous day. She had wanted to know what he was going to do about the problem of homelessness and mental health issues here in Quebec City and to hear he hadn't got all the answers had initially taken her by surprise, but the more she thought about it, yes, he might be the Prime Minister, but he was only one man. She was impressed with the fact that he took the time to listen and his story of what he did when faced with a difficult matter when he was a similar age to her struck home. She began to think maybe she could do something with a lot of help from friends, but what precisely? At least he didn't just smile and move on down the line like most men in his position would have invariably done.

She had never really talked to her friends about her mother and what happened and why she lives on the streets drugged and drunk off her head most days. What would she tell them? She didn't understand herself why her mother had, so to speak, fallen off the planet? Maybe she, like Mr Trudeau, needed to seek out local organisations that try to support people like her mother to talk to them so as to get an understanding and listen to the people that find themselves on the street. Get her friends to come along. If it's a matter of money, perhaps she could talk to the school council, get them involved by adopting a local homeless charity and make them the school's charity of the year; get them to come into the school and talk to the students about the work they do and agree a suitable working program. Maybe get the local community on the island here to donate money each time they play a game of ice hockey. As she lay there the ideas were flooding in and her head was becoming awash with all the ideas. Yes, this was going to be her task for the immediate future. She was grateful for what Prime Minister Trudeau had said and quietly thought to herself what an inspiring man he is. She would talk with her father in the morning for his views. With those thoughts, she turned over in bed; the pain that shot through her ribs was excruciating but that would fade over the next few weeks. But for the time being she added a reminder note on her phone to make a discreet visit to Bec City School and kick that little lassie's ass hard for all the discomfort she was in.

YESHE

Autumns on the high Tibetan plateau, often referred to as the roof of the world, were dry, cool and pleasant. The grasses were still green and fresh from the summer rains and not yet covered by the harsh winter snows. For Yeshe's family, their nomadic way of life was hard as they followed their herds of yak, cattle, sheep and goats. Every few weeks the family would pack up their belongings and move to better pastures.

Yeshe's people were known as Drokpas simply for the nomadic lifestyle they followed. But for Yeshe's generation the traditional ways of his forefathers were disappearing as modern life, with its technology and globalisation, seeped deeper into Tibetan customs. What Yeshe wanted from life as an eleven year old boy and what his parents wanted for him were very different, which led to numerous family conflicts. The bright city lights of Lhasa and the world beyond had started to call and what they had to offer him, in stark contrast to a simple yak tent herding yaks and goats, had no comparison. A compromise was needed and that came in the form of a split agreement. For six months of the year, mainly late spring through to early autumn, Yeshe would live with his parents and younger siblings high in the Tibetan plateau around the Tanggula Mountains in the Nyainrong County tending the livestock, but for the rest of the year he lived with his elder brother's family in a second floor flat in the Jia Malinka district of Lhasa.

The small group of ten families that owned the various livestock had lived side by side for years; each family had their own tent made of black yak wool that was tied and draped around wooden poles. Yeshe was always amazed how quickly the family home could be dismantled and erected, loaded and unloaded on and off the trailer pulled by two of their horses. Every time they assembled their home it would be set out in the traditional way. An earthy fireplace positioned in the middle would be the sole source of providing heat and the means to cook. Rugs and blankets would be scattered all around the floor. Sleeping arrangements were simple; men on the left side of the circular tent, women on the right. At the back, mainly on the men's side, a small space was put aside to create a shrine area where the family statues of Buddha and other local deities they worshipped were displayed. Any pieces of traditional jewellery would also be put on show.

Yeshe woke early; he had spent the night, as he usually did when the weather was fine, huddled with his friends under a pile of brightly coloured woollen quilted blankets under the open skies. Sitting up for a few brief moments before tossing the blankets aside, he looked at the Tanggula Mountains in the near distance; they were majestic as they rose high above the plateau. Their peaks, still covered in snow, had the odd thin wispy strands of cirrus cloud floating above them. The herds of yaks and cattle had spread themselves far and wide over the plateau. With an extensive yawn and a stretch he got to his feet; as he got up he shook the family dog that was lying to his left as if to say, '*if I'm up then so should you be*'. Tibetan Mastiffs were large powerful dogs bred to protect the family and the livestock from unwanted visitors, like the occasional Chinese authorities trying to confiscate their jewellery and animals in lieu of taxes, and the local wildlife predators like the square-faced Tibetan fox from attacking the sheep and goats. Your average Tibetan Mastiff was not a cuddly pet that you could toy around with; they were working dogs that had a fearsome reputation, so commanded respect. The snarl and growl followed by a sharp cuff across Yeshes' lower back legs from a large paw was a clear message of disapproval. Yeshe winced; looking down he saw the inflicted gashes. The drawn blood had started to trickle down the inside of his leg. Scowling with rage, Yeshe quickly scanned the ground to see what sharp object was close to hand that could be hurled at the dog as a means of a swift retaliation. Still enraged and not being able to place his hands on a suitable weapon, he merely glared at the Tibetan Massif before stomping off to the nearby stream to clean his wounds. There was no point complaining to his father, for all he would say is that he shouldn't have aggravated the dog. As he headed off to the stream, he stopped briefly to pick up his clothes that had lain strewn around the ground in the exact place where he had discarded them the night before.

Walking back from the stream, Yeshe could see

that his mother was up and had lit a fire, evidence made clear by the wisps of smoke emerging from the smoke hole at the top of the tent. Other nearby tents were showing signs of early movement as more and more wispy trails gently billowed into the light morning breeze. Today, for this small group of nomads encamped on the high Tibetan plateau, it was a strategic day as the decision had been taken to move the camp and all the livestock further south near Nagqu. It would take a few hours to dismantle the tents and load all their belongings on to the wooden trailers. With the women attending to the tents, Yeshe and some of his friends, along with their fathers, embarked on rounding up the various livestock. The wild horses, with their free spiritedness coursing through their veins, would prove to be the most challenging to round up; even for the most experienced horseman among them it would take cunning and skill to catch them and keep them under control over the next few days. Yeshe was excited, as he was bored here. This simple but hard way of life wasn't for him; he wanted to be back in Lhasa with his real friends at school, to be able to log on to his laptop to see what was happening in the world.

There was an air of urgency among the clan, an eagerness to be on the move; it wasn't the prospect of fresh pastureland that was creating this vibrant buzz, but the excitement of the Nagqu Horse Racing Festival that was three days away. For Yeshe there was an added incentive to go, for after the festival he would not return to the Drokpa nomadic lifestyle but head off with his brother to Lhasa.

The new camp was a day's journey; the site, like most of the places the families temporarily settled in, were well known to them – as their forefathers that went before them had once put down brief roots. The new site was more sheltered and below fifteen thousand feet, thus less exposed to the plateau's most extreme weather cycles. The journey would give some of the men time to polish the horse riding skills they had been working on over the last few weeks as they raced their horses alongside the moving herds. Yeshe watched his father putting his stallion through his final paces in preparation for the big race at the festival in a few days time. It had been a glorious sunny day, but as evening approached the new temporary settlement site came into view. Dismounting from his own horse that he loved to ride bareback, Yeshe unloaded the tent from the wooden trailer. Within a matter of hours all the tents had been erected and the various livestock settled on the surrounding pastures. The topic of discussion around each family fire would no doubt turn to the forthcoming festival.

The day of the festival had arrived. Tens of thousands of people from all around Tibet had converged around Nagqu for the seven-day festival. Thousands of tents had sprung up on the golden grasslands, creating a small tent city. Paintings of Buddhas and colourful prayer flags were displayed everywhere. After the opening ceremonies, a week-long series of festivities including horse racing, yak racing, wrestling, dance, live music, archery and other such activities would ensue. For Yeshe this was a time of great excitement, watching his father in the horse racing, taking part in the tug of war competitions and watching his mother and sisters winning prizes in the cookery and dance events. Yeshe thought it was good for his family to let their hair down and watch the smiles return to their faces and for a few days forget about the harshness of life. He was only glad that he didn't have to leave the horse festival as an unwilling volunteer to go back to watch the herds like his other friends had to. It had been a wonderful festival; Yeshe had met new people whom he promised to stay in contact with; the chances of that happening was slim. In reality he would probably not see them again. With the festival over, the thousands that had attended started to pack up their belongings and make their way home, be that on horse or for rich Tibetans car. For Yeshe it was on the back of his brother's gleaming new red motorbike. With the family embraces completed, Yeshe departed for Lhasa with his elder brother, but he was intrigued about an envelope his father had handed to his brother.

Helmet fastened, bike leathers on, Yeshe gripped the metal handlebars under the seat. The five hour pillion ride to Lhasa would be enthralling; he even remembered how to lean with the bike as it twisted and turned along the roads. Yeshe's brother put the keys into the ignition and pressed the starter button. The powerful engine roared into life, and with a gentle pull on the throttle they were off. The G109 south out of Nagqu for the next few kilometres would be busy with the thousands of festivalgoers heading home; the road would be littered with cars, tractors, herdsmen on horseback, people on foot and livestock of various descriptions. It didn't take long for the powerful motorbike to weave its way through all the congestion and head for the open road, a road that would take them across the roof of the world. It was a beautiful day, with not a cloud to be seen in the deep azure blue sky. With the wind tearing at his leathers and tugging at his cheeks, Yeshe was enjoying the thrill of the ride. Sweeping across the high plateau at an alarming speed, tearing through the small villages that where dotted along the way, Yeshe and his brother soon came to Guluzhen. From thereon in the high plateau gave way to the steep valleys, narrow gorges and mountain passes that cut through the mighty Himalayas. A few kilometres further along the route was the small modern town of Danquka; here Yeshe and his brother stopped for light refreshments and fuel. The Kaihen Tea House on the main road was busy and it was a little while before their hot sweet tea with yak buttermilk arrived at their table. Sipping the hot tea was a welcome relief for Yeshe; as it slipped down his throat a warm glowing feeling began to spread throughout his body and eventually he could feel life coming back to his feet. It might have been a glorious day outside, but up at fifteen thousand feet on the back of a motorbike in the middle of the Himalayas with only bike leathers to keep you insulated from the cold thin mountain air that sucked the very life out of you was a cold experience.

Refreshed, Yeshe and his brother hit the road again. A few kilometres along they turned left onto the S202, which was the scenic mountain pass road and would shorten their journey by at least an hour. The tiny mountain road at times was nothing more than a single lane dirt track cut into the mountainside. Yeshe could sense that his brother was enjoying the thrills and spills of the ride as he pushed the bike to its limits, tearing up the road in front of him; sometimes he thought his brother had forgotten he was sitting behind him. There were moments when Yeshe was convinced his heart was in his mouth as the back wheel occasionally spun out of control, with inches to spare before the bike could have easily tipped over the precipice, free falling thousands of feet to the fast flowing rivers below. They would be dead on impact and nobody would discover their bodies for days; there was nothing he could do except to say his prayers and cling on to the bike for his life. The mountain scenery was spectacular, but his brother's reckless disregard for their lives had started to frighten him and spoil the day.

With the mountain pass Grand Prix over, Yeshe's brother slowed the bike down, indicating right at a forthcoming junction on the outskirts of Lhasa. With the bike at a complete standstill waiting for a break in the traffic, Yeshe scrambled off the back, removed his helmet and placed it in his right hand before proceeding to batter his brother with it, at the same time expressing his views with angry, sharp words. His stunned brother simply looked him straight in the face with an expression of disbelief, as if to say *'what's your problem?'* Infuriated with his brother's attitude, he clambered back onto the bike, having given stern instructions to slow down; with his helmet fixed in position and securely fastened again, he thumped his brother on the back as if to say he was ready to go, but he would continue the argument with his brother when they got to the home apartment.

The main streets of Lhasa were busy with the hustle and bustle of modern life. The shops and cafes were teeming with people and Yeshe was glad to be, what he called, back in civilisation. Lhasa, the former capital of Tibet, was now the provincial capital of the Tibetan Autonomous Region of China. Life in Lhasa was a far cry from the nomadic lifestyle of the Drokpa people, sitting in a tent oblivious to the outside world. Yeshe couldn't understand why the friends he had just left didn't want to follow him? Why they didn't have his vision to become a doctor and see the world? Why did they want to choose to live in the past? He couldn't grasp their thinking. At times he found them exasperating, but came to the conclusion it was their loss if they chose to live in the past.

Sitting at a set of traffic lights at the junction that was the end of the S202 and the start of

Linkou N Rd, Yeshe observed the number of teenagers that were riding bikes with no protective helmets; he thought to himself what stupid idiots they were, or was he just being old and boring for his age? With the lights changing to green he was only five minutes away from his brother's second floor apartment. In a few moments they would turn left onto Niangre Middle Rd and as they turned the Potala Palace, the former winter home of the fourteenth Dalai Lama, would appear to their right along with the Tibet Peaceful Liberation Monument, the two most significant buildings in Lhasa. Turning right onto Jinzhu E Rd and immediately left to cross the bridge that spanned the Lhasa River, Yeshe had arrived on the small river island. N Ring Rd rang along the river's edge and the apartment block that his brother and wife lived in with their small baby daughter was located here. The view from the second floor apartment was impressive; from his room Yeshe could look directly at the peace monument with its surrounding parklands, and the imposing historic Potala Palace complex that dominated Lhasa's skyline with the mighty northern Himalayas in the background.

Yeshe slammed his bedroom door having had a second spat with his brother over the daredevil bike ride antics he had endured a few hours ago. Throwing himself onto the bed, he reached underneath and, fumbling around with his right arm, he managed to locate the orange cloth bag which had his laptop and smartphone in along with the various chargers. Having carefully retrieved the bag, he proceeded to switch his laptop and phone on. Great! No charge or sign of life in either of the devices. Why didn't his brother charge them up? Knowing that they would take several hours to fully charge, he stomped out of his room and muttered something inaudible to his brother as he headed out of the apartment. Bounding down the steps, he knew he was behaving like a spoilt brat. His plan to catch up with his friends by video link on his laptop, letting them all know he was back from no man's land, had gone awry and he was now going to have to walk through the myriad of streets to his Chinese friend's house.

Jinhai was a little taken aback when he opened his front door to see Yeshe standing there.

"Why! What are you doing here? Why didn't you text, call or email me to let me know you were back?"

"No charge on my phone and the laptop was dead."

Sitting on one of the stone benches in the parkland close to the peace monument, Yeshe and Jinhai spent the next few hours catching up with each other; the last few months had been pretty uneventful as far as Yeshe was concerned. Jinhai, on the other hand, had been to Beijing and The Forbidden City, along with a flying visit to Shanghai, where his family came from. As opposed to Yeshe's family, Jinhai's family were comfortably well off. His father was a judge who was ordered here by the Chinese Authorities, sent to ensure Chinese rule was followed to the strict letter. It was a strange friendship and one that neither family encouraged. Many of the older Tibetan generations had not forgotten or forgiven the Chinese for invading their country in the middle of the last century and saw the Chinese community that had settled in Lhasa as unwelcome guests. Tensions still existed between both communities and, while there were those that actively encouraged full integration, there still remained a hardcore minority who were fiercely opposed to the Chinese People.

Jinhai looked at his watch. Turning to Yeshe he said:

"I have to go, see you at school tomorrow."

Collecting the paper wrappings up and the empty plastic cups that had hot sweet tea in from the nearby fast-food café, Jinhai headed off home. As he passed a nearby litter bin he hurled the remains of his and Yeshe's takeout meal, briefly stopping to make sure the screwed up package had landed in the trash can, not like other people's rubbish that was strewn around the bin's baseline. With a final turn and wave to Yeshe he left.

Yeshe remained for a few further moments. He was glad to be back in civilisation. Looking at The Potala Palace, Yeshe quietly reflected and thought to himself how imposing the palace was as it sat perched on top of Red Hill. Rising three hundred metres from the valley floor, the palace dominated Lhasa's skyline. At its base the walls were estimated to be three metres thick, and molten copper was rumoured to have been poured into the foundations, giving some support to the massive structure against the violent earthquakes that struck the area. The palace was probably one of the most significant buildings to be constructed in Tibetan history; started in sixteen forty five by the 5th Dalai Lama, the palace had been the winter home of Tibet's Buddhist spiritual leader until nineteen fifty nine, when Tenzin Gyatso, the present and 14th Dalai Lama, fled to India in fear of his life from China's powerful authorities that sat in Peking – now known as Beijing. The palace was reputed to have over a thousand rooms, including the Dalai Lama's living quarters, priceless murals, chapels, tombs, ten thousand shrines and a staggering two hundred thousand statues. The palace today is a museum and a world heritage site.

Walking back to his brother's, Yeshe started to wonder what was in the letter his father had handed to his brother and why all the secrecy. As he reached the apartment Yeshe could hear voices from within. As he opened the door his brother stood up, but Yeshe's eye was immediately drawn to the tall, slim Buddhist monk dressed in the traditional habit of red and yellow. Yeshe glanced back to his brother, who gestured at him to sit down; Yeshe could feel his heart starting to pound faster and faster in his chest. As he slowly sat down he read the letter his brother had handed to him; it was the very letter he had seen his father give to his brother earlier that morning. Reading the contents of the letter to himself over and over, the message and significance of the contents slowly unravelled in his head. He was to be handed over to the monks to start the life of a Tibetan Buddhist monk. The letter was his father's authority. Yeshe had heard strong rumours that it was sometimes a father's choice to hand over as a gift a child to the monasteries to follow the life of a Buddhist monk. Yeshe's heart had almost come to a halt; he didn't want to enter into a monastery to become a Buddhist monk. Tibet was full of monks; Yeshe had a clear vision for his future. He wanted to be a doctor or a lawyer, something that would earn him a lot of money and take him around the world. The life of a monk was not on his radar. What annoyed him most as he sat reading the letter again was the fact his father didn't have the courage to talk to him about this but left it to his older brother to handle. He looked at his father's pathetic simple signature at the bottom of the letter and he knew that the Lama was here to take him away.

Several days had passed and Yeshe found himself sitting in a compound full of novice Buddhist students. Gone were his T-shirt, jeans and trainers; replacing them was the traditional orange robe with a yellow tie around his waist. Sitting hunched in a corner with his back against the wall and his arms wrapped around his legs, he looked up from underneath his thick eyebrows at the other young students that were milling around. Were they feeling despondent, angry, betrayed? Or did they simply accept the situation they found themselves in? Yeshe sat quietly, making no attempt to communicate with the other students that were close by; a few tried to make polite conversation with him but Yeshe just grunted back at them, making it quite clear he was in no mood for small talk. Questions and thoughts continued to whizz around his head; he needed to get in touch with Jinhai, but with all modern means of communication temporarily put beyond his reach making contact with him would be a challenge – a challenge he was determined to overcome. Yeshe was going to have to come up with an ingenious escape plan. Yeshe had heard the tales of previous students that had hatched escape plans only to be thwarted by the senior monks, resulting in them being confined to their cells and closely monitored. Those few that managed to escape were invariably tracked down and returned to face strict punishments. A small minority successfully absconded, but often had to face the consequences of family dishonour and that could be brutal. Yeshe also knew that many young Tibetans chosen by their families for the monastic life of a Buddhist monk relished the idea and devoutly followed that life. But Yeshe knew in his own mind that this way of life was not for him and he was going to take the necessary steps despite the consequences that would ensue.

Snapping out of his teenage mood, he got to his feet and began to mingle with the other students, starting by making apologies for his impolite recent mannerisms. Confronted with his new surroundings and circumstances Yeshe, over the course of the next few days, managed to get the general groundswell of feeling that prevailed from his fellow students; he quickly established that a small group of slightly older monks that had been in training for the last few years controlled the monastic compound and meted out relevant punishments to wayward minded fresh students. Yeshe needed to be careful so as not to give anything away.

Over the forthcoming days Yeshe's observations quickly established that small groups of students were allowed out of the monastery compound to visit and learn more about the Jokhang Temple, believed by most Tibetans to be the most sacred and important Buddhist temple in all Tibet. One of the most significant artefacts to be found in the temple is a gold statue of the young Buddha. The temple, now a UNESCO world heritage site, was on Barkhor Square, a few streets away from the monastery complex. Enquiring of the Lama he had been assigned to, the visits were for conscientious, well-behaved students keen to learn the teachings of a Buddhist monk; Yeshe's whirlwind analytical mind went into overdrive. He could do well-behaved, appear enthusiastic and show willing.

Weeks of extolled virtue had earned Yeshe accompanied visitation rights to the Jokhang Temple with his Lama. These organised outings would soon become a regular occurrence, and with each trip Yeshe added ideas to his escape plan. It was on one of these visits Yeshe had the brilliant idea of how he could contact Jinhai without drawing his Lama's attention and the attention of the other students that accompanied him to the temple. Yeshe knew that Jinhai and his friends hung out at one of Lhasa's infamous tea houses and that the tea house was en route; making his excuses for urgent toilet requirements, he darted into the tea house. Quickly scribbling a note on the reverse side of a serviette he thrust it into the hand of one of the waitresses who knew Jinhai; she looked at the note and, with a puzzled look on her face, asked:

"What's this about?"

"Never mind!" retorted Yeshe. "Just make sure he gets the note."

With that he dashed out of the tea house, not forgetting as he reached the door to turn back, smile at the young waitress and at the same time toss the pen he had so abruptly snatched out of her hand moments ago back at her.

Over the next few days and after more urgent trips to the tea house gents', Yeshe had got a reply back from Jinhai. He looked at the note and merely added a date and a time. With that his escape plan had been formalised; all he needed to do now was carry it out.

Yeshe was pleased with his plan and his running away plot would no doubt give his father embarrassment and dishonour. Next time his father and family had any ideas about his future they should include him in the discussions.

The day had come for Yeshe to execute his

meticulous game plan, but this time he added a final twist to the scheme. Instead of making a toilet stop on the way to the temple he would offer to fetch a tea for his Lama on the return journey, knowing that this would take longer. He even suggested, so as not to keep his master Lama waiting, he would bring the tea back to the school, thus creating sufficient time before his disappearance had been commented upon and a search party established.

Jinhai was in the precise spot Yeshe had stipulated by the small water fountain that was surrounded by dwarf yellow and pink dahlias that sat in their individual clay pots neatly arranged in circles. The fountain occupied a small, quiet area of the Norbulingka Palace gardens, the former summer residence of the Dalai Lamas. The summer palace was only a short distance to the south west of Potala Palace, the main residence of the Dalai Lamas.

There was a look of surprise on Jinhai's face as Yeshe raced up the pale white block paved track in his bright orange outfit, the yellow waistband that kept his outfit together was half undone and blowing around in the wind. Yeshe gave Jinhai a huge hug:

"Why are you in a monastery?"

Yeshe simply replied; "It's tradition. My father wants me to become a Buddhist monk."

"And you agreed!"

"I had no choice in the matter; my father signed a letter of consent handing me over to the monks. I don't want to be a monk. I respect those that want to be monks, but that life is not for me, so I have escaped."

"I tried ringing you, texting you, even facebooking and WhatsAPPing you, I even called round at your brother's flat but he wouldn't say what had happened to you."

"Sorry, mate, but I had no means of contacting you until I had access to the tea house. Have you got all the stuff I asked for, Jinhai?"

"Yes, but..."

"Don't ask; the more you know, the more trouble you will get into. Here's an envelope; open it and hand it to your father in three days' time. I'll pay you back the money as soon as I can. Promise me, three days."

Jinhai reluctantly nodded.

"You better; I stole the money from my father's safe. He doesn't know that I knew the combination. He'll blame my mother."

Yeshe gave a final hug to his closest friend before heading to the train station. Stopping off at a fast food outlet, he changed into the clothes Jinhai had managed to buy; it was so good to be back in jeans and a T-shirt with new designer trainers and a new smartphone. As he left the fast food outlet he discreetly placed his orange tunic into one of the many swing bins that had been strategically placed to stop the pavement becoming littered with polystyrene cups and food boxes.

Yeshe swiftly negotiated the busy streets of Lhasa that led to the train station. The station itself was high-tech and modern; the white and red colour scheme on the exterior walls correlated closely to the white and red of the Potala Palace. The large square directly in front of the station was full of people; a small stone seat near the main entrance suddenly became available as a small group of Chinese students that had temporarily occupied the seat vacated having sorted their luggage and got their trappings in order. Sitting on the stone bench, Yeshe placed the bright red rucksack between his legs; quickly undoing the buckled straps he rummaged around to check to see that Jinhai had packed everything he had asked for – a few items of clothing, money and his passport. How Jinhai had managed to get his passport he didn't care, the important factor was he had got it. Yes, he had asked Jinhai to get US$. Why? He wanted to create an impression to any enquiring official that he was a tourist, thus minimising any questions re his intentions and why he was heading for Beijing; so paying for his train ticket with US$ and flashing his passport at the ticket official wouldn't raise any suspicions. Yeshe knew the station would be busy and security minimal; he had watched, when waiting in the past for Jinhai returning from Shanghai, how people merely held up their ID documents to the security officials as they brushed by; most of the times the officials didn't bother to look, merely gesturing with their hands to hurry up.

Taking a deep breath, Yeshe headed for the ticket office. The queue was long but he had plenty of time to catch the high-speed train to Beijing.

As envisaged, the lady behind the screen at the ticket office merely gave Yeshe's passport a cursory glance. She was more concerned with working out the exchange rate so as to charge the right amount of dollars. Yeshe handed over 113 US$, equivalent to 720 Chinese Yuan. With his ticket bought with relative ease, Yeshe headed off to the appropriate platform. Looking up at the electronic departure board, Yeshe could see that the hi-speed train Z22 Lhasa to Beijing was expected to arrive shortly and depart on time. The 41-hour train journey would take him right across China and into the heart of the Chinese capital. He was glad he had booked a hard sleeper cabin, and wondered whom his travelling companions would be – would he get on with them over the coming days? Having boarded his train, Yeshe was excited but at the same time somewhat apprehensive. Looking out from his window seat, in his mind he waved goodbye to Lhasa as the train slowly and quietly slipped out of the station en-route to Beijing.

Yeshe continued to stare out of the window, watching the landscape float past him; he began to wonder had the monastery started looking for him yet and how long would it be before they got in touch with his brother? At this precise moment, nobody in the world knew where he was. The three Chinese students that sat across the way from him? Well, they knew where he was, but knew nothing about him and what he was doing sitting alongside them in the tiny compartment.

The alarm had gone off in the mindset of Yeshe's

Lama. His tea had not arrived and upon further questioning a couple of the students whom he thought had befriended Yeshe immediately realised that Yeshe had disappeared. A new student breaking free was not unheard of, and the monastery had a well-rehearsed routine in place to deal with this situation. Yeshe's elder brother was forthwith notified of his younger brother's escape; he knew Jinhai would be involved somehow and immediately set out to scour the nearby streets in search of him. He had a rough idea where Jinhai lived and the haunts he and his friends hung around in. With the word out on the street, Jinhai soon learnt that Yeshe's brother was looking for him. He knew why, so decided to lie low for a couple of days. He was intrigued as to what was in Yeshe's letter that he had hidden at the bottom of his school bag, but a promise was a promise and he wouldn't open it for three days.

Yeshe's brother contacted the local radio stations and the police, but they were initially hesitant to start a full-scale search and put out broadcasts; it was well-known fact young novice monks that had been handed to the monasteries as a family tradition ran away as an act of rebellion and that the monasteries had their own grapevine network tracking them down. Invariably they simply turned up back home cold, wet and starving. The decision was taken to delay any further action for a couple of days and let the monastery network take the lead.

The weather that accompanied Yeshe's train

journey was, for late autumn, simply stunning; beautiful blue azure skies dominated the entire route as a slow moving high-pressure weather system crossed over China, creating the glorious sunny days. Yeshe had never left Tibet before, more widely known nowadays as the Tibet Autonomous Region of China, so seeing for the first time the vast open spaces of China was in Yeshe's young eyes awesome. The route took him from Lhasa through Nagchu, Golmund, Xining, Zhongwe, Taiyuan and eventually to West Beijing. Alighting the train, Yeshe found himself in the middle of a large concourse surrounded by tall grey buildings and for the first time the reality of what he had done struck home to him. For a split second he wanted to turn around and get straight back on the train, but doing that simply defeated the aim of what he was trying to accomplish. This was about defying his father; even at the tender age of eleven, all alone in one of the world's biggest cities with a population of over twenty-one million inhabitants, he was going to have a say in his life. Walking out of the train station, he sent a text to Jinhai to say he was in Beijing and that he could open the letter.

Jinhai was stunned when he had read the contents of Yeshe's letter; why Beijing, he thought to himself? Had he missed something here? Jinhai sat quietly on his bed contemplating the letter; he couldn't recall Yeshe ever talking about Beijing and his interest in The Forbidden City. Jinhai opened his laptop and logged into Skype; within minutes he was chatting with his friends and showing them the letter. The general consensus amongst his friends was to tell his father and admit his role in the matter. The consequences! Well, he would simply have to face them. Beijing was a dangerous place for a lonely eleven-year-old boy, and unscrupulous people with no morals could harm him. With the letter in his hand Jinhai went down stairs and showed his father. Jinhai handed the letter to his father. Having explained what had happened, his father scanned down the short letter. Jinhai stood patiently in front of his father, becoming increasingly fearful of his father's reaction. His father put the letter gently down on the table; Jinhai could see the look of anger across his face and felt his knees wobble under him, but he managed to stay upright. Looking at his son with rage building inside of him, his father said:

"This is not the time for retribution, Jinhai, but believe you me it will follow. Do not think you are going to get away with this. I need to think what is the best way to handle this matter."

"Perhaps we need to tell the police, father!"

"Absolutely not!"

"But…."

"Jinhai, you have no idea the position you have put me in."

"What position, father?"

"Jinhai, I am a senior judge here in Lhasa. I'm here to ensure that the strict letter of the law is upheld. My son, you that is, have broken the law by aiding a young child to escape. I'm fully aware that you didn't understand the consequences of your actions and that your intentions, although naïve, were well-intended. I understand that you had no idea of your friend's full intentions; nevertheless this is highly embarrassing for me. Let me spell it out to you. This is what the local newspaper headlines will be if the press find out. *'Son of judge helps friend to escape monastery.'"*

"Aah…that's not good, father! Sorry…"

"Plus, Jinhai, that was a family matter which you should have never become involved with. Jinhai, the Buddhist way of life is steeped in Tibetan traditions. Next time talk to me, and don't think for one moment you're off the hook here. Now leave me alone for a few minutes. I need to figure out what is the best way forward here, for Yeshe and us."

Jinhai could hear his father on his smartphone in the next room, which acted as a study as well as a small library; it wasn't long before he emerged, shouting at Jinhai to get his coat. Jinhai dashed upstairs, threw on his coat and shoved his feet into his trainers, making no attempt to tie his laces; apparently it was cool and trendy to leave them untied, something his father didn't quite understand but hey… whatever.

Moments later two of Jinhai's father's protection officers appeared at the door; being a judge it was necessary at times for his father to have bodyguards, particularly when he was hearing a case that involved violent criminals. The officers looked at the letter and suggested a photocopy would be more appropriate to take to Yeshe's brother, ensuring no fingerprints could be traced back to the family. With that in mind, the officers used Jinhai's father's photocopier and took a copy of the letter. Jinhai was about to go out the front door when the secret phone Yeshe had told him to buy pinged in his right coat pocket. Looking at the phone he saw a text message with a photo attached; it was Yeshe. He had taken a photo of himself standing next to a police officer outside The Forbidden City entrance on Tiananmen Square in Beijing.

"Whose phone is that?" asked one of the bodyguards.

"Yeshe asked me to get two new phones so that we could communicate with each other."

Avoiding eye contact with his father as much as he possibly could, he handed over the phone.

"So, Yeshe thinks you are the only person who knows about this phone and that any messages he sends or gets is communicating with you and you alone?"

"Yep."

"Take the protection officers to Yeshe brother's apartment, Jinhai."

"That won't be necessary, Judge. Just give us the address and we'll make sure everything is taken care of. We'll get an unknown source to drop the items off with a small explanation attached."

"Aah… yes, that would be a better idea. Thank you for your discretion, guys."

"No problem, Judge."

With that the officers disappeared and Jinhai slunk back upstairs to his room.

Yeshe was completely unaware that he had been rumbled and that the attached photos and messages he was sending giving his whereabouts were going direct to his brother and that the communications back were not Jinhai himself.

The unknown source had made contact with Yeshe's brother, making it clear that neither the police nor the monasteries are to be involved. A small envelope containing enough money in cash for the necessary train fares was sellotaped to the phone. A private undisclosed donation; source unknown.

Yeshe's brother boarded the train and, for the time being, kept his end of the bargain by not involving the authorities. This was a family matter and he would resolve it. The three-day train journey would give him ample time, disguised as Jinhai, to communicate with his brother. He had already established that Yeshe's actions were a means of punishment for the decision taken by his father to send him to the monastery and that he fully intended returning once his family had tracked him down, but for the time being he was going to enjoy the sights of The Forbidden City.

Tiananmen Square was busy, not that Yeshe minded; his fascination with The Forbidden City and the Chinese Dynasties had long captured his imagination, but it was something that he could not share with his family as they had not, like most Tibetans, forgiven the Chinese for invading their country back in the 1950s. Yeshe had learnt about small parts of Chinese history at school, when he was allowed to attend. The Forbidden City was the palace of the Chinese Emperors during the Ming and Qing dynasties; it was located at the heart of Beijing, covering an area of 178 acres with 90 separate palaces and 980 buildings with just short of 9000 rooms. It was called The Forbidden City as no one could enter it without the express permission of the ruling Emperor of that time. The ancient walls of the city were 26ft high, protected by a moat approximately 170ft wide. The yellow tiles on the roofs of the various buildings symbolised the colour yellow, which was the colour of the numerous Emperors. Today the city was known as the Palace Museum and anybody could visit it.

Yeshe had spent several days going around some of the famous sights of Beijing, still thinking he was talking to Jinhai. He was intrigued when he got a message, *'Where exactly are you at this precise moment?'*

'Why do you want to know that, Jinhai?'

'Just curious.'

'Sitting on a wall near the north gate of The Forbidden City known as the Divine Might gate.'

'OK, see you in a couple of minutes.'

Yeshe was completely thrown by the last message; confused and perplexed he sent another message.

'Are you here, or are you just winding me up?'

'I'm here, look up I'm walking towards you.'

With that he looked up and with total astonishment and bewilderment written all over his face he saw his brother walking towards him, brandishing a smartphone in his right hand. Yeshe stood up, still somewhat aghast but at the same time pleased to see his brother. He was disappointed that the chain of events had left his control; yes, he wanted to be found, but not quite so soon. Yeshe could see the relief in his brother's eyes as they went to give a hug to each other. Sitting back down, Yeshe could sense an inquisition so decided to kick start the conversation:

"Does father know I am here?"

"No."

"I suppose you have worked out that Jinhai was involved by the message responses on the phone?"

"Yes, and before you say any more I understand why you ran away. What I can't get over is the fact you chose Beijing, so far away."

"I wanted to punish father for doing what he did."

"I get that; I did the same."

"What?"

"I did the same, but I only had the courage to hide away in a friend's house. Father did exactly the same to me; maybe if I had become a monk he wouldn't have pushed you down the same route."

"I didn't know that."

"Well you do now, Yeshe."

"Why didn't you say?"

"I agreed with him never to discuss the matter with anybody. We reached a compromise; I was to continue my religious studies and attend the monastery on a regular basis, thus creating an image to others that I was kind of following in the Buddhist ways. But at the same time he allowed me to become a teacher at the school. I knew what was in the letter; he asked me to write it, I knew one day he would sign it and hand it back to me. Yeshe, what is important to our father is tradition and honour, and as long as we work within certain boundaries he will be prepared to show flexibility. He might be a simple nomad, but he knows the world is changing and what he wanted as a child and what we want for ourselves are different. Yeshe, you and I just need to work with him and respect him. That's all he wants."

'*Hmm…*' thought Yeshe

"Let's go home and work this out. But while I'm here let's have a look around; the next train to Lhasa is not for a couple of days. I can't believe you had the courage to come here. Wow."

Yeshe couldn't believe that it was only a few days ago that he was sitting on a train looking out of the window as the train slipped out of Lhasa station bound for Beijing, and here he is again sitting on a train looking out of the window but this time sneaking back into Lhasa station. Waiting on the platform was Yeshe's Lama.

"Welcome back. How was Beijing?"

Yeshe looked at his brother. As he did so, his brother merely said:

"Remember what we discussed."

Yeshe was rather surprised with what his tutor had to say; the prospect of a new adventure culminating with meeting the Dalai Lama himself.

"You know, Yeshe, running away from things isn't always the best approach. Sitting down and talking about them I have always found helpful. The monastery has been given an allocation for so many students to go to Dharamshala to hear the Dalai Lama talk about a Buddhist monk's life. Would you like to go?"

"Where is that?"

"Dharamshala is in Himachal Pradesh region of India. It is the present home of the Dalai Lama and the Tibetan government in exile. Maybe listening to the great man himself might help you to decide what is right for you. Interested?"

"Oh yes."

"Good. We start the trip tomorrow; we'll follow the very route the Dalai Lama took himself back in March 1959 when he escaped from the Chinese authorities in fear of his life."

Yeshe recalled the story his father often talked about, how on the 17th March 1959 the Dalai Lama slipped passed the Chinese authorities disguised as a simple soldier, travelling by night on horseback across the Himalayas so as to avoid detection. With him was a small entourage including some of his family; the fifteen-day arduous journey into Northern India was accomplished with the then Indian Government agreeing sanctuary for the holy man and his companions.

Yeshe was excited that he was going to follow in the steps the Dalai Lama had taken all those years ago; for an eleven year old he was an accomplished horse rider and he was used to trailing the high mountain passes of The Himalayas, so a journey of this nature would be a relatively easy trip.

The scenery along the route was breathtaking; the snow-capped, high peaks were magnificent against the backdrop of clear azure blue skies. As he crossed over into Northern India via the mighty Brahmaputra River, Yeshe listened to his tutor's teachings, but like any young adult he was eager to reach his destination.

Having rested at Towang Monastery for a couple of days, the small entourage moved onto Dharamshala. Yeshe was excited. He was about to meet the 14th Dalai Lama, a holy man he had heard so much about. Sitting cross-legged on the grass, Yeshe listened intently as the Dalai Lama talked to the large crowd that had gathered in the grounds of his house complex. Having talked for the best part of a couple of hours on the life a young Buddhist monk and what that entailed, the Dalai Lama stood up and mingled amongst the crowd, his bodyguards keeping a watchful eye as ever. As the Dalai Lama approached, Yeshe stood up, bowed respectfully and shook his hand. The brief conversation he had with the Dalai Lama would remain private with Yeshe for the rest of his life.

Whether he becomes a monk or an international human rights lawyer travelling the world, or a doctor, which were Yeshe's initial thoughts, we will have to wait and see.

Have a safe journey home, Yeshe; catch up with you shortly.

KYMANA

A chill wind blew down from the mountains, sweeping across the valley floor and signalling the early arrival of Yellowstone's autumn season. Already the leaves of the cottonwoods, aspens and maples had started to turn from the bright vivid greens of summer to their spectacular Fall colours of scarlets, golds and coppers. The Yellowstone National Park, situated in the Rocky Mountains of America and occupying large parts of the states of Wyoming and Montana, was home territory for Kymana and her two-year-old wolf Three Socks.

Kymana was thirteen and lived with her father and older brother in Riverton, near The Wind River Shoshone Indian Reservation in Wyoming. Her father was the head park ranger for The Yellowstone National Park. Every Saturday he would take Kymana, her Cheyenne friend Dyani and Three Socks with him to the visitor centre, where Kymana and Dyani both had weekend jobs. Occasionally, if Kymana had finished early, he would bring her along with him as he visited the different parts of the park to see for himself what was happening on his patch. He found going out and about and speaking to the local rangers was the best approach.

Kymana loved walking and going with her father around the various park sites, but occasionally her father would say to her that he was too busy and would she like to take her Cheyenne friend, Dyani, along with her for company instead of him and that he would be back as soon as possible to take the two girls home.

Kymana recalled that it was on one of those days, two years ago, when her father made it clear that he was too busy with park matters to go walking with her and that he would arrange for one of the rangers to take herself and Dyani wherever they wanted to go. Kymana and Dyani had a particular favourite spot down by the Yellowstone River and, having been dropped off by one of the young rangers, they set off on a mini walkabout. It was by a small creek that fed into the Yellowstone River that they came across Three Socks for the first time. She was wandering around all on her own, whimpering for her mother. Her mother had abandoned her at four months old as she had a deformed back leg. In the wilds of Yellowstone only the strongest survive – any wolf pups born with a weakness and out of the comfort of the maternal den were simply abandoned and left to die. Harsh as it sounds, that was nature's way of ensuring the strongest pups survived and the pack thrived. Kymana remembered the arguments she and Dyani had had on the way back to the main office, where the park rangers based themselves, about who should keep the little wolf pup and what name would they give her. Naming the little wolf pup wasn't so much of an issue for either of them, and the obvious choice was Three Socks as the little pup had three white paws that looked like socks. With regards to who should keep Three

Socks, that led to heated arguments and constant fallouts between the two girls over the ensuing days.

The two girls had known for some time about the small cluster of outbuildings that were close to Kymana's father's office; Kymana also knew that the furthest building had a storeroom at the back, which could easily be accessed by an old wooden door that was covered in peeling green paint. The key to the old door was in a battered red tin box that belonged to her father's assistant. The red box, for some bizarre reason, was always found next to the office kettle in the rangers' staff room. The key to that had been lost for years, so the red tin was forever open for all and sundry to rummage around in. Kymana would often ferret through the tin while waiting for the kettle to boil to see what she could unearth. The storeroom key was always lurking at the bottom, buried deep under piles of weird objects and old jawbones belonging to various dead animals.

The storeroom was dry and out of the view of prying eyes. It was here Kymana had suggested to Dyani that they put Three Socks until they had come to some agreement as to what was best for her. For the time being, the storeroom was to be Three Socks' new den. Over the next few days, Kymana and Dyani took it in turn to check up on Three Socks, bringing food, blankets and a large cardboard box. Dyani had the brilliant idea of getting a duplicate key organised, so as not to raise any suspicions among the park rangers and office staff with constantly going in and out of the administration building for the key.

Several days had gone by since Kymana and Dyani had adopted their wild wolf pup. Kymana found herself in her bedroom, lying on her bed watching a YouTube video on her laptop about the ancient ways and customs of the Shoshone people, of whom she was so proud. As she lay there she knew she would have to tell her father about Three Socks, but choosing the right moment was going to be difficult. She knew her father's views on not interfering with Mother Nature's ways were quite strong. His judgement would have been to let Three Socks go the way of the wild, even though that decision would come across as appearing cruel at the time. With the YouTube video finished, Kymana put her laptop away under her bed. Getting up to pull her curtains closed, she stopped for a few brief moments and, looking out of her window, she glanced up at the full moon. As she pulled her curtains she gave the man in the moon a wave, like she used to do when her mother tucked her into bed all those years ago. Still staring up at the nightly array of stars and galaxies, Kymana began to wonder what it would be like to fly in space and visit other planets. Was there life out there? She often wondered. Climbing into bed and pulling her duvet around her, she reached to turn off her bedside lamp. As she did so, she looked at the photo of her mother in full traditional Shoshone costume. Picking the photo up she gave her mother a little kiss. Kymana never forgot the night her father told her that her mother had been killed in a car crash; but like most things in life, time marched on. Snuggling down into her bed, Kymana subconsciously made the decision to tell her father about Three Socks at the weekend. She would tell him when they were walking close to Old Faithful, the famous geyser that attracted hundreds of tourists and visitors. The lecture she would get wouldn't be so direct as there would be no end of people around them. *'Good choice,'* she thought. With that she switched the bedside light off and went to sleep.

The next morning Kymana discovered that her father had left early for work; the note propped up against the cream coloured milk jug in the middle of the kitchen table simply read: *'Gone to work early got a problem with a herd of pronghorn near Beartooth Mountains. Get yourself off to school. Your packed lunch is in the fridge. See you tonight. Love Dad x.'*

Kymana's father had called an early morning staff meeting of the local rangers in the staff kitchen to discuss the issue of the pronghorn; with a plan briefly outlined, they all set off, but before he left he remembered an old Shoshone trick that his own father had taught him and that the small piece of equipment he needed was in the storeroom in the far outbuilding. Rummaging around the red tin box, he fished out the key and headed straight for the storeroom. Giving the old green door a nudge with his right shoulder, as it had become slightly swollen over the past few days with all the rain, and switching on the light, he started to scan his eyes around the shelves but was getting distracted by the whimpers and scratching noises coming from a large cardboard box shoved against the wall at the far end. Carefully lifting the cardboard box lid, he gingerly peered inside and was stunned to see a wolf pup staring back at him with a timid expression on its face. Instantly recognising the old Shoshone Indian blanket that once belonged to his late mother, Kymana's father immediately knew that his daughter was involved here. What was she up to? He would find out when he got home later that evening, but for the moment he had a small wolf pup to deal with. Carefully reaching in, he lifted the little pup out and placed her on the concrete floor; he could see a yellow piece of string had been tied around the little pup's neck, attached to which was a white luggage label with the words *Three Socks, girl,* written in purple felt-tip.

With the little wolf pup tucked safely under his arm, he closed the storeroom door behind him and headed back to the admin building, where he gently put the little wolf pup on his assistant's desk. The assistant looked up in total amazement. His boss had dumped many things on his desk over the years, but never a wolf pup. Three Socks was shaking and snarling, for she was scared.

"What do you want me to do with the wolf pup, boss?"

"Call one of the local vet teams to come and fetch her. Instruct them to check her over thoroughly and find out exactly what is wrong with her back leg."

"This looks like your daughter's writing on the label."

"I'm well aware of that, Simon. I'll be broaching that little matter with my daughter later this evening. Oh, if she calls, you can tell her I have found the wolf pup. If you need to get hold of me I'll be on the usual radio channel – other than that I'll see you tomorrow. Thanks, Simon." With that Kymana's father headed to the Beartooth Mountains.

Kymana remembered the conversation she and her father had that night two years ago. He was right. Kymana knew the rules of the wild. She and Dyani should have left Three Socks, but in her heart she knew something could be done for the little wolf pup. A wonky leg could be fixed and she had had every intention to reintroduce Three Socks back to the wild. Kymana agreed with her father that she and Dyani would learn more about the lives of the animals in the park. She understood that Three Socks could not live with her like any other normal domestic dog. Living in a residential street in Riverton, Wyoming, close to her college, wasn't the ideal location for a wolf to grow up in, and of course there was the added complication of the neighbours, who probably would have objected to the idea of a wolf living on their street. The small matter of whom was going to own or be responsible for Three Socks worked out rather well; both of them would take on the role. With the help of some of the park rangers Kymana and

Dyani built an enclosure behind the outbuildings where they had originally tried to hide her. The work Kymana and Dyani did to train Three Socks was a task they undertook with great enthusiasm most weekends and, over a period of time, their hard work and dedication was starting to pay off.

During the week, when the two girls were at school, Kymana's father would take Three Socks with him around the park. She proved on several occasions to be quite an effective guard dog, warding off other wolves or large male grizzly bears, thus giving him some form of security. At the weekends it was mainly Kymana that looked after Three Socks with Dyani, who lived with her family in the Cheyenne Reservation in the state of Montana, supporting as best as she could. As for Three Socks' wonky leg, that was now, after several operations and long periods of recuperation, almost fully restored. She would always have a limp, said the park's main vet; apart from that she was a healthy young wolf enjoying life. With regards to Three Socks' chances of returning to the wild, that was out of the question. The local wolf packs, the largest being the Truid pack, would probably kill her and by now she was so used to being fed and following the ways of man that training her to hunt and survive in the wild was simply not feasible. Kymana's father would often turn to Three Socks as he was driving around the park and say to her, "How many wolves do you know that travel around in a 4X4? You should be trotting and keeping up with those guys over there;

they're proper wolves." Three Socks would give him a quick glance, as if to say '*Whatever*'.

Three Socks was now two and a fully-grown wolf in her own right. The previous two years had been a challenge for Kymana and Dyani, having to learn wolf ways, but they overcame lots of issues with the support of Kymana's father and his rangers. Kymana's father loved to take Three Socks with him when he went out and about all over the park, and had become rather attached to his little wolf friend.

Yellowstone in early October was a busy time for the park officials, as thousands of visitors from all over the world would arrive to experience and observe the goings on in the park, migrating herds of pronghorn, bison and deer preparing to leave as chilling winds started to blow down from the mountains carrying flurries of snow, indicating winter was around the corner. Pine squirrels and Clark's nutcrackers gathered up the last of the season's nuts, making sure they remembered where they had stored them. Mother grizzly bears with this year's cubs started looking for suitable dens to hibernate the winter months away, beavers put the finishing touches to their dams and gathered the last of this year's new tree growth, making sure their underwater larders were well stocked. The local wolf packs started to emerge from their summer retreats now that their pups were fully weaned – winter was their time in the park. They had the upper hand as snow and the bitter cold weakened their prey, making it easier for them to catch. The cottonwoods, aspens and maples put on a final dazzling display of autumnal colours as they prepared to drop their leaves over the next few weeks as they shut down for the winter. It is this magnificent change in the park's life that attracted so many visitors to Yellowstone in the Fall, along with the magical splendour of the gushing geysers dotted all over the park. Old Faithful, the most famous of the geysers, attracted thousands of tourists every day, sending five thousand gallons of water up to a hundred feet into the air every hour.

Kymana and Dyani continued to work mostly at one of the nearby visitor centres, close to where Kymana's father based himself. Dyani would get a bus every Friday afternoon when school had finished; the bus ride from the Cheyenne Reserve in Montana to where she lived in Riverton, near Wind River, would take slightly over an hour depending on the weather. Kymana always made sure she was at the bus stop to meet Dyani and to check what bus she was on; Kymana would send a text message every Friday morning asking Dyani to confirm the bus times. Without fail Dyani would reply, but for some unknown reason she didn't respond to Kymana's message on this occasion, which puzzled her. Waiting at the bus stop, assuming that Dyani had caught the usual bus, Kymana was relieved to see Dyani get off.

"You didn't reply to my text message, Dyani! You alright?"

"Yep, really sorry. I had no charge on my phone and then I realised I'd left my charger back at home this morning. Sorry."

Having given each other a hug, the two girls headed off to their usual fast food outlet, where they spent the next hour catching up on girly chit-chat over banana milkshakes, fries and chicken nuggets.

"Oh, my brother has given me the information about which websites to go on concerning the best training programmes and courses you need to do to become an astronaut, Kymana."

"That's so cool, Dyani! We'll have a look later this evening."

"And he has a friend who works for NASA who might be able to arrange for you to visit the space centre so that you can have a look around."

"Really? Wow!"

Kymana's fascination with space was starting to become an obsession. She often found herself late at night sitting gazing up at the stars, wondering was there life beyond earth? What did they look like? What did they eat? Were there really Martians on Mars?

The visitor centre was really busy for a Saturday; both Kymana and Dyani were rushed off their feet with people wanting to know all about the activities, events and where the best places were to see the wildlife. The outdoor clothing shop and the café behind the reception desk were doing a roaring trade. Dressed in their traditional costumes from the Shoshone and Cheyenne native Indian tribes, Kymana and Dyani were often asked about their native American background, but to watch people's reactions to Three Socks as she followed Kymana around was interesting to say the least. The various looks ranged from unease to total fascination, but no matter what individual people's thoughts were, Three Socks got a lot of attention and drew in the crowds, which was good for business.

With the busy day done, Kymana and Dyani walked the short distance from the visitor centre to Kymana's father's office. As they did so they could hear the cries of the nearby wolf packs howling to each other; what messages or warnings they were sending out to the world neither Kymana nor Dyani could differentiate, but Three Socks could. She stood with her ears pricked, listening intently to the messages that resonated across the surrounding mountains and valleys.

Looking at her phone Kymana read the text message from her father. '*Running a bit late will be with you within the hour. Make sure Three Socks is secure in her compound before you leave.*'

Sitting on a small outcrop of rock, Kymana could hear the gurgling waters of a nearby stream. That stream fed into Yellowstone River, which ultimately flowed into Yellowstone Lake, where in summer she would swim with Three Socks watching closely from the shoreline. Wrapping her orange fleece tight around herself, she once again looked up at the clear night sky, gazing at the trillions of stars that were sprinkled across the stratosphere. What was beyond the stars? And what were other galaxies like? Her imagination was starting to run away when Dyani nudged her with her right elbow.

"How long is your father going to be? It's cold sitting here... my bum cheeks are starting to turn into blocks of ice."

Kymana called her father, but his phone went straight to voicemail. She left a message. As she hung up her phone pinged; looking at her Messenger App she read the note from her brother. He was on his way to pick Dyani and herself up as father was held up attending to an urgent matter somewhere in the wilds of Yellowstone Park. Kymana hoped that her brother had remembered to light the big log fire in the lounge; it was going to be a cold, cold night ahead. Kymana often wondered how her Shoshone ancestors endured the bitter winters of Wyoming. They only had traditional tepees with bison fur and campfires to keep them warm. No log fires or central heating.

It was getting close to midnight when Kymana's father finally arrived home. As he pulled onto the drive, he could see Kymana's bedroom lights were still on. The purple curtains had only been partially drawn. He knew exactly what the two girls were up to; they were watching a video on YouTube and at the same time posting silly messages on various social media sites. Standing outside Kymana's bedroom door he took a few moments. Having briefly thought about what he was going to say, he knocked before pushing the door ajar; he'd had a busy day and was in no mood for Kymana's excuses. With a few stern words he closed the door;

as he did so he could hear the computer being shut down and the two girls crawling into their beds.

Kymana was up early the next morning. As she came down the stairs she could hear her father in the kitchen rustling up some breakfast. There was already a small pile of thick pancakes stacked on a large plate in the middle of the breakfast bar. Kymana sat on one of the tall stools and, while pouring freshly squeezed orange juice into a yellow tumbler, she watched her father beating some eggs in a bowl.

"Morning, Sweet Pea. How was your day yesterday?"

Sweet Pea was a term of endearment her father had called her since she was a small child. At times she found it embarrassing, but when it was just the two of them alone she quite liked it.

"Father."

"Yes."

"What–"

"One moment, Sweet Pea."

The microwave pinged several times. Opening the microwave door, Kymana's father took out the bowl of beaten eggs and with a nearby fork gave the eggs a quick stir before placing the bowl back in the microwave for another thirty seconds. Clearly her father had watched and remembered her mother making scrambled eggs this way in the morning.

"What would you say, father, if I told you that I have a dream to become an astronaut?"

"Well? I'd say go for it."

"Really?"

"Yes, really."

"Father, you're so cool."

"Well, that may be so, but this cool father of yours has a busy day ahead of him, and like you needs to get his butt out of the door in the next half hour. Where's Dyani?"

"Dyani!" Kymana screamed.

"What!" retorted Dyani as she walked into the kitchen.

"You're up."

"Well, yes, apparently so. This isn't a ghost you're seeing."

Dyani wasn't a morning person. Unlike Kymana, she tended to be rather grumpy at the start of a day. Sitting at the breakfast bar, pushing her scrambled eggs on pancakes around her plate, Dyani simply stared at Kymana, who was bouncing around the kitchen telling her all about the fact her father had told her to follow her dream to be an astronaut.

"Yeah! Whatever. Can we talk about this later?"

"You're such an old misery guts in the morning, Dyani."

"Yep! Now can I finish my breakfast in peace?"

"Ooooh! Make sure your skinny ass is outside the door in the next twenty minutes; if not you'll be getting the late bus to work."

"Whatever!"

It was a beautiful Sunday morning as Kymana, her father and Dyani set off for the national park. Bells from a few of the local churches of different denominations rang out across Riverton, reminding people that church services were about to start.

Three Socks was walking around her compound when Kymana and Dyani arrived; she was delighted to see both girls, jumping up all over them and licking them to death. With the daily chores of making sure Three Socks' compound was clean and tidy, Kymana and Dyani – with Three Socks in tow – hitched a lift on the back of the park ranger's 4x4 jeep to the visitor centre to face another day of curious tourists and visitors alike.

Normally on a Sunday both girls only worked until lunchtime, as they had schoolwork to attend to and Dyani had to return home to the Cheyenne Reservation in Montana. Visitors loved to see the two girls dressed in their traditional native Indian costumes and hearing about the Shoshone and Cheyenne tribes' histories.

Most Sundays Kymana's father would take the girls out to lunch in one of the nearby cafes, but on this occasion he wanted to know more about Kymana's ambition to be an astronaut. He arranged for Kymana's brother to collect Dyani and put her on the bus home while he drove Kymana in his park jeep with Three Socks in the back up to the Beartooth Mountains. The Beartooth Mountains were located deep in The Yellowstone National Park itself and the journey there and back would take several hours, giving him and Kymana enough time to talk. The journey up and along the narrow mountain tracks would also give him the opportunity to show Kymana parts of the park she had not seen before, plus enable him to catch up with the local park rangers to find out for himself what was happening in their allocated areas. Kymana's father was keen to get to the Beartooth Mountains, as the local rangers had reported that a family of cougars (mountain lions) had moved into the area and were attacking the local deer population with devastating consequences, along with a large herd of bighorn sheep that were destroying the surrounding vegetation. Kymana's father had received a call that morning saying there had been a fresh sighting of the cougars by local hikers out walking the mountain passes and that two male cats had attacked them. While it was rare for attacks of this nature to take place, Kymana's father needed to investigate and resolve the matter before the local and social media got wind of these so called attacks. Kymana was looking forward to seeing cougars in the wild and the big male bighorn rams in the rutting season, fighting amongst themselves for the rights to mate with the females.

Several days had passed since Kymana and her father visited the Beartooth Mountains. She was disappointed not to have seen a cougar, but on the other hand watching the bighorn rams in the rutting season headbutting each other with such brutality was amazing. The discussion she and her father had about her dream of being an astronaut was interesting. The harsh reality of the training programme and understanding that it took a special breed of person to become an astronaut had started to sink into Kymana's mindset. Clearly her father had done his research and put the hard facts to her.

It was Kymana's birthday in a couple of days and she wondered what her father had bought her. She was slightly disappointed to see a plain brown envelope on the breakfast bar; normally she got a large parcel with lots of nice surprises inside. Opening the envelope, she tried hard to conceal her disappointment; her father could see the look of despondency written all over her face.

"Open the envelope, Kymana."

Continuing with tearing the envelope open, spilling the contents on the breakfast bar, her facial expression changed from despondency to sheer excitement within seconds as she stared at the two airline tickets to Orlando in Florida, coupled with passes to The Kennedy Space Centre. Kymana could hardly contain her delight as she jumped off the stool to hug her father, but the mug of coffee she knocked over in all her excitement spilled all over her handwritten school assignment that she had to hand in that morning; her mood in the last five minutes had gone from despondent to excited and now to utter despair. Frantically picking up the brown soggy papers, she looked at her father as if to say, '*Now what do I do?*'

"Put them on the radiators to dry out. You'll just have to explain to your tutor what happened. Take a photo and show him that you have done the work and ask if you could have extra time to rewrite your work."

"Oh yeah, father! Do you really think Mr Henderson is going to buy that excuse? You should hear all the excuses the other students come up with as they try to wriggle their way out of why they haven't done their assignments."

"Try it."

The weekend had arrived and Kymana found herself sitting alongside her father in the departure lounge of Casper Airport. The short drive from Riverton to Casper, Wyoming's state capital, had taken just over an hour, but the United Airlines flight to Orlando in Florida would take up to six hours. She was rather looking forward to the flight and watching whatever films the airline company were screening that day. Kymana had thanked all her friends for the texts and Facebook messages she had received over the last few days. For the weekend visit she had packed shorts and T-shirts, for despite being late October the weather in Florida was still warm compared to the chilly days in Yellowstone.

The Kennedy Space Centre visitor complex on Merritt Island just off the main Florida coastline was busy. Kymana had made a list of the zones she particularly wanted to visit. She was excited to see the new Orion EFT-1 multi-purpose crew vehicle that was being developed with the aim of bringing about deep space exploration. The astronaut hall of fame simply inspired her, to see the names of the astronauts that had gone before her and the missions they had undertaken, especially Neil Armstrong, the first man on the moon on the Apollo 11 mission. Looking into the crew capsule of Apollo 14 she got an understanding of how small it was inside in real life. Seeing the space shuttle Atlantis for the first time and numerous other rockets blew her away. The whole experience was beyond her wildest imagination. Learning about Mars, The Red Planet and the explorations that may happen in the near future caught her attention in particular. The story of the international space station, that on a clear night could be seen with the naked eye as it passed overhead, fascinated Kymana. She could see herself waving back down to Yellowstone as she passed over it, but for the time being all this was a dream she had locked inside her head.

Kymana was quiet on the flight back to Wyoming, for she had been awed by what she had seen and experienced over the weekend. The thought of going in a rocket up into Earth's orbit and beyond was frankly mind-blowing to her. Would she fulfil her dream? Well, we'll have to wait and see, but for the time being it was back to school, back to work and back to her beloved Three Socks.

Kymana wondered what Three Socks would make of her becoming an astronaut and quietly thought to herself, *'Probably not a lot.'* But her early Christmas present from her father of a return trip to the Kennedy Space Centre to watch a live rocket launch was going to be an experience of a lifetime for her.

FADL

The Gulf state of Oman, on the south-eastern coast of the Arabian Peninsula, was home to twelve-year-old Fadl. Officially the country is known as '*The Sultanate of Oman*', with the reigning monarch being The Sultan of Oman. This Arabian state has its borders with The Yemen, The Kingdom of Saudi Arabia and The United Arab Emirates. Muscat is the capital and it is here that Fadl lives with his family in the wealthy coastal suburb of Qurm.

Over the past few decades, Fadl's family had amassed considerable wealth; his father was an adviser to Sultan Qaboos Bin Said on matters relating to oil and other mineral exploration projects, as well as managing a global corporation company that dealt in oil and diamonds. The diamond mines his father and uncle had heavily invested in were in South Africa; as for the oil, well, that came from deep below the deserts of Oman. The family's vast wealth was a far cry from Fadl's forefathers, who were nomadic Bedouin Arabs living in tents in Oman's desert lands, trading in camels and Arabian horses. Fadl knew he came from a privileged background – the servants, bodyguards, yachts, Arabian racehorses, several homes scattered around the world in the Bahamas, south of France, London and Manhattan in New York – yet he remained considerate to those that were not as fortunate as himself. Looking at the horrifying images on his TV and smartphone of the suffering children of his own age had to endure in nearby Yemen and Syria was painful to watch. He was extremely glad he didn't have to face what they had to face on a daily basis, something his mother often reminded him of when he was having a teenage strop and being rude to one of the servants over trivial matters.

A good education was vital to a young person's future, something his father had instilled into him from an early age. Fadl knew much would be expected from him in the future, mainly to take over from his father in running the family business empire; to do this he would need a diverse education. Fadl and his father had often talked about Eton School on the outskirts of London; he didn't want to go and leave his friends and family here in Muscat, but his father had made the decision and next week he would leave for the UK. For the remaining few days he had left in Muscat Fadl was determined to have fun.

It was early in the morning and, being late August, the temperature on Fadl's smartphone weather app was showing 30c. It was going to be another hot day. *'Perfect,'* thought Fadl. He tapped on to the home control page of his phone and instructed the TV to come on, the air con system to kick in and the blinds on the windows to go up. Sending a message to the kitchens with his breakfast order, he got out of bed and walked across the marble floor to the sliding doors that separated his bedroom from his balcony. Standing on the balcony for a few moments, he admired the beautiful manicured gardens that lay below; the neatly-arranged flowerbeds that the house gardening team meticulously worked on throughout the year looked amazing. Lifting his head up slightly, he could see the cliff edge and beyond that The Gulf of Oman; the different shades of the blue waters sparkled in the early morning sun. A young lad from the kitchens gave a discreet cough to draw Fadl's attention to the fact he had arrived with breakfast; slightly startled, Fadl turned round to face the young boy and instructed him to put the tray on the small table on the far side of the balcony. Returning to the view, he could envisage a great day in the waters around Muscat, snorkelling around the coral reef and swimming with the dolphins. Fadl had asked his father at dinner the previous night if it could be arranged for the family super yacht, the sixty-five-metre vessel along with several crewmen, to be prepared. Fadl walked across the balcony to the table where the servant had carefully placed the breakfast tray; he noticed a small note was tucked under the ornate silver milk jug. Lifting up the jug and opening the folded piece of paper, he read what his father had written. *The yacht is all yours today, enjoy. However, I want you to take Lefa with you.*

Hmmm, thought Fadl. Lefa was the same age as him and was the youngest son of a wealthy South African diamond mine owner who lived in Cape Town. Lefa was here with his parents, who were in Muscat discussing a new business venture with Fadl's father. Fadl might be twelve but he understood that when his father was entertaining future business clients, his instructions had to be obeyed. Fadl understood the tone of his father's note; no Lefa, no yacht, no snorkelling and no swimming with the dolphins. Fadl sent a text message to Lefa, informing him that a car would arrive at his hotel within the hour.

Fadl was excited. He was determined to enjoy the last few days he had here in Muscat before leaving for London and a different life. Lefa had arrived and was downstairs in the main hallway. Sliding down the bannister, which annoyed his mother no end, Fadl greeted Lefa.

"I hope you enjoy swimming Lefa, because we are going snorkelling and swimming."

"That suits me fine."

Despite the family's vast wealth, Fadl loved his battered old bike and wouldn't part with it for anything; with the bodyguards in tow Fadl and Lefa headed for the Marina Bandar Al Rowdha, where the yacht was moored. The cycle ride would take the two boys along Al Qurm St, onto Bab Al Mathaib St, which merged into Al Bahri Rd, and eventually onto Al Saidiya St, which was the coastal road to the marina. Turning into the marina Fadl knew precisely where his father's super yacht was moored. The yacht was his father's pride and joy, over sixty-five metres in length and costing a cool eighty-four million US dollars. *Fadl 1* was ready to set sail as soon as he and Lefa had arrived. Cycling across the floating walkways was fun; arriving at the yacht the two boys abandoned their bikes on the jetty for one of the bodyguards to pick up and throw into the back of one of the 4x4s that had been part of the security convoy. The ten man crew that had been carefully chosen by his father to sail the super yacht all over the world were ready to cast off and set sail out into the Gulf of Oman. While the crew did the last-minute checks, Fadl showed Lefa around the boat that had been named after him. Fadl simply allowed Lefa to have a cursory glance at the luxury air-conditioned cabins with their beautiful Persian rugs and American walnut panelling as they passed their way up to the swimming pool on the fourth deck. The purpose of taking his father's yacht out wasn't to show off the family's immense wealth to Lefa, but to show him the wonderful array of marine life that lay beneath the deep azure waters of the Gulf.

The shipping lanes of The Gulf were busy, but Captain Morgan, who was from Australia, had managed to find a secluded bay not far from the coastline. This bay was famed for its marine life and it was this that Fadl had wanted to show his South African friend. Sitting on the side of the lower deck, fitted out with the latest snorkelling gear and with their legs dangling in the warm gulf waters, Fadl and Lefa waited for the go-ahead to dive. As they sat patiently, Fadl pointed out the Al Hajar Mountain range that dominated the skyline behind Muscat, the place Fadl called home, but as he started to talk Captain Morgan gave the go-ahead to dive. Accompanied by two members of *Fadl 1*'s crew who were expert divers, Fadl and Lefa jumped into the crystal-clear waters. Immediately they could see the pale pastel colours of the coral reef that was only a few metres below them; the bright reds, purples, yellows and deep orange colours of the shoals of fish that were darting around made the whole scene amazing. The green and leatherback turtles that were swimming amongst the massive balls of baitfish completed the spectacle that unfurled before them.

Clambering back on board the yacht, Fadl and Lefa headed for the top deck; from there they would have a better view of the schools of common, spinner and bottleneck dolphins that were chasing the boat as it powered out to sea. It was amazing to watch the dolphins leaping into the air and crisscrossing under and around the yacht. A little further out Captain Morgan switched the yacht's engines off; as the yacht bobbed up and down in the water, it wasn't long before what Fadl had come to show Lefa appeared on the horizon; whales. Pods of humpback and sperm whales had gathered to feed on huge balls of baitfish. Watching these enormous marine mammals haul themselves up from the depths of the Arabian waters was an awesome sight. In the distance Fadl had spotted a small pod of about six killer whales chasing through the waters after a bottleneck dolphin that they had managed to separate from a nearby school. Fadl and Lefa watched for a few brief minutes before the commotion and splashing of the sea's waters came to a sudden halt with the six killer whales reappearing at the water's surface. It appeared the bottleneck dolphin had given the whales the slip and managed to survive another day. A small school of spinner dolphins circled the yacht. Fadl, shouting at Lefa to follow him, scampered down to the lower deck. Both boys started to get excited as the thought of jumping into the sea and swimming with the dolphins was about to become a reality. Pausing momentarily at the edge of the lower deck, both boys looked at each other before pinching their noses and hurling themselves into the water. Swimming with the spinner dolphins had been an electrifying experience, although brief, as the dolphins soon tired of the boys' antics; as fast as they had appeared they simply vanished into the great blue yonder.

Several hours had passed and, with it now being late afternoon, Captain Morgan turned the yacht around and headed back to the marina. As the super yacht pulled into the jetty Fadl noticed two very small baby leatherback turtles floating on the surface. Clearly they had lost their way. Jumping into the water, Fadl snatched the two turtles up in his hands, knowing full well that if any of the local fishermen had spotted them they would have been scooped out and most likely be someone's dinner in a few hours time. Fadl insisted the emergency motorised dingy be released from the second deck of the yacht and a crew member take him back out to sea where he could return the turtles. Lefa wanted to come with Fadl, but Fadl said no and gave instructions to one of the waiting bodyguards to take Lefa home.

That evening Fadl and Lefa reflected on the day they had had, and Fadl explained that he had another day of excitement lined up for them both. Tomorrow he would take Lefa to Bawshar Sands to ride quad bikes up and down the sand dunes, followed by an excursion to the Wahiba Sands, where he had planned to ride his Arabian stallion across the desert with Lefa seated behind him. The thought of the hot desert wind and sand blowing in his face was exhilarating and he assumed Lefa would enjoy the experience as well. In the evening Fadl had arranged for a camel ride on a nearby beach and ended the day with a small falconry display of his father's magnificent birds of prey.

Fadl had enjoyed the last few days, having had someone of his own age to go around with. Driving the quad bikes up and down the dunes at Bawshar Sands was great fun, as was throwing themselves off the tops of the dunes and rolling all the way to the bottom, ending up with sand in every bodily crevice possible. Being the only child of a rich, busy family, Fadl often felt lonely, surrounded by older people in his life, so spending time with Lefa had been fun. A knock on his bedroom door by one of the servants brought Fadl around from his reflective state of mind; he had started to think about his new life at Eton College, which would start next week. The young servant boy merely reminded Fadl that his father was waiting downstairs to go to the Mosque, with it being

Friday, the Muslim day of prayer. Fadl followed the young servant boy down the marble staircase; he could see the agitated look on his father's face as he waited anxiously at the main door.

"Hurry up Fadl, we're going to be late for prayers."

"I'm coming," said Fadl in a slightly miffed tone.

"And we'll have less of the attitude, young man."

"Whatever."

"Excuse me...!"

"Father, we have got loads of time."

"That might well be the case, but I said I would meet up with some of the elders beforehand."

"Well! How was I supposed to know?"

"Enough of your lip, Fadl. Get in the car."

Fadl sat in the back of the chauffeured Rolls Royce with his father. The short drive to the Sultan Qaboos Grand Mosque was an opportunity for Fadl and his father to talk about Fadl's time at Eton College and what both of them expected in terms of academic achievements.

The mosque was busy, with twenty-thousand worshippers expected through its doors. The pale Indian sandstone that made up the exterior walls of the mosque looked striking in the early morning sunshine. Fadl entered the main Musalla (*Prayer Hall*) and as usual his eyes were attracted to the huge fourteen-metre Italian chandelier that hung in the centre of the high dome. The eleven hundred lamps would bathe the cupola in a magical light and at night the dome could be seen all around Muscat and beyond. Kneeling down in his usual spot, Fadl liked to run his fingers over the magnificent Persian carpet, the colours of which mesmerised him. But he hadn't come to admire the décor; he had come to pray, to pray for his future and a safe flight to London tomorrow.

Oman Air flight number WY0103 touched down at London Heathrow half an hour earlier than expected. Fadl had been warned that the weather in the UK was very much on the inclement side; nevertheless the cool breeze that hit him in the face as he exited the main airport terminal buildings came as a bit of a shock. Zipping up his fleece, Fadl followed his cousin to her car. He was a little taken back, as he was used to servants carrying his bags and chauffeured limousines waiting for him, so having to carry and push his own luggage and walk half a mile to a nearby car park was somewhat of a rude awakening. For Fadl life was about to change; gone was the heat, gone were the servants and gone were the bodyguards.

The next morning Fadl drew back the curtains of the tiny bedroom he had been given by his aunt. The small three bedroom terrace in Camden town was a far cry from his own home back in Muscat. Fadl's aunt was his mother's youngest sister and it was quite clear that this side of his family didn't have the wealth his father's side had. The decision to put Fadl with his cousins was his mother's; he recalled the arguments his parents had about where Fadl should stay in London. Yes, they could have bought a house in Chelsea and employed servants to look after Fadl, but that was not the point; his mother wanted to show him that the lifestyle he had in Muscat was the exception, not the norm, and that he should experience a different way of life, a life away from servants, bodyguards and luxury. Fadl went downstairs and what could only be described at best as an organised mess stood in the small kitchen; his aunt gave him a big hug and asked him what he wanted for breakfast. Being unsure what breakfast consisted of here in the UK, Fadl merely looked at his aunt and asked what the usual thing was people ate for breakfast here.

"Cereal and toast, Fadl."

"That sounds OK with me."

"Cereals are on the table, milk is in the fridge and the bread for the toast is in the blue breadbin on the worktop over there. Bowls and mugs are in the cupboard above the sink, help yourself."

Fadl stood slightly embarrassed, for he had no idea what to do; his pretty older cousin who had picked him up from the airport yesterday snarled at her mother.

"Oh for goodness sake mother, the boy is a guest in our house, you can't expect him to help himself straight away. He needs to adjust and get used to us. Fadl, let me show you how things are done around here."

With breakfast over and having had a brief tour around the house, Fadl went back to his room and sent a text message to his mother. *'Wow things are very different here, not sure I like it here in London. Miss you.'* The reply from his mother was swift. *'I know life is going to be very different for you there in*

London, but your father and I think the experience will be wonderful for you and you will soon make friends. I have sent your aunt some money so that she can take you to the shops in Knightsbridge to get some new clothes, but I have also told her to take you to Camden Market to get bits and bobs as well. I will call you this evening love Mum x.'

Fadl's stay at his aunt's house over the last few days had been an eye-opening experience for him; but today, Thursday September the 7th, he was off to Eton College. Fadl had visited Eton College's website on several occasions over the last few weeks, and noted that the minimum entry age was thirteen; he was only twelve but assumed he met the minimum age requirement as he was thirteen next week. All the other requirements he more than met for a school of this prestigious calling and reputation.

The weather had improved as the day went on, and by the time Fadl arrived at Eton the morning drizzle that had persisted had given way to a glorious sunny autumnal afternoon. Fadl had been allocated to Godolphin House, one of the many schoolhouses the college owned; he even recalled turning up on Common Lane in his aunt's rather old 4x4 jeep and meeting his housemaster for the very first time and thinking what an odd place this was. Dragging all his stuff up three flights of stairs to his room with other boys staring at him was a new experience for him; normally the servants would have sorted all this out.

Several weeks had gone by and Fadl was

beginning to settle into his new life and surroundings, although the cold chilly days he would never get used to. His mother had read on the school website about the community work the school was involved in, especially with the local charity shops; in a recent Skype conversation she encouraged him to look into this area. Fadl took note of what his mother had suggested and so, every Friday afternoon with a newfound friend, Paul, he would walk to a local charity shop and help sift through all the sacks of unwanted clothes people had left. As the two lads left each week, having sorted the clothes into the right categories – age, sex and so on – they would call into a small café on the way back for coffee, cake or whatever took their fancy . The café was a small, family-run affair, not one of the multinational chains that you saw on most high streets throughout the country. It was here Fadl met Harold for the very first time. Harold was a Down's Syndrome young man aged thirteen, slim build, not your usual plump stature associated with a Down's person. Most days after school Harold would walk to his mother's café to help with the washing up and clearing away of the tables as the customers left. Harold loved to flirt with the lady customers, no matter how old they were; he would always give them a big cheesy grin and for the regular ladies that called in for afternoon tea, well!! They got an extra hug. Harold knew how to play the scene and, oddly enough, he got the most tips out of all the staff that worked at the café. Furthermore, those tips somehow never quite managed to find their way into the staff tip bowl that was by the till. Strange how the tips ended up in Harold's pockets, '*hmmm!....*'

Harold was a young man living with Down's Syndrome of a high-grade tendency; he stayed with his mother and older brother in the flat above the café. Each day, that is Monday to Friday, he attended mainstream schooling with the support of his special needs one-to-one tutor. Harold, like most Down's people, had a warm loving, caring and trusting nature, but at the same time could be stubborn and mischievous when he didn't get his own way. At the weekends Harold loved to play rugby with his brother and other local lads on one of the nearby parks. On the odd occasion, if Harold misbehaved during the week, his mother would threaten to confiscate his boots; that threat always worked, as Harold knew no boots meant no rugby at the weekend, so he would change his ways and behave himself.

It was a wet Friday afternoon in October when Fadl and Paul, soaked from walking the short distance from the charity shop where they had spent the last few hours sorting out all the plastic bags of clothes left by people over the previous days, popped into the café. Looking at the menu board both of them plumped for mango and passion fruit coolers, cheese and tomato toasties warmed up, and sticky toffee puddings with gooey sweet treacle sauce drizzled all over, again warmed through with large dollops of vanilla ice cream plonked on top. '*Hmmm... yum! yum!*' thought

Fadl. As the two boys were wolfing down their food Fadl turned to Paul and said:

"That lad standing over there staring at us, looks... different."

"Yeah, that's Harold. His mum owns the café. He's a Down's Syndrome lad."

"What's one of them?"

"I'm not sure, Fadl mate."

Fadl reached for his smartphone, logged on to the Internet and searched Down's Syndrome. Scrolling through the text Fadl kind of got the gist, but he would Skype his mother to talk about this.

Having scoffed their food, Fadl and Paul stood up; as they did so Harold walked over to them and, looking at Fadl, asked;

"Everything alright, lads?"

"Err... yeah! Hmmm… Harold, is it."

"Yeah, that's my name. What's your name mate?"

"Fadl."

"Oh! That's a funny name. Where do you come from?"

"I come from Oman."

"Hmmm… Where's that?"

Fadl was slightly thrown by Harold's presence and started to feel a little uncomfortable; looking at Paul as if to say *what do I do now*, he clumsily shuffled everything into his rucksack and made a feeble excuse to leave. As the two boys scarpered out the café, Harold shouted, "You've not paid. See you guys next Friday, eh!?"

The café on the Saturday afternoon was busy.

Fadl sheepishly crept in and sat down at a small table in the corner by the window, trying hard to be inconspicuous, burying his head into the menu sheets. Fadl had spoken with his mother the previous night via Skype and what she said stunned him; to learn that Harold would be the most trusting, caring and loving person as a friend he would ever meet. Fadl didn't always follow what his parents said or suggested – he had a mind of his own and made his own choices. Harold simply intrigued him; he had never met a person before with learning disabilities and yesterday's reaction to run didn't sit well with him. His mother's words *'Do not talk down or at him, speak and treat him like any of your other friends, but bear in mind he might on occasions need a little support'* stuck firm in Fadl's mind; as did the words *'Ask him or his mother what is best for you and him.'*

"Hello mate, you didn't pay me yesterday. I think that was rude, don't you?"

"Err… yes, Harold, it was very rude of me. I'm really sorry. I…"

"That's okay, mate, I get that quite a lot. Do people stare at you as well?"

"Not really, Harold. Why, do people stare at you?"

"Oh, some people see me as a little different."

"Well that's rude, Harold."

"I know. They can't help themselves."

Fadl quickly scanned down the menu, stopping at the pizza section; with much deliberation and finger hovering, he finally opted for the egg, spinach and triple cheese on a thin crust. '*Hooray,*' thought Harold; at last the guy had made a decision.

"Oh! Harold, could I have a large hot chocolate with two marshmallows and no sprinkles on top?"

"Sure."

"Who are Leicester Tigers?"

"You don't know who Leicester Tigers are, mate!?"

"Nope."

"They're the greatest rugby team in the world; my dad takes me and my brother to the matches. We're going up to Leicester tomorrow; with a bit of luck we might win. My mother and father can't stand the sight of each other, so my old man lives in a council flat down the road."

"Oh. Sorry to hear that, Harold."

"No worries mate, with the old man down the road they can't scream and shout at each other so much. Lol. Do you play rugby?"

"Err… I never heard of the game before."

"Really!" uttered Harold, looking totally aghast.

"No."

"Oh! Do you not play rugby where you come from?"

"No."

"Where is it you come from again?"

"Muscat, in Oman."

"Mmmuscccaatt in Oooomaann… sorryyyy sometimes I get aaa stttuttttter."

"You okay?"

"Yep, sometimes when I get a bit nervous I start

to stutter; sorry about that."

"I've just remembered my friend Paul plays rugby for the school."

"Which school is that?"

"Eton College."

"Oh the pppposh school, my dad says that's a school for rich brats. Are you a rich brat?"

"Yes, I'm rich…"

"Very, vvvvvery rich?" interrupted Harold.

"Yes."

"That's cool, mum will like you. I'll tell her my new friend is from that posh school and is very, very rich."

"Does it really matter, Harold, if your friends have money or not?'

"My old man says if they're rich then they can afford to take you out, milk it my son. If they're poor and you end up paying for them, well that's plain daft son."

"So if we became friends, from your point of view the friendship would be based on the fact that I have money and could afford to pay for you if we visited places. Well I think that's not nice; you should pick your friends for who they are, not how much money they've got."

Harold's mother, who had overheard their conversation as she was clearing away a nearby table, turned to Fadl.

"Well said, young man. Harold knows that as well; unfortunately Harold's father clearly has different views, with which I strongly disagree. I can reassure you Harold picks his friends for who they are. Thank you for chatting to him. Oh, the pizza and the hot chocolate are on the house."

"That's no problem, but I will pay for my meal as well as the meal myself and my friend had yesterday but failed to pay for."

Harold gave Fadl a cheeky smile as he blurted out the following words.

"If I had said it's on the house mate, I'd be for the high jump."

Fadl didn't understand what Harold was getting at, so Harold's mother explained that he would be in trouble.

Over the last few weeks Fadl and Harold got to know each other more; Harold was fascinated with the photos on Fadl's laptop that showed an insight into Fadl's life: the Grand Mosque, the marina, the Arabian horses, the fabulous sea life in the Gulf of Oman and the amazing homes he lived in all around the world. Fadl, on the other hand, was learning about people who were living with Down's Syndrome; he even started to realise that his life up to now was one of wealth, privilege and that his way of life was the exception as opposed to the norm. Listening to his mother on Skype most nights, having talked to her about what he had experienced that day, he was starting to get a glimpse into his parents' lives and their thinking; for his father life was about business and getting on in the world and sending his son to Eton was part of a career plan he had in place for Fadl. His mother agreeing to send him to Eton was about getting him away from his father's influences, giving him freedom to experience new things and letting Fadl start to make his own future based on his own experiences and not those imposed on him by his father.

Fadl was starting to enjoy his new life at Eton; he loved going with Harold and his brother to the rugby games on the local parks around Windsor. He had even joined the school U14 rugby team along with his friend Paul. The hard knocks and bruises he picked up along the way he learnt to accept as par for the course. Seeing Harold laugh at him when he had made a complete fool of himself on and off the rugby pitch was a joy. Harold often told Fadl naughty jokes and the pair of them would laugh their heads off.

One Friday afternoon in late October, with classes finished for the day, Fadl was getting himself ready to go as usual with his friend Paul to the local charity shop to sort out the sacks of clothes that had been brought in that week. A knock on his door took him by surprise; opening it he was slightly taken aback to see Harold standing there.

"What are you doing here, Harold?"

Harold ignored the question and shouted at Fadl to come quickly.

"Harold, I'm off to the charity shop to sort the sacks out. I'll meet up with you afterwards at your mum's café, alright?"

"Oh, forget the sacks! I want you to meet someone."

"But Harold…"

"But nnnnothing, follow me! Come on."

Harold grabbed Fadl's arm and started to push Fadl out the door.

"Okay, I've got the message. I'm coming, but let me text Paul to say I will be late."

Racing down the three flights of stairs of Godolphin house at breakneck speed to catch Harold up was scary to say the least. Shutting the door at the bottom of the stairs and emerging out onto the street, Fadl paused for a few seconds to catch his breath and glance either way up and down the road to see which way Harold had gone. Looking up the street, he caught sight of Harold's light teal coloured fleece. Sprinting two hundred metres and narrowly avoiding knocking down everybody he had passed along the way, Fadl finally caught up with Harold; grabbing him by the shoulder Fadl managed to stop Harold in his tracks.

"Harold what is all this about? Who is it that you want me to meet? And why the rush?"

"Wait and see. Come on, we'll be late."

"What's in the bag, Harold?"

"I'll tell you later."

With that the two boys headed off around the corner. At the far end of the road Fadl could see a small crowd of people standing on a corner near the main entrance to Windsor Castle. Harold pushed his way through the small crowd and, having reached the metal crowd barrier, leaned over and tapped the police officer on the shoulder. Turning to see who had tapped him on the shoulder, the police officer smiled as he looked down and saw Harold; lifting the barrier slightly he hinted at Harold to squeeze through.

"How are you, Harold?"

"I'm alright PC Joe, you?"

"Fine. Mam will be along shortly."

Harold looked back at Fadl behind the crowd barrier; with a cheeky smile he said,

"Watch."

With utter astonishment Fadl watched as a fleet of black official cars swept around the corner. The second car in the cavalcade stopped. As it did so Harold walked towards it, and as he approached the back window slid down, revealing Her Majesty Queen Elizabeth II. Harold knew that The Queen spent most weekends at Windsor Castle and had a rough idea what time her entourage would arrive most weeks. Harold bowed as usual and, leaning against Her Majesty's car, handed over the small bag he had been clutching for the last hour. With the brief chat over, The Queen headed off to the castle, leaving Harold to squeeze through the metal barrier and give Fadl a high five.

"So that's what all the rush was about? Well! I have a friend who knows The Queen of England. That, my son, is impressive."

Fadl had only been in the UK for a couple of months and already he was beginning to know and speak the local sayings.

"So, what did you say to The Queen?"

"That's ppprivate, mate."

"Okay, what was in the bag?"

"Ah… never you mind."

"Oh! Is that a big state secret as well?"

"Yep, between me and her."

"Are you one of Her Majesty's secret service guys working for MI5 or 6?"

"You taking the pppiss?"

"Would I… Hope The Queen enjoys her chocolate cookies."

"How did you know they were chocolate cookies?"

"I didn't, merely guessed, Harold."

"You're too smart for your own good, you are."

"Really! Harold, so what's on next week's menu? Orange and ginger cookies? On the house as well?"

Fadl couldn't help sniggering to himself; he loved winding his best friend up.

"No, salted caramel. I… shouldn't be telling you."

"Of course not Harold, 'BIG STATE SECRET'."

"You're taking the mick now, be off with you. I thought you had some sacks to sort out."

"Harold!"

"What?"

"See you back at the café later. Oh, and Harold? Two chocolate cookies on the house."

"Ha, ha, ha…very funny. Whatever! Clear off! I suppose you want a mug of hot chocolate as well, two marshmallows and no sprinkles."

"That would be good, and on the house?"

"Don't push your luck, sunshine."

Fadl texted his mother as he ran to the charity shop, telling her what had just happened and the exchange of banter he had had with Harold. His mother replied straight away. *'OMG that's amazing. I knew you would have a different life at Eton away from the constraints of home and your father's influences. I'm proud of you. Maybe one day I will get to meet Harold. Mum x'*

Fadl had experienced so much over the last few months, learning new things at Eton, making new friends, especially Harold – he could never have imagined in his wildest dreams that one day in his short life a young man living with Down's Syndrome would have such an impact on his life. Back in his own country he had not heard or seen anybody with Down's Syndrome and he wondered why. Fadl knew he led a privileged lifestyle, but he didn't realise until now how his life in Muscat was the exception and not the norm. Harold had taught him so much, so let us see what decisions Fadl makes for himself about his future, be that following in his father's footsteps or taking a different route. But one thing he definitely wanted to do was to invite Harold and his older brother to Oman to show Harold where he came from. That question he would put to Harold and his family over the next few weeks, but for the time being he needed to knuckle down and get on with his studies at Eton, or the posh school as Harold called it.

See you soon lads.

ACKNOWLEDGEMENTS

Alex Davis for all his tutoring, editing skills and patience.

Mark Bell for his wonderful character illustrations.
markbellillustration.com

Joe Clark for the professional photo.
joeclarkphotography.co.uk

Pete Mugleston for his technical skills on the webpage.
One of the best friends a guy could have.

CONTACT

Please feel free to let me know what you think to the stories.

Twitter: John Thomas Crowley @jtcrowley187

Website: www.jtcrowley.com

Facebook: Jtc Crowley

Printed in Poland
by Amazon Fulfillment
Poland Sp. z o.o., Wrocław